ANONYMITY

Margie Gosa Shivers

ANONYMITY

By Margie Gosa Shivers

Writers Club Press
San Jose New York Lincoln Shanghai

Anonymity

Writers Club Press
an imprint of iUniverse, Inc.

For information address:
iUniverse, Inc.
5220 S. 16th St., Suite 200
Lincoln, NE 68512
www.iuniverse.com

ISBN: 0-595-24817-9

Printed in the United States of America

To my son, Patrick Cook, his wife, Shalon and my precious grandchildren: Shayia, Devin, Chantiera and Little Pat; my father, Jessie Gosa Sr., and all my sisters, brothers, aunts, uncles, cousins and friends, with love!

CHAPTER 1

Cara Fleming stared at her reflection in the mirror. What she saw was not unkind. At twenty-eight, she still had the figure of a young girl and the fresh, exuberant looks to go with it. Now, if only she could get her marriage back on track. The familiar anxiety returned. Mario had been acting strange lately. He'd been staying out late and returning home with alcohol on his breath. One time she noticed makeup on his shirt.

Barring unexpected rain, or worse, a typical Chicago blizzard, Cara drove north on Lake Shore Drive heading to the Loop. Her goal was to buy a *to die for* outfit she would wear tonight at a Luther Vandross concert. She wanted to re-ignite the passion in their marriage. Luckily, it was a mild 68 degrees. Windows rolled down; she breathed fresh air on a mid April day. Piercing through pockets of thin clouds, the sun gleamed a tender haziness over Lake Michigan.

Three hours later, she arrived home with the most perfect outfit. A flowing sleek golden duster pant set with sparkling white embroidery and bugle beading. It was sensually feminine, and showed off her naturally tanned skin and five-feet six, hourglass figure. Surely Mario wouldn't resist her.

Feeling sensual and stepping from the tub an hour later, she rubbed a peach fragrant lotion all over her body, leaving no area untouched. Dressed in the new outfit, she brushed her long dark brown hair as far as her arms could stretch. Then she applied a soft honey beige foundation to her high cheeked, oval face, and delicately dotted a melon-flavored gloss over her small lips.

To set the mood, she selected a Barry White CD and poured chilled champagne into two flutes. The last song played and she checked her watch. It was 6:00 p.m. Darkness would soon claim her private view of the lake. Where was he? He had promised to be home at 5:00 p.m. Had he been in an accident?

Purging the thoughts, she refused to let fear and doubts ruin the evening. On the edge of the sofa, she sat remembering what their life had been like: Eating at elegant restaurants, going to plays, museums, movies and blues concerts. Just three months ago, that had changed. Most disturbing was the rut of occasional candle-lit dinners at home, watching a rented video, making love for five minutes and then falling asleep. She tried to calm her nerves by watching a popular game show, but that didn't help.

She walked to the full-length window, and peered into the darkness of the night. It was a little after seven. Suddenly, she heard keys rattling at the door.

"Cara Slater," His voice was loud enough to wake up a dead man. She knew something awful had disturbed his goat. The last time Mario called her that was the day he married her.

She rushed down the hallway, and seeing Mario, she stopped abruptly. His evil and drunken face frightened her. He edged his five-ten lean body, clad in an orange T-shirt, white shorts and gym shoes closer to her.

Instinctively, she stepped back, and put her hands against the wall for support. "Mario, what is wrong with you? You're late, we're going to miss the concert."

"Forget the frigging concert," he spouted, throwing his keys on the glass top table in the foyer. You've been cheating on me. Miss Angel, Miss Goody-Two-Shoes."

Cara's breathing shortened and she tried to swallow, but her mouth was dry. Mario walked past her, eyes watery, the dark eyebrows and thin moustache on his handsome medium tan face slanted in a frown. He stopped in front of her, stretched his broad shoulders and then he sauntered off to the bar in the corner of the living room. He poured a shot of Wild Turkey, and almost fell over when he tilted his head back to toss down the golden fluid. He stumbled to the sofa and plopped down. She knew he had over consumed and was afraid for the first time in their six-year marriage. Why would he turn on her like a mild mannered dog, gone mad?

"So, the lady wants to know what's wrong? I'll tell you, Miss Lady. While you were out, the anonymous caller told me the sordid details. From all he said, one thing convinced me he wasn't lying. Oh, and the jerk explained why he wanted me to know." He sprang from the sofa and walked toward her, stopping to sip his drink. "The evidence speaks for itself, Miss Lady."

"What evidence?" Cara screamed. Tears drenched with mascara trickled down her face. What did the caller tell you?"

"Enough."

"Enough about what?" Cara stared at Mario and remained silent.

"Why should I tell you what you already know? Anyway, you want to know what ripped my heart out? That the two of you are planning to get married." He turned around in a flash to face her once more. "And, another thing, I don't believe you were a virgin when we met. You want to know what else I don't believe?"

"No, why don't you surprise me?" Cara had thought that nothing could ruin this day for her, but now she'd immediately lost all feelings of being sensual and rekindling their marriage. Her world had changed from euphoria to primal fear.

"I don't believe Ashley is my child."

"Do me a favor, please, stop calling me Miss Lady, I have a name, remember?" she replied in a raised voice. "And, you could never be more wrong about our daughter. You were the first and only man I've been with, and you know it."

"Wanna know why?" he snapped at her. "Because you didn't bleed like virgins supposed to. Back then, I figured I was wrong to look at it that way. I didn't make a big deal about it at the time."

"I can't believe you just said that." Icy contempt flashed in her eyes, as she shook her head, trying to ignore the sting of pain that knifed through her. "Anyway, virgins don't necessarily bleed."

"Yeah, right. Is that according to the bible of Cara? I know you're sleeping with another man. So, stop lying to me."

"I am telling you the truth," she spouted the words slowly.

Suddenly, he put his glass down on the bar and stormed off toward their bedroom. Taking short steps, she quietly followed, and watched him remove his gun from the drawer. Without waiting around a second longer, she ran for the front door and dashed out into the long hallway. She took off her heels and fled with all the speed she could rally. Realizing that the elevator would slow her down, she opened the door leading to the stairway. Trumping down two steps at a time, she was in the lead, at least by four floors.

When she reached he fifteenth floor, she realized the silence behind her. Still running like a bat out of hell, she started to think he'd stopped to rest or he was too drunk to continue. Maybe he went back to the condo. Worst, he would take the elevator down and catch her on a lower floor.

Without wanting to, she slipped on the tenth floor landing. Whisked in a surge of energy she got up and ran some more, ignoring the pain that writhed through her tired body and aching feet. It wasn't long before she saw the sign on the back of the door below that told her she was about to reach the first floor.

Stepping into the lobby, she took a deep breath. Her face felt flushed, hair curls dangled loosely across her forehead. To her left, the voices drew her attention, where people sat in the lounge watching the big screen television. A lady stood alone peering through the window.

She took a deep breath and crossed the lobby. Cara noticed the tall and circular desk guarding a paneled wall with closed doors. Her high heels pierced the marbled floor, alerting the security guard, wearing a dark blue shirt and badge. That's it, she thought. He can protect me, hide me in the back room, and call the police.

Without his permission, she walked behind the tall security desk and kneeled to the floor.

"Hey lady, you can't play hide and seek here," the guard chuckled.

Index finger over her lips, she whispered, "This is no game. I can't let my husband find me. Help me, please."

Meanwhile, Mario rushed through the lobby calling her name. He ran outside, looked up and down the streets, and didn't see her.

"Hmm, stay down and don't move." The guard's lips compressed. He watched Mario run back inside the building and heading toward the security station. He got up and stood at the entranceway, shielding Cara.

Mario nodded a hello to the guard and edged closer until he stood directly in front of the guard. He looked down at the floor.

Doggone it, Cara thought, as she looked up at Mario.

"I looked all over for you," Mario said, holding both hands out to her. "It's okay, I'm not gonna hurt you." His tone was civil.

Cara stood, looking briefly at the guard. "This is my husband, Mario." She tucked her hair behind her ears and let him take her hand. They walked to the elevator as if nothing was wrong.

Mario pushed the button and she looked back at the guard as the elevator door opened. The guard removed his hat and scratched his head. Two black women and a white man got on behind them. Mario let go of her hand once the door closed. He watched her and it made her feel uncomfortable. The other passengers tried not to stare. Afraid to rouse his anger again, she pressed her lips closed, and breathed deeply.

When the elevator stopped on the twenty-seventh floor she let him lead the way to their apartment.

Inside, she sat on the sofa and quietly thanked her guardian angel for sparing her life.

"We need to talk about this." Mario said, and sat down in the loveseat facing her. "I'm sorry. I was so angry. I wanted to shoot myself. Don't you know I'd never harm you?" He held his head down and she started to sense his regret.

"Read my lips, Mario, I was scared. How was I to know your intentions?

Too exhausted to argue anymore, she stood up and walked out on the private balcony. She held onto the iron railing, body still flushed in warmth, undaunted by the coolness of the night. Dappled light fell across the Devil Ivories and Philodendrons hanging from the balcony. Sounds of water splashed against the cement wall bordering the Lake. She stared at the sky, black and dotted with millions of sparkling stars. The night view was spectacular. Even that couldn't erase the desolation that swept over her, and the fact that they had missed the concert. Plans for the evening vanished. Thoughts of what could've been, now floating in the wind.

She let her mind drift back to the allegations and the put-downs. Could someone have actually told Mario such a lie? Oh sure, Mario was capable of lying and cheating on me, but never to lie about something such as this. He was immature, jealous, self-centered easy to anger. But this time he had done too far, she thought.

"I need the truth," Mario said, walking out on the balcony. "You hurt me, can't you understand that?"

Looking around at him, and filled with disgust, she brushed past him and went back inside. He followed her inside to the living room.

Slowing her steps to face him, she said, "Considering your track record, I find what you just said, amusing."

"Throwing mud in my face again?"

"Not exactly." she said, without a blink of the eye. "After what you just put me through tonight, it was the perfectly logical thing to say."

He pounced to his white, gold trimmed bar, poured another shot of bourbon and stared at her. The longer he stared, the more he poured.

Cara realized she could no longer endure his mistrust and unproven allegations.

She walked toward him and stopped. "*You can believe this buster, if nothing else. I don't do adultery. That's your style, not mine!*" She turned around swiftly and marched to the guest bedroom and locked the door. Not long after, she heard him rush down the hallway and shut his door. Amid long moments of quietness, finally she slept.

At exactly eight the next morning, she woke up. It took more than ten minutes to move her body out of bed. Instantly, she realized it was Sunday and she got up and showered. Mario had left the condo. It was his regular day to be on the tennis court.

By 10:00 a.m., she was dressed in a two-piece oyster white suit, her hair neatly coiffed in a French roll held with a gold bejeweled pin. She grabbed her long chestnut brown leather coat from the closet and quietly shut the door behind her.

Cara arrived at church an hour later. Sitting on her favorite pew, she prayed and recalled their life in Memphis: Cara had been honored with the teacher-of-the-year award. Mario had received numerous field and track awards for his outstanding coaching. Low wages, his spendthrift habits, and a young bubbly daughter, to care for, forced them to pursue better wages in Chicago.

She found herself standing and singing the opening hymn. She thought about their daughter. Hundreds of miles apart, she missed Ashley. Cara wanted to feel Ashley's short arms draped around her.

When services ended she eased past everyone, not in the mood for small talk, and greeted those she recognized with only a friendly smile. She got in her car and drove home. It was a sunny cool day and there was little traffic on the streets.

Arriving home an hour later, she realized Mario wasn't due to arrive for another three hours. She undressed and changed into a sleek leopard caftan and matching ballerina shoes. She opened the drapes, checked her phone, email messages, watered the plants, paid the household bills, and baked a cake.

Following a long nap, Cara woke thinking she heard Mario come home. She got up and pushed his bedroom door open hoping to talk to him. She checked the kitchen, the bathroom and balcony. He must have come in and left again.

❧ ❧ ❧

The next day, Mario was stuck in rush hour traffic on the Ryan Expressway hoping to get home before Cara. He reflected on the way she had talked up to him, intimidating his male ego. How could she do this to me? What a fool I've been, he thought.

Then he remembered his torrid affair with Paula Coles, a married woman. Cara thought he was in Dyersburg, Tennessee attending a teaching seminar. When the credit card bill came in the mail a month later, Cara pointed out a one-night charge at a Holiday Inn in Memphis. Her words still rang in his head. "The hotel clerk said you checked in under the name of Mr. & Mrs. Mario Fleming. Since I didn't go with you, it's obvious you had another woman with you." Her eyes were set ablaze like cackling wood burning in a fireplace on a cold winter night. She spent two weeks in their guest room until he broke the ice and begged for her forgiveness.

Somehow he believed the magic would work this time. It didn't. Now, the shoe was on the other foot. He started to think: She's in the hot seat now and won't admit her guilt like I did. Maybe she just forgave me, and didn't forget, he thought.

At 4:00 p.m., he parked his white Thunderbird in the underground garage. Feeling completely worn, he walked into their semi-dark, quiet apartment. Mario's thoughts had left a bad taste in his mouth, so he headed straight to the liquor cabinet. A double shot of gin over ice, will clean my palate and numb my brain, he figured.

He lit a cigarette and turned the television to Channel 7 Eyewitness News. The male reporter was interviewing an alderman apparently about a good deed he'd done for the people in his ward. Mario barely caught the name, Alderman Giles Bennett. He lowered the volume and sipped the rest of his drink and smoked like a chimney. He hardly ever smoked around Cara.

He looked at his watch thinking Cara will walk through the door in an hour.

Fifteen minutes later, relaxed, though, still not at ease, he heard the door open. She placed a basket of clothing on the kitchen floor. Did she take the day off? Maybe, she called in sick again, like the caller said.

"Hello, Mario," she said without expression and put the basket down on the floor.

"What happened? You and lover boy get your signals crossed?"

Here we go again, she thought. She knew it was best to keep quiet and not respond. If she didn't respond with one of her smart remarks, maybe he'd leave her alone.

He got up and walked to his room.

She breathed a sigh of relief and put the neatly folded clothing away. Then she started preparing dinner, a Pepper Steak with steamed rice and a tossed salad. She washed the tomatoes, lettuce and cucumbers, thinking it was going to be nearly impossible to get along with him if he continued to believe that she was having an affair. If I leave him, how will I support myself, she wondered.

An hour later, Cara stood outside his bedroom door. "Mario, dinner is ready."

He slowly came out a few minutes later and sat down at his end of the table. He acted hungry and didn't wait for her to bless the food. The silence was unbearable until halfway through the meal.

"So, how was your day?"

"Not so good," he replied, and continued to eat. "But I got through it. Yours?"

"Same here," he replied, without looking at her.

Cara sipped her white zinfandel. "Have you called your parents?"

"Just my father."

"How're they doing?"

"Fine, they're doing just fine," he spat, eating the rest of his food like he had to get somewhere in a hurry.

"Spring is here. I suppose Bradley's going to be busy," she said, trying to fill the silence with small talk. Mario's father had owned a successful landscaping company since he was a young child. He'd expected Mario to keep his promise and take over the business when he passed on.

"You got that right," he replied, checking his watch. He dropped his napkin on top of his dirty plate. "Thanks for the food."

She watched him stand abruptly. "I made a pound cake yesterday while you were out. Can I get you a slice?"

He walked away from the table without removing his plate, grabbed his light jacket, and walked out the apartment.

Still fearful but without intimidation, she got up and locked the door behind him. As she stood outside his bedroom, she wondered what had the male caller told him that was so convincing? Who was this man? Why were the facts a big secret? How will I defend myself against such blatant allegations? She wondered.

Cara dashed into his bedroom and located his gun. She walked to her bedroom. Mario had left her with but one option.

CHAPTER 2

Mario drove away heading to his favorite watering hole, the *Due Drop Inn*. Thunder roared like a rumbling disaster in the sky. Raindrops covered the windshield. He slowed down and started the wipers. He decided to call his tennis buddy, homicide detective Lester Miller.

After several attempts, he left a message: "I'm at the end of my rope. Meet me at the Inn."

At thirty-seven, Lester stood six-feet and was ruggedly handsome with light skin, dark wavy hair and perfect straight teeth. Considered by some to be Chicago's best-looking Afro American cop, he had compelling dark brown eyes and a generous smile.

Lester entered the lounge at 7:20 p.m. Mario appeared to be mesmerized by the bubbles that moved gracefully in his glass. Lester tapped his buddy on the shoulder and sat down on the high legged bar stool.

"What's up? You look like hell has run over you, twice."

"Yeah right," Mario replied and finished his beer. "Glad you could make it." He wiped drops of moisture from his forehead.

"Your message sounded urgent. What's wrong?"

"Man talk. Things that you can only talk to your best friend about," Mario stammered. "I've got major problems at home."

"Hate to hear that buddy. What's this about?"

"Cara is sleeping with another man."

"Whoa, come again? Lester asked. The bartender placed a beer in front of Lester and quietly disappeared.

"You heard me, don't make me repeat it," Mario snapped.

"How did you find out?" Lester asked, popping the can open. "What exactly did he tell you?"

"A lot," Mario uttered. And, he had his facts straight. I got madder than a junkyard dog. I wanted to grab him through the phone and kill that son-of-a __." Mario told Lester the caller had described the appearance and location of her peculiar birthmark. "He left an envelope for me at the security desk."

"What was in there?"

"Three pictures of Cara standing close to a man with curly hair." Mario slammed his empty glass on the counter.

"Hold that thought," Lester said and rushed to the men's room.

Soon afterwards, Mario decided to join him.

Three minutes later, Lester walked out alone. Mind still heavily on Mario, he slowed to shake hands with some people he knew as he moved through the crowd,. He remembered a snapshot of Cara that Mario showed him. He thought she was a very beautiful woman. Not once had Mario introduced them. Lester had come to believe that Cara was a good woman who mostly stayed home, out of the streets, unlike some women he knew. According to Mario, she wasn't the type who would cheat on her man. Now he wasn't so sure. What went wrong with the model couple? Lester wondered.

Mario returned to the bar.

"Feeling better?" Lester asked.

"Hell no." Mario paused for a moment. "Are you ready to kick it up a notch?"

"Sure, count me in, I'm off duty," Lester joked, and ordered another round for them both.

Mario gathered his thoughts. "Oh, yeah. I'd had way too much to drink before I got home. She was expecting me to take her out to a concert. I walked through the door and blew off like a nuclear missile. She saw me take out the gun. It wasn't meant for her. Before I knew it, she ran out the door, and down the stairs faster than a track star."

Lester stared without blinking.

"Don't give me that look. I was mad enough to shoot me, not her."

"Well, I'm glad nothing happened," Lester replied. Wouldn't want to be the one to take you to jail. So, what did you do?"

"I'm ashamed to tell you." His brows set in a straight line. He realized that Lester was keenly attuned to everything he'd said thus far. Then, he decided to tell Lester everything about that night.

❧ ❧ ❧

"So, you let your anger get the best of you. Obviously, she thought you were chasing her with your gun."

"Yeah, I can see that now. I said some awful things to her, half of it I don't remember."

Lester shrugged his shoulders and put his arms around Mario' shoulder. "If she's having an affair, my heart goes out to you, buddy. But if not, you could be facing trouble you never dreamed."

A waitress filled the jukebox with a handful of coins. A Bobby Bland tune, For Members Only played. Some of the people got up to dance and soon the crowd grew larger as did the noise.

Mario sipped some of his drink and changed the subject. "How're you getting along with your new girlfriend, Barbara?"

Lester glanced at the ceiling and turned to look at Mario. He remembered his date with steady girlfriend, Barbara Rhodes. After two cancellations in a week, he figured the relationship was over.

"I have yet to find a woman who has everything all wrapped up in one package," Lester said.

"Still on the prowl, uh?"

"Maybe, but then you're the romantic type. You believe in love and following your heart, right?" Lester asked.

"Hey, what can I say? I came from the good ole birds and bees country. It doesn't take much to fall head over heels in love in the south. In my case, it took just one beautiful woman and a colorful butterfly. Man, I was up and away in love. Out of all the women on campus, I knew Cara was the one."

Lester leaned back and laughed. "Mario, you never cease to amaze me. Why don't you give it a break? Don't throw away what you have with your wife. If it helps any, I envy you. Remember, the Irish cliché? Hope springs eternal," Lester added, giving him a pat-on-the back.

"We'll see. Anyway, thanks for listening."

Deep down Mario knew his marriage would never be as good as it was. Although Cara had put forgiven his past sins, he wondered if there was a limitation on guilt.

"So, what's your next move?" Lester asked.

❧ ❧ ❧

Cara had removed the bullets and put the gun back inside the third drawer underneath a pile of sweatshirts. She hated that he had it but went along with the idea for their personal safety.

Mario unlocked the door shortly after ten that evening and entered the living room as though he feared what she'd do or say. "We need to talk." His voice was almost a whisper now.

Looking up at him, she said, "Sure. You go first." She sat up and closed the book. Bourbon reeked from his body. She regarded him with impassive coldness. Not in the mood to talk to him about anything, she studied his face unhurriedly.

"Why can't you admit you've done me wrong? I'll forgive you." He said.

"I want you to listen and listen good," she said and stood up. "For the last time, I'm not having on an affair. Realize it, Mario, someone framed me."

Suddenly, he spun around and left the room.

Cara picked her dignity up off the floor. She'd thought long and hard about her decision. She knew it would be a struggle to divorce him and there would be hardships, but she was up to the task. She believed she could make it on her own, the old fashioned way. If I have to eat Black eyed peas, pinto beans, ham hocks and cornbread for the rest of my life, I'll do it, she thought.

When he came back inside, she pushed herself to a standing position, hands clasped together in front of her.

"A few minutes ago, you wanted to talk. Well good. Because there's something I need to say to you."

"All right, talk to me," he blurted, standing a few feet from her.

"It seems we've found ourselves on a dead-end street. The No-Detour sign is staring us smack in the face." Her voice had depth and authority.

"I don't believe you just said that," he said.

"Sometimes it's harder to close a door than it is to close a window." She breathed heavily. "By your actions and behavior, you've somehow made it easy for me. This time," she paused to take a deep breath, "It's really over!"

"Oh, I see, so you want out?"

Cara looked at him, blinking away the tears.

"Answer me, is that what you want?" Mario walked closer to her.

"Yes. As much as it hurts, I can't live with someone who demands I confess to something I'm not guilty of."

Mario slammed his hand on the wall and his voice raised an octave. "Bullshit. I want your ass out of here! The sooner the better!"

Cara walked slowly down the hallway, head bowed, and fully aware she lacked the time she needed. She'd hoped they could come to a harmonious solution giving her time to save enough money to start over. She walked slowly into her room, locked the door, and sat down in the chair to think.

❧ ❧ ❧

Two weeks later on a Saturday morning, everything that wasn't nailed down was packed and ready to go. Her mail had been forwarded. Mario was on the tennis court and he knew she was leaving him. They had agreed to split everything, including the money. She'd withdrawn half of the joint savings: a mere three thousand dollars after moving expenses.

She took her final cup of coffee and walked out on the balcony to capture a last look. The sun gently streamed down on the perfectly blue water on Lake Michigan rendering a peaceful warmth and calmness. She started to feel sick inside wondering what could've been, if this dreadful lie hadn't come between them.

It occurred to her that she was leaving without word between. Not once since he told her to get out had Mario tried to get her to change her mind. She went back inside and wrote him a letter.

Mario:

I'm leaving. Believe it or not, I've been framed. I have no clue why anyone would do this. What I do know is that I'm innocent. I've been totally faithful since the day I met you, and you were my first. Even though I've stood by you through thick and thin amid all of your flaws, you have put me through hell because of this mess. You couldn't even give me the benefit of the doubt and trust me. If you don't believe Ashley is yours, get a paternity test. Obviously, you know more than you're willing to tell me. But, somehow, someday, the truth will come out. But then, it'll be too late. Life goes on, and so shall I.

Cara

CHAPTER 3

Cara's two bedroom unit located on Seventy-Seventh and Exchange, was if nothing else, affordable. Here and there, windows were boarded up and cars parked bumper to bumper along the curb. It was not uncommon to find used condoms, broken glass, and discarded litter resting on street corners. At best, it was minutes away from large grocery stores, fast food establishments, a commercial Laundromat, and public transportation.

By 8:30 that morning, she had showered and dressed in black leotards and a white baggy T-shirt, hair pulled in a ponytail. Taking a sip of her coffee, she walked to the large bay window in the living room. She felt blessed to have a roof over her head. She paced the living room floor some more and glanced at the surroundings: the sofa, two lamps, a Zenith color television, a brass floor lamp, a tall Weeping Fig tree, a bushy spider plant and several Philodendrons that amply filled the octagonal-shaped living room. A portrait of Martin Luther King and Harold Washington and two of her favorite oil paintings graced the living room walls. Glancing at the windows void of curtains or blinds, the white shades will have to do for now, she thought.

Walking into the smaller bedroom turned into a workspace, she said, "Oh, yeah, my Compaq Presario will be my friend. The computer won't break my heart, cheat or lie on me." Knowing that she could surf the Internet anonymously without emotional entanglements, she created a new screen name, *Current Wife*.

Finally, she entered her bedroom and eased her body on top of the peach and green floral comforter and stared at the bare walls thinking, I must call my parents. But, how I'm going to break the news to my mother? She wondered.

Naomi, fifty-five, half Cherokee and Afro American, was a woman who believed in staying married for better or worse, richer or poorer? Open and honest communication between them had ceased when she turned fifteen. She often thought about her mother's brand of sex education and took delight in the humor. She knew her mother had done the best she could. The words still rang inside her head: "Every month, Cara, you're going to bleed for a few days. Remember to never let the boys ride on you like a horse or else you'll come up pregnant with a baby." She was forced her to learn about her body, sex and babies from reading library books.

I hate to disappoint my parents. But why prolong the inevitable, she thought.

She reached for the phone and dialed their number. "Hi, mom."

"Hello, Cara," Naomi said. "It's about time we hear from you. How're you doing?"

"I'm okay. I miss my daughter," she said in a low tone. "How is Ashley?" Cara had tormented herself daily over leaving Ashley with her parents. Besides, Frank, fifty-eight, and a master carpenter, believed Chicago wasn't safe enough for their granddaughter and had insisted on it.

"She's fine, and looking more like you everyday." Naomi boasted. "You sound different. Is everything okay? How's Mario?"

"I don't know."

"What is that supposed to mean?"

"I've left Mario." Cara's voice broke miserably. Momentarily pausing, she bit her lip to stifle the outcry.

"No! You left Mario? Why?" Naomi screamed. "Where are you staying, for God sakes? Are you okay?"

"I'm fine, Mom." Cara said, still hesitant to spill the details.

For a few moments there was complete silence on the other end of the line.

"Mom, are you still there?"

"Barely," Naomi replied and paused for a moment. "Why did you leave?"

Cara's father had been listening. "Baby girl?" Her nickname since she was six years old. "What's this I hear about you leaving Mario?"

"Dad, he accused me of cheating on him. Can you imagine that?" Cara stammered.

"I swear before Chicken Gizzards. If that don't beat all I've ever heard!" Frank, a normally mild tempered fellow woofed.

"What would make him believe such a thing?" Naomi joined them.

"Oh, Good. You're both listening. Hope you're sitting down. It's a long story.

Cara told them everything. What she didn't do was repeat the words Mario thrashed at her: *I want your ass out of here.* The sting lingered in her heart. It had been awful to hear the words and difficult to repeat. Not even to her parents. What would they think about me? That I've been a bad wife and deserved to be thrown out by my husband? She thought.

"The nerve of that man, thinking you would cheat on him. What's gotten into him?" Frank asked, spacing the words evenly. "Well, I've got one better than that. He better not hurt you."

A heartbeat of silence followed in which Cara could almost hear the thoughts spinning through her father's mind. He wouldn't lift his hand to hurt a fly. For her, he'd kill and regret it later. "Luckily, daddy, that didn't happen. I ran for my life that night."

"Still, I don't like it one bit. I wonder what his father would have to say about the way he behaved?" Frank asked.

Cara had wondered the same thing.

"It's just you and me," Naomi said, after a long pause. "Your father has heard all he wants to hear." Naomi said.

"Is dad okay?"

"Yes. Try not to worry about us. It's you we're concerned about now. You're a Slater woman, a tough cookie. I'm glad you didn't compromise your principles."

"I can thank you and daddy for that. A marriage based on deception and infidelity can't thrive on such shaky grounds. All your hopes and dreams for a peaceful secure life become impossible expectations," Cara preached.

"That-a-girl! Listening to you talk such wisdom at your young age is remarkable. I couldn't have said it better," Naomi trumpeted.

By that response, Cara was relieved to know that she could finally talk to her mother. Her parents had lived in pursuit of relative few pleasures: living decently, owning a house, having good friends, great southern food, and going to church. She'd learned being a parent was one of the true legacies in the world. It's what you passed on that really matters, she thought.

"I want you to promise me," Naomi paused.

"Yes mom?"

"Promise me that you'll be careful up there. You're alone and don't have a husband to look out for you anymore. For God's sake, keep your cellular charged and with you at all times. Get a motor club card in case you have car problems. Just be careful."

"I promise!" Then Cara remembered the rest. "He's disowned Ashley." Cara blurted, scarcely aware of her own voice.

"What?" Borrowing one of her father's southern cliques, Naomi blurted, "I swear before Baking Powder. Has Mario lost his mind? Why does he think that he's not her father?"

"Would you believe, because she looks like me and nothing like him?"

"He actually said that? Well, he's not the same man you married." Her voice was heavy with disgust."

"He's not, Mom. Somehow, he's changed.

"I'm disappointed your marriage couldn't have turned out differently. But I do applaud your decision," Naomi said. "I'll pray that he'll come to his senses and soon. That child needs her father, even if he doesn't want her. Now that you've left him, what are your plans?"

"I'll take one day at a time, Mom. *I'm no quitter.*"

"Good girl. Remember, when it comes to Ashley, we're like an insurance company. She's in good hands. Just take good care of yourself. Remember, you have a home here with us."

"I'll keep that in mind if all else fails. But, Mom, I'm going to make it the old-fashioned way. I'll work hard and earn my way. You'll see," Cara said, and hung up.

For a while she sat and thought. Going back to the south is out of the question. It's not because I don't cherish the good things about living there—the fresh air and food, or being able to Ashley on a daily basis. It's why we came to Chicago. Better wages and a new life, she thought.

Cara's career was very important to her and being in control and being able to make choices about her life had always been a priority. Her present position offered no room for growth, neither an appreciative salary in the near future. Government funded programs were low on the totem pole when it came to paying employees, not to mention considerations for their dedication and services. The paperwork required to document compliance, had enough rules to fill a book. Yet, she could reach out and touch the lives of the less fortunate. Being able to help others meant a lot to her.

Panic welled at the thought that whoever framed her was lurking around somewhere in Chicago and soon the savings would be gone, but she let the determination to make it on her own give her courage. I need a friend to exhale with, she decided.

She met her only girlfriend, Jennifer Tate at a church function. Right away, they became friends. Until now, Cara hadn't discussed marital issues with her.

Jennifer was twenty-nine, a high school math teacher, fairly attractive, and she had beautiful unblemished chestnut skin. She exercised often to maintain a size 10. Jennifer's husband, Duncan worked in the City Comptroller office. They were childless and owned a modest priced three-bedroom home in Pill Hill, an affluent, south side neighborhood.

Cara reluctantly dialed her number.

"Hello," Jennifer answered.

"Hi, it's me."

"Hey, it's been awhile. How you doing?"

"So-so," Cara's voice dropped two octaves.

"You sound different. What's going on?"

Cara could hear Jennifer's rapid breathing. "Well, let's say it's something I'm not proud about. I've moved out of the condo. Mario and I are separated."

"No, please tell me you're joking."

When she'd finished giving Jennifer the details, she broke down and cried.

"Oh my God, I'm so sorry. How could Mario possibly believe you'd cheat on him? Damn him. The nerve of that man."

Cara's crying eased some. "I was framed."

"Oh no, you got to be kidding."

There was a long silence as Cara gathered her composure. "What's worst is I don't know who framed me or how to prove my innocence."

"My goodness! I hate this happened to you. Are you all right?"

"Yes, I'm okay, for now."

"Good. Jennifer paused. "Think about it girlfriend. Maybe, it was someone who had a score to settle with you?"

"Actually, I don't have a clue? I've tried so hard not to make enemies."

"What if Mario lied? Think about it. He refused to tell you about this so-called evidence. Why? Cause there isn't any! Sounds like some intelligent, cooked-up shit on his part, if you ask me. Oh that, I rest my case."

"I heard that. Right now, I'm tired of thinking about what happened and the reasons why."

"Whatever. I'm just mad as hell for you!" Jennifer declared. "Living all alone has got to be rough. Do you need anything?"

"Right now, just be my friend and most of all, keep this to yourself. Lend me your ears and shoulder when I need to cry."

"Sure. I won't breathe a word," Jennifer promised. "Remember, I'm here for you. All you got to do is pick up the phone."

"Thanks. You're a wonderful friend." Still, Cara wondered if Jennifer would keep her mouth shut.

CHAPTER 4

While watching a rented video, *Random Hearts*, Cara suddenly pushed the stop button. For some reason and maybe because she needed to think about who would possibly have a motive to ruin her marriage. Recalling the darkest moment in her life a year ago, she remembered her run-in with Paula:

Driving home from a doctor appointment, she waited for the light to change. Engines running, windows rolled up to keep the cool air inside. She glanced at the black car next to her. Then she focused on the youthful looking woman behind the wheel. She had short tinted hair, very attractive, and her dark lashes set off her medium brown skin.

At that moment, the woman turned and looked directly at Cara. It was as if she had thrown a harpoon through Cara's heart. The wounds from just a few weeks ago re-opened, and Cara's anger was without restraint.

"Ah, ah!" Cara screamed. It's, it's, it's you isn't it? Paula Coles, the bitch, she thought. Cara felt her nostrils flare. She gripped the steering wheel as if she were wringing Paula's neck. She continued to glance at Paula and Paula looked over her and she watched Paula's eyes widen with concern. "You're that conniving bitch of a woman who slept with my husband. You slut!" It was so unlike her, but she couldn't restrain her pent-up feelings and past anger. In fact, she felt better looking the woman in the eye and screaming at her.

The light changed. Cara accelerated slowly and veered into Paula's lane, directly in back of her. They were bumper to bumper driving down the road. Cara had just wanted to tap Paula's bumper, exerting her female power. If she could just get close enough. Cara remembered pushing on the pedal and the car had moved close enough to ransack Paula's rear end. But before the slight impact, Cara saw Paula look in her rear-view mirror. In a split second, Paula sped out of Cara's sight. It's a good thing, Cara thought. I probably would have killed her. Cara knew she wanted revenge, but that was illogical thinking. Better to pull off the road and cool down.

Finding the strength not to cry, she was glad that Paula got away. She prayed out loud, "I was so mad. I just wanted to scare her, not to harm her." And, yet she continued to spat. "Women like that need to wake up and realize that they can't f__ around with any woman's man. I don't play that s__." In the next breath, she asked for God's forgiveness for her choice of words. "I don't know what I'm doing, I don't know I'm saying. Please help me. Help me please." She bowed her head and continued to pray.

Finally she felt like her prayers had removed the venom inside her and she realized something about herself. She had another side to her. More surprised than frightened, she discovered that she could be tough, especially when it came to protecting anything she felt belonged to her. If someone stepped on just one of her toes, she'd break all ten of that person's toes. Still she felt somewhat vindicated, but glad that no harm came to Paula.

An hour later Cara remembered pulling into the driveway. The phone was ringing when she walked inside the house. She picked up the phone and said, "Hello."

"You could've caused an accident," Paula sniffed.

The anger returned, more powerful than before. "You shut up, you married bitch."

"You don't have to talk like that. And, you had no right to scare me half to death," Paula railed.

"I was angry, but maybe, you're the type of woman incapable of understanding how it feels to be cheated on. Well, it hurts, Mrs. Coles."

"You should be thankful that you have a husband who loves you more than anything. I feel so badly about this. I, I just want to clear the air and make sure you're okay, Cara."

"Really, how can you possibly do that?"

"If you let me, I can come to your house and we'll talk. I won't take much of your time."

"You're not only a low-life, you got guts, too!"

"I can take anything you throw at me, because I deserve it," Paula admitted.

"Oh really. So, what do you expect to accomplish coming to my house?"

"After today, I'm scared this thing will escalate until someone gets hurt. Until you get it all out of your system, you'll never heal, and we'll both suffer in the long run."

Cara hesitated for a moment. "All right, come on over. It's your life." She hung up and let out a long breath, while pacing the kitchen floor. I must be out of my mind to do this, she thought.

Not long after Cara had answered the door and gave Paula the cheesy non-approval look from head to toe, she said, "Come in." Somehow thoughts of getting even with Paula were banished.

"Hi," Paula said, with a humble smile on her face. "Thanks for letting me come."

They both exchanged a polite, simultaneous smile. Paula sat at the kitchen.

"Can I get you anything?"

"No, thanks." Paula fumbled with her hands. She moved about in her seat, crossing her legs and stared at Cara.

"Why don't you begin?" Cara sat down and leaned forward in her chair.

"First, you need to know that your husband loves you very much and never meant to hurt you."

"Don't give me that. The truth is, he never meant for me to find out."

"I'm sorry about that. Wish I could make it all go away, but I can't," she said, apologetically. "I've caused you pain and I'm sorry. If you call me everything under the sun, it won't erase what I've done to you."

Cara got up and poured a glass of water for herself. "Are you sure you don't want anything?"

"I'm sure. But, thanks anyway."

Cara sat down and slowly drank her water. "I'm curious. How did you meet my husband?"

"At the mall," she stammered, not able to go on.

"Don't mind me. Please continue."

"Do I have to? This is very difficult. Telling you more would only make it worse for you."

"Let me be the judge of that!" Cara pushed the empty glass in circles on the table, "You know that old saying, *what goes around comes around?*"

"Yeah, sure. Why you ask?"

Cara shook her head and took three deep breaths and thought about monogamy and how some men need more than one woman. Societal rules require that women stay monogamous or otherwise wear the label of slut or whore. Men who sleep with other women were casually considered as playboys, or just oversexed or couldn't help it. I never would've believed Mario would turn out to be that kind of man. Neither am I ready to do a double standard act, and cheat on him. Adultery no matter who did it was wrong. Two wrongs don't make a right!

"If it's forgiveness you're asking for," she said, calmed down. "Get on your knees and pray."

Paula shrugged her shoulders and twisted her lips. "I will. Oh, just so you know, I'm going to Europe to be with my husband, Howard at the military base. He's been hounding me for the past three years to come and be with him."

"Really? When are you leaving?"

Cara started the movie again, and thought: Paula is a ghost from my past. After the affair ended, Mario had changed. Except for going to work and playing tennis, he was at home with me.

She had believed their marriage was more important to him than risking it for an occasional romp in bed with some other woman and she had marital peace with him until her world came to a shocking end in Chicago.

CHAPTER 5

Surprisingly, another weekend had come and gone too soon and for the first time she realized even though she was alone, she wasn't lonely. Dressing for work, she suddenly sensed a chilly ache in her stomach: "*I want your ass out of here.*" His words wouldn't go away.

Cara checked her watch. It was 8:15. She grabbed her brief bag, the packed lunch consisting of a can of tomato soup and a ham sandwich, and her keys. She locked the door behind her.

During the drive to her office, she considered another possibility: Mario has met another woman. He fell in love with her. Someone who satisfied him like I no longer could. He needed to be free of me. Divorce was the logical answer, only I was a good wife and he had no grounds. He labels me the adulterer this time. Bingo, that gave him sufficient grounds for divorcing me, only this time he didn't have the proof, like I did about his affair. He knew I loved him and was in the marriage for keeps. He gets drunk and stages a vicious argument hurling enough allegations to make me hate him. He adds fuels to the fire, stomps off saying he is mad as hell, and frightening me with that gun.

By then she steamed like a pot of water about to boil over. Slowing down in the far right lane at the intersection of Seventy-First Street and Stony Island, she felt a sudden jolt to her neck. Blood rushed through her veins and a plummeting sensation overtook her. "Oh no. My car." She thought she was going to retract her breakfast. She looked at the driver who hit her. He shook his head back and forth probably thinking, dumb slow driving broad, she instantly thought.

Onlookers suddenly stopped along sidewalks. Traffic slowed. She just wanted it to be over and to get out of view of gapers stopped to see the ruins of an accident. She seemed all right. Nothing was broken, no bruises or the sight of blood. Worry about her dwindling savings account, swirled throughout her body like sand tossed about in a storm.

Minutes later, lights flashed, and police officers converged.

Cara got of her car and the driver approached her. He was a dark skinned gentleman, medium height and he wore sunglasses and a crisp white shirt was large enough to cover his belly and brown slacks.

"Hi, I'm sorry about this, are you okay?"

"I seem to be. How about you?" Cara replied, heaving a sigh.

"I'm fine. The name is Joe Michaels." He slowly removed his sunglasses, riveting her with his liquid dark brown eyes hooded like a hawk.

"I'm Cara Fleming. What happened, Mr. Michaels?" She clamped her jaws firmly shut, making no protest as he stood giving her a flighty gesture.

"To tell you the truth I had a lot on my mind."

Cara thought, you and me both. "Well, we should both be grateful for that," she said.

"You got that right," Michaels replied, turning around to face his car.

They exchanged the required information.

"Well, Ms. Fleming, take care of yourself. Again, I'm sorry for the damages to your car." Joe Michaels sauntered off to his car.

Returning to her car, she used the cellular to call her office and left a message on the secretary's voice mail: "I had an accident on my way to work. I'm okay. I'll return to the office tomorrow." The police had found him at fault. She folded the paper and tucked it inside her bag.

Expecting a visit from Jennifer any day now, she stopped at the Walgreens store on Seventy-First Street and Jeffrey, and bought two bottles of wine: white and red zinfandel.

Twenty minutes later, she parked at her building and noticed the first floor neighbor peering out the window. She waved a friendly hello, grabbed the mail and went inside her apartment.

By 11:00 a.m., Cara had accomplished a lot over the phone: reported the accident to her insurance company, and settled on taking her car that afternoon to Turner Auto Collision & Repair. To her surprise, the owner offered pick up and delivery service.

Afterwards, she wondered what else could go wrong? I've got be strong. I won't give in to the forces of evil. Peace and happiness are the rewards.

With nothing else to do that day, she decided to relax and reflect some more about her life. Sitting on the sofa, she had a flashback of her storybook wedding four years ago. The wedding was perfect, but the honeymoon left her unsatisfied as a woman. Sex was something for the man to enjoy and not necessarily the woman. Little did I expect that my husband would ever cheat on me? Loyal? Yes. But more than that, very naïve! She figured.

She finished the wine, picked up the daily Sun Times newspaper, and turned to the Jobs section. The doorbell rang. It was three o'clock. She looked through the peephole and saw the first floor neighbor. She was obviously someone who cared about her appearance and she seemed friendly. She was medium height, a little on the stocky side and she appeared to be over sixty-five. She wore a pretty, aquamarine polyester pantsuit. Her partly graying hair worn, wrapped in a thick ball on top of her head.

Right away she'd felt relieved. It's about time someone broke the ice. It's so unlike me to be unfriendly and shy away from people, she thought. She opened the door.

"Good afternoon," she said, greeting the lady with a smile.

"Hello, my name is Thelma Walker. I'm your downstairs neighbor. It took me awhile to say hello, but here I am."

"Hi, it's nice to meet you. I'm Cara Fleming. Please, come in for a while?"

"Well, okay, but not for long. Didn't want to let anymore time pass without stopping by to say hello."

"How thoughtful," Cara said. "Make yourself comfortable."

"What happened to your car? Mrs. Walker sat down in the chair facing the kitchen. "Are you okay?" She asked, taking little peaks at the surroundings.

"A man in a bit of hurry hit my car as I was about to turn right on red." She's not so bad, a little nosey maybe, but mostly concerned about me, she figured.

"Well, I'm glad you're alright."

Cara got an overview of everything from the building to the neighborhood: An even mix of singles and married folks lived there: They stayed mostly to themselves. A few strange ones, but they didn't bother anybody.

Cara got up and walked to the kitchen. She returned with two glasses of cold lemon flavored tea she'd made the day before.

"Thanks dear." Mrs. Walker sipped her tea and smiled. "Let me tell you about Louis, the guy above you. If you haven't met him, you shall. Anyway, every time I turn around, Louis is packing or unpacking," she couldn't seem to resist telling her about him.

"Why is that?" Cara remembered bumping into him on her floor a day ago. He'd spoken to her and kept walking. He'd seemed to be the I-mind-my-own-business-type of a fellow.

"Well, he has a place down in Florida. People like Louis do that sort of thing when they retire. Not me, I like it here. I never go down for the winter like some people do. Oh, sometimes, his lady friends come to visit him: Young and bony looking. They all dress like they're hustling him for money."

"I see, good for him." Cara let her mind wander about Mrs. Walker. Was she as nice as she appeared friendly? Could she expect unannounced visits in the future?

"I hope you like living here," she said.

"So do I," Cara replied, tilting the glass to her lips.

"One thing I want you to know about me is," Mrs. Walker said, twiddling her fingers, "I'm very independent, and never ask nobody for nothing. So you don't have to worry, I won't bother you. Just want to be neighborly."

"Oh," Cara threw her a warm smile. "Well, in that case, you'll find me to be the same."

"Good." They exchanged phone numbers and Cara showed her Ashley's photo album.

"Call me if you need anything or feeling lonely. Believe me, I know what it's like to be alone. In your case, you're too young to suffer like that."

Well, Cara thought, raising her eyebrows inquiringly. She's done her homework.

"It was nice to meet you. I'm sure we'll get along just fine, there's nothing like a good neighbor," Mrs. Walker said and put her glass on the coffee table.

Following the brief visit, Cara closed the door and returned the glasses to the kitchen. Her thoughts were still on Mrs. Walker: Friendly, and she seemed protective. She was a bit gossipy, but she's someone I believe I can count on, she thought.

In the past, Cara had been friendly and open with others about her personal life. She got stabbed in the back with gossip that never seemed to quit. She remembered that day in the ladies room at her school in Memphis. How she wished she hadn't been in the right place at the wrong time when she overhead: "If she and Mario are so happy and in love like Cara claims, you would think he wouldn't find other women so interesting." Another one said, "I don't quite understand how a man can play around on a wife as pretty as she is." Then a third voice spoke, "Seems to me, men need more than a pretty face and a pencil thin body to keep them satisfied." When her silly coworkers had stopped giggling they walked out. Cara was left in tears. She got wise and learned to deal with folks who put her down. Especially, the ones couldn't get their own life in order.

Her memory had brushed back over mistakes she'd made as a result of sharing too much of her personal life with so-called friends. She didn't have any male friends outside her marriage. She became a social recluse living her life on her terms. It wore on her like a habit that she hadn't been able to break. Now, more than ever, she thought, I need to keep to myself. No character assassination, probing questions, or opinionated advice.

It was around five-thirty that afternoon and she was hungry. She opened the brown lunch bag, poured a glass of skim milk and ate the lunch she prepared to eat that day at the office.

Later, she went on online and e-mailed Jennifer. Then she clicked on her favorite places, and searched Monster.com for potential jobs. Realizing her chances for getting a better paying job were slim to none, she felt like screaming. But instead, she decided to do the crossword puzzle in the Sun Times newspaper.

By six thirty, she'd finished the puzzle when the phone rang. She started to reach for the phone. "I won't answer another hang-up call." But, after four rings, she answered.

"Hello."

"It's Bradley Fleming calling." His voice was unusually cold. At 58, he was a proud, leading businessman in Memphis, respected by important people, including the mayor. Since the day Mario introduced her, she'd felt adored and considered as a daughter, rather than a daughter-in-law. She even remembered how Bradley would often say nice things about her to his friends: That she came from a loving, Christian family, that she was a good girl who didn't sleep around. That he was glad Mario had chosen her. He boasted about she'd worked hard to earn a college degree on a student loan and part time work-study program.

"Hi Mr. Fleming, how are you?" Cara said, trying to sound upbeat.

"I'm disappointed in you." His tone was low and he paced his words. "You had me and everyone else fooled young lady and now I think you are immoral and unfit. I feel sorry for my son. You've ruined his life. I promise you, that I'll see to it that you lose custody of my granddaughter. You are unfit to raise that child," he said, as his mood veered sharply to anger.

Why do I suddenly feel like the scum of the earth? "You're so wrong about me," she answered, struggling to get the words out. "There's another side to this story."

"Listen, young lady," he interrupted her, "Don't even try to deny it. Mario told me everything."

At that moment, all she could think of was, as far as Bradley Fleming was concerned, she was *shit* to him now! Trying to hold it together, she said, "I'm sorry you feel that way about me, sir. I'm not like that. One day the truth shall be told." After a long pause, he hadn't come back at her with more of his wrath. By now, she couldn't figure him. Feeling nauseated and fed up to her eyeballs, she lacked the words to continue. "I can see you're unhappy with me. Perhaps, it's best we end this conversation, so, I'll say goodbye." She hung up no sooner than she said the words.

Well, she thought, this call lets me know where I stand with Mario's parents.

She leaned back in the armed chair, hands shaking. "Oh, God, what have I done to bring such misery upon myself? When will it end? *Could it be that it's my turn to be the victim of what goes around comes around?*"

CHAPTER 6

Bradley's eerie phone call was still on her mind when she woke the next day. That she could manage to put aside. What she couldn't understand was that a month had passed since she left Mario. Did he care at all how she was doing on her own? Was he moving on with his life?

At 6:30 a.m. she felt excruciating pain in her neck and shoulders. Later, she managed to shower and dressed for work. She went to the kitchen to make some coffee and remembered she had only instant coffee in her cupboard. The gas stove hissed at her, and she finally had to light it with a match. She put a pot of water on to boil and thought about what she wanted to eat. More ravenous than ever before, she cooked two strips of bacon, scrambled an egg, and browned a slice of wheat bread.

She sat down later at the table, poured a glass of orange juice and savored the harmonious flavors. Suddenly the pain in her neck and shoulder lingered making it difficult to suddenly continue. She took a sick day.

Jennifer called around eight that morning. "Why don't I come by later to check on you?" She asked, in a bit of a hurry.

"That would be nice. When shall I expect you?"

"I'll come by right after work."

"Sure, I'll see you then." Cara hung up the phone and flushed down two Excedrin with a glass of water, and slowly drifted off to sleep on the sofa.

It was exactly 1:00 that afternoon when the doorbell woke her.

A few seconds later, she looked through the peephole. A gentleman wearing a beige and brown uniform stood, face grim and body still.

Cara slowly opened the door. "Yes, may I help you?"

"Are you Cara Fleming?"

"Yes," she uttered. She let in him in and he handed Cara the clipboard.

At first glance, the words DIVORCE PETITION grabbed her attention. Her thoughts, jagged and painful like an old wound that ached on a rainy day: So, he actually filed for the divorce. The grounds for the divorce were there, as clear as day and night: *Adultery*. At least I know where I stand. He wants it over, and right now. But why am I not surprised? Mario hadn't cared enough to call to check on me, yet he managed to find out where I moved and get a lawyer.

Motionless, she just stood and continued to read.

The officer interrupted her seemingly in a hurry to get out of there. "I need your signature, ma'am." It hadn't occurred to her that she didn't need to read the document before she signed it. She signed the form and handed him the clipboard.

"Okay, you have a good day," he stated and turned around to walk out as calmly as he'd entered.

She locked her door and scanned through the petition. Mario had taken the upper hand and had wasted no time. This changes things, now more than ever. I've got to defend myself, but how? Hiring a lawyer would be costly. Should I tell my parents about Bradley's call? Now what? If I get one more piece of bad news, I'm going to scream my fool head off, she thought.

Still in pain, but ready to explode into a zillion pieces, she forced herself to get busy making the apartment look presentable for Jennifer's visit. Slowly, she made the bed and pushed the vacuum over the living room carpet. The weather report had the temperature around eighty-five but the humidity was vicious. She turned the control up one notch on the air conditioning. Afterwards, she sprayed a cinnamon flavor air freshener around the apartment. Then she brushed her hair into a ponytail, swerved it to the right side of her head and held it together with a yellow cloth band. She slipped into a pair of yellow short-legged pants cut just above her knees and a white pullover baggy shirt tucked at the waist. Seeing Jennifer again brighten her spirit.

While she waited, Cara got busy on the computer. First, she played Free Cell for about an hour. Just as she grew tired, she clicked on *Statistics* and noticed she had six hundred wins versus two hundred and ten losses. Winning was very important to Cara, no matter what she involved herself in doing. And it was no question that Free Cell had become an easy target for relief and accomplishment. That and surfing the Internet kept her mind charged and ready to think, plan and decide what was best for her.

Alderman Giles Bennett finished writing a speech for his friend, Alderman Horace Tucker. Bennett, thirty-six, was a light brown brother, and slightly heavy at five feet eight. He'd replaced the incumbent two years ago.

His office was furnished in a manly fashion. Ultra modern lights in the ceiling, the glass fronted bookcases, the leather chairs around a granite-topped table. The huge space on the third floor was where he spent most of his time. The walls were papered with an earth tone striped paper, tapered from top to bottom and set off by oak baseboards. On one side of the room, the walls were lined with books and art objects. Three dieffenbachia trees thrived in large hand-painted clay pots. He kept a small refrigerator stocked with diet sodas, beer, bottled water and wine to share with his friends. Those who knew him hadn't understood the absence of pictures of his family. Neither did they broach the topic with him.

He was holding a soda pop when his deputy chief, Joe Michaels appeared at the door.

"Hi Joe. Come on in and pull up a chair."

"Good afternoon, Alderman, how's it going?" Joe Michaels remained standing, belly thrust out for balance. He took a pair of glasses out of his pocket, shook them open, and set them on his short nose and sat down. He'd had a full day helping to solve problems: trash pickup, meetings and organizing a picnic for the people in Bennett's ward. He wanted this day over and quick.

"I'm finished." Bennett put the papers inside a large brown envelope. "Take this to Alderman Tucker on your way home."

"Sure."

"By the way, how did it go with the church member?" Alderman Bennett asked.

Michaels boasted, "Oh, yeah, that went quite well. All that's left is to wait for the lady to take the leap."

Bennett's eyebrows raised a fraction. "Good. I'll need you to keep an eye on that situation. Remember, it's really important that it doesn't get linked to me."

CHAPTER 7

When the bell rang at 4:45 p.m., Cara perked up. She pushed the buzzer and opened the door.

"Hi, come in. It's so good to see you." She embraced Jennifer with a sisterly hug. Jennifer's hair now worn in long thick braids showed off her cute round face with perfectly high cheekbones. Her white sandals showed off her toenails, painted bright red to match her sleeveless dress. Gold looped earrings swung from her ear lobes.

"You look great," Cara said, checking her over.

"Thanks, and so do you. How do you keep yourself so together in all of this?"

"Oh, I don't know." Cara wrinkled her nose some. "Mostly eating healthy, drinking plenty of water and getting proper rest. So how've you been?"

Jennifer walked grandly to the sofa and sat down "Can't complain. Gee, it sure feels nice in here." She squinted peering around the room.

Cara soon joined her. "I'm sure. Now that you're here, I feel better already."

Not long after, she showed the apartment. Jennifer seemed impressed as she toured the clean, scarcely furnished apartment. Walls freshly painted off-white, floors carpeted in a light tan color.

"It's small, but nice and clean. I like it," Jennifer said, as they walked into the kitchen.

Cara laughed softly. "Hey, I'm happy here. Hopefully, one day I'll do better."

Cara took out the bottle of chilled wine.

"Care for something to drink?"

"You know me. It's the best way I know how to unwind after work."

Cara poured the wine. They raised and clicked the wine glasses together in a silent toast.

"Cheers," Jennifer said, taking a good sip. "Wish I could be so brave. I envy you."

The two ladies walked to the sofa and sat down again.

"I'm only that way because I have to be." Cara hesitated, her brow dimpled. "Lately I'm starting to expect to be surprised or startled by some unpleasant event."

"Really, why you say that?" Jennifer lifted the glass again to her lips.

"Other than getting rear ended in traffic by some strange man yesterday, my father-in-law called me hours later. It wasn't pleasant. He called me sleazy things and he threatened to help Mario get custody of Ashley. Can you believe that?"

Jennifer relaxed her back on the sofa and she shook her head. "Seems old man Fleming doesn't know that Ashley is a disclaimed member of the family." She grinned at her words and looked at Cara. "Joking aside, she asked, wiping the smile abruptly, "How did you manage listening to that man?"

Cara took another sip of her wine. "I got through it. What he doesn't know is that I'll fight to keep my daughter." Cara suppressed her anger.

"I'm sure. Have you heard from Mario?"

"Funny you asked that. I was served with divorce papers today. As you can see, I have a lot on my plate. If one more crisis erupts, I'm going to call it a platter."

"What's his hurry? Seems to me, he's got other plans, don't you think?"

Cara shut down on her and got quiet.

Jennifer stated, changing the subject, "I picked Duncan's brain about this Joe Michaels. He's the alderman's top man.

"Really? How about that? The alderman is a member of my church," Cara said, and sat up straight. She sipped some more of her wine.

"You should sue him for some whiplash money."

"No, that's not my style." She sighed. "Besides, I'll be all right."

"Just a thought." Jennifer stammered.

"With all due respect," Cara smiled, "I thank you for your concern. One thing for sure, Mr. Michaels needs to slow down or one day he'll hit the wrong person. Someone who'll take him for all he's worth."

"I heard that." Jennifer downed the rest of her wine and she darted off to the kitchen for a refill.

A few minutes later, she returned holding her filled glass and the half empty bottle. It had surprised Cara that Jennifer drank a lot. Putting that aside, she figured Jennifer had something heavy on her mind.

Cara said, turning the heat on Jennifer. "I'm curious, what have you been up to lately?"

"Oh, nothing much," Jennifer responded quickly. Her eyebrows flickered a little. "Oh, you should come by and see my flower garden. It's simply beautiful this time of the year, if I may say so," she said, and finished another glass of wine.

"I'd love to," Cara replied. Some of your red peonies would work well in my living room."

"Great, I've got another great idea. Come work out with me at the YMCA. I get one free pass each month."

"Sounds like fun. When?"

"How about this Saturday?"

"It's a deal."

"I'll come by around 9:00 a.m., if that's okay."

"I'll be ready," Cara replied.

"Now tell me, how does it really feel to be single and free?" Jennifer probed.

"What can I say? I felt lonely a lot. But I'm getting used to it. Sometimes, I feel like crying. When I'm not feeling sorry for myself, I find so many other things to do."

"Have you considered getting out and meeting new people?"

"At times, but I'm not ready. A new man in my life is the last thing I need right now."

"Not that you have to go to bed with him. I thought it might be good just to talk and laugh and do fun things together," Jennifer spouted.

Cara grinned. "Sounds appealing, but not now."

"There's something I've learned about you tonight."

"Really, what's that?" Cara asked.

"You not only respect yourself, you know how to turn the favor. I like that about you."

"Thanks for the compliment. And, thanks for being my friend," Cara replied. She sensed something was wrong about Jennifer, but couldn't put her finger on it. For the moment, she had enough mess in her own life to work through.

Suddenly, the cheeriness in Jennifer's face swiftly died. She checked her watch and quickly turned to Cara.

"Hate to leave like this. There's something I've got to check out."

❧ ❧ ❧

Jennifer sped way in her maroon Skylark knowing she'd been totally dishonest with Cara. Yet Duncan was all she could deal with. She knew her husband was up to no good. She needed to prove it wasn't just her imagination. His excuse not to come home for dinner tonight was a political meeting.

Fifteen minutes later, she drove past Alderman Horace Tucker's ward office.

Duncan had lied again. The area looked like a ghost town.

Lately, Duncan showered before going to work splashing a new scent over his body. Before that, a bath the night before seemed enough. Now, he created reasons just to get away during the evening.

CHAPTER 8

Cara lifted the divorce petition papers from the kitchen counter and sat down at the table. She read the six-page document twice. Uncertain about the outcome, pain and isolation resurfaced. She thought, I know Mario's position about Ashley, so I won't worry about Bradley's threats. The one thing I want from him is child support.

She went to the computer room, clicked on Notepad and started to write in prioritized order, her immediate goals: *Find a lawyer. Find another job. Prove my innocence.* She thought, all are equally important, and yet more than ever I've got to find another job. The attorney must be paid.

Then as Cara always did before bedtime, she signed on AOL under her master screen name, CaraNchgo. She clicked the mouse once, twice, three times and the icons on the computer screen opened and departed at her command. Junk mail was deleted before reading her messages

Seconds before she switched screen names, she heard, You Got Mail! The message was from someone called, Green Lawn.

Opening it, Cara read:

"Just got a personal computer at home. Seems like everyone has one. I know that you left Mario. It's hard for me to believe any of the crap he told

Bradley and me. I care about what you have to say. This is my private e-mail address. Call me when you get this message."

Mary Lee Fleming

❦ ❦ ❦

Around 2:00 p.m., the next day at work, Cara ended her meeting with Teresa Peyton, a twenty-one year old mother desperately looking for her birth mother. Raped when she was sixteen, Teresa abused drugs and she prostituted for a living. Cara's heart wept for Teresa and she pledged to search the Internet to help her. Helping others is definitely the antibiotic. No one will know the despair I feel, she thought.

The phone rang, interrupting her thoughts.

"Good afternoon, Parent Child Care Agency, Cara Fleming speaking."

"Hi, this is Barbara Rhodes."

"Hello and how are you?" She asked thinking how odd it was to get a phone call on the job from the administrative assistant to the pastor.

"Oh, I'm fine," Barbara cheerfully responded. "Can you come by the office on your way home. I've got something to show you."

"Okay." Cara wondered, was it church related or what? She didn't belong to a church organization and was satisfied at the time being a bench member. Maybe she wants to ask me to join the Usher Board. "Can you tell me now?"

"I think it would be better not to talk about this over the phone."

And on those words, Cara panicked, hung up, grabbed her purse, tote bag, and hurried out the door at 2:45 p.m. They weren't exactly friends but they did see each other at church, however they really didn't know much about each other.

Still, Cara wondered if it had to do with her marital situation. Her spotless reputation meant a lot to her.

Stopped at the traffic light, she noticed the driver ahead of her refused to donate some coins to a soliciting homeless. As the man walked toward Cara's car, she noticed his dirty and torn clothing, and his stringy salt and pepper beard. Cara lifted two dollars from her purse and put the money in his hand. It hadn't mattered that she had only twenty dollars left and that payday was a week away.

He looked at her, smiled and said, "Bless you madam."

"May God bless you too, sir," she replied and smiled.

Thirty minutes later she parked her car in front of the church. The sun was still high in the sky, streaming through the windows. It seemed more like high noon, than 3:15 p.m. Before entering she stopped to say hello and shake hands with the church custodian and security guard. She walked up to the second floor slowly. Cara remembered Barbara's office was the corner one. She stood and took a deep breath and knocked once on the door, dreading the thought of what she'd learn.

✤ ✤ ✤

For the past twenty minutes, Barbara's thoughts had been on Lester Miller, the man she'd been madly in love with for more than a year. She had believed he was Mr. Right. Twice she'd seen him on dates with other women. A week ago, she finally broke off the relationship.

Suddenly she remembered she'd heard a knock at her door. A good hour too early for it to be the deacon, she thought. She opened the door and saw Cara Fleming who wasn't expected to arrive until after five.

"Hello. Come in." They gave each other the customary church-member hug.

"Hi, Barbara. I'm early. Do you mind?"

"No, don't be silly. Come in. Make yourself comfortable."

"It's good to see you." Cara sat down in one of the chairs facing the desk, hands folded. "How've you been?"

"Really well, and you?"

"Busy. Thanks for seeing me. I'm sure you're busy," Cara said, sounding apologetic.

"No problem. My next appointment is less than an hour from now. What I want to share with you is not earth shattering."

Involuntarily, Barbara recalled Joe Michaels' visit to her office yesterday. The look in Joe Michaels' eyes screamed serious business. Make sure that a lady named Cara Fleming knows about the job opening at Human Services. Do not mention the source of this information. Urge her to apply by August 15.

That a politician had gone to such trouble to help Cara caused her to want to know more. Was she married? Not once had she seen Cara at church services with a man. Lester cancelled a date to help a friend in trouble. His name was Mario Fleming. Could there be a connection?

Cara sat motionless. "Am I in trouble or something?"

"No," Barbara replied, pondering how she'd handle the matter with discreetness. "Someone who knows your credentials and work ethics asked me to tell you about a top-level job opening at Human Services. You should submit a resume right away."

Cara's eyebrows lifted. "A job with the city? You're kidding me?" she said, realizing she'd been wrong about Barbara's urgent phone call. She didn't know anyone in high places. She racked her brain and couldn't think of anyone who'd want to do her a favor. Maybe, this is the blessing I've been praying for, she thought. With God on my side, how can I lose?

"As elated as I am about this opportunity, who shall I thank?"

"I don't believe you know the person." Barbara reached for the ad Michaels had left with her, and handed it to Cara.

Still stunned, Cara quickly scanned the paper. "I _I thank you." She had wanted to but couldn't tell Barbara the real reason for her jubilation. That she'd left her husband and needed to make more money.

"If you're wondering who your benefactor is, don't ask. Some things are better left unknown. Besides, what does it matter anyway? Be happy and go for it."

"Yeah, maybe you're right," Cara said.

"Good. Try not to think about the messenger. Focus on the message. It's not everyday that the chance of a lifetime falls in your lap. I hear that the city pays really well, not to mention the benefits," Barbara said.

"I suppose. But since it's no secret that only a powerful politician can get someone a city job, do you honestly believe I'll get the job?"

She shrugged. "Your chances are probably 50-50, but don't let that discourage you."

"All right, I won't. Tell you what, I'll give it my best shot and then say a big prayer. Prayer changes things you know!" Cara said.

"Halleluiah, you go girl. By the way, mind if I ask you a personal question?"

Feeling the pressure, Cara asked, "What do you want to know?"

"I'm preparing invitations for our pastor's anniversary. It just occurred to me that we don't have your husband's name on the records."

Why am I surprised to know you weren't finished with me? Cara thought. "Oh, he's not a member," she replied, thinking Barbara would've known that. "His name is Mario."

"Good. Now the invitation will be addressed properly."

"I forgot to give you the new address and phone number," Cara said, covering her tracks.

"Really, I can record the information now." Barbara turned on the computer and updated the information. Then she faced Cara and said, "I'm glad you remembered to tell me."

Otherwise, the invitations would've come back here."

"Right," Cara said, checking her watch. Abruptly she stood up. "I've taken up enough of your time. Thanks a lot for the information."

"Sure, and God bless. Please, keep in touch, okay?" Barbara said, and walked her to the door.

"I'll do that, and thanks again."

After Cara left, Barbara's thoughts drifted back to that night Lester had to meet his buddy. As small as the world had seemed at times, she figured that this person had to be the same Mario Fleming. Lester postponed their date because of him. Cara and Mario aren't together anymore. Now, a politician is helping her anonymously, she concluded.

While driving, Cara noticed a man in a white sedan following her. Later on, he had vanished. Relieved, she reflected on how well the day had gone for her. It was a good day. Barbara gave her reason to be hopeful.

She stopped at the Food Exchange on Seventy-Ninth Street. Just as she stepped out of her car, she observed what looked like the same white car stop along the street. The driver, who she couldn't recognize, continued to sit inside with the engine running.

Cara's heart seemed to beat in her throat. "For some reason, someone is following me," she said and quickly drove to her apartment.

CHAPTER 9

It was a quarter to seven that evening when Mary Lee Fleming sat staring at the welcome screen on American Online. The home computer and private lessons had been a gift from Bradley. Worrying about Mario, she shut down the computer she called *Sweet Pea* and reflected on a phone conversation she had with Mario a week ago:

"Hello, son. I've been trying to reach you."

"Hi mama. Just walked in the door when the phone rang. So how're you doing down there in Memphis?"

"I'm fine. Your dad's fine, I suppose. So tell me what's going on? I worry all the time about you."

"Not much to tell. What's up with daddy?"

"Funny you asked. He's not himself lately. I suspect it has to do with your breakup with Cara."

"Oh, really?"

"Does your father know something I don't?"

"Can't keep nothing from you, can I? Dad knows all about Cara's affair. I told him the day after I discovered the truth," Mario said.

"I don't believe that she'd do something like that. Not the Cara Slater-Fleming I know."

"The caller told me things that he could only know if he'd seen her naked. What do you think about that? Still think she is an angel?"

Mary Lee remembered closing up on him and didn't respond.

"Did you hear anything I said?" he asked.

"Yes." Her voice drifted into a hushed whisper. "I need to ask you something. Did you think to check out this man's story? Or, whether she took off sick from the job, when and how often? Did she change in anyway at home and with you? Things like that?"

"Well, now that you mentioned it. No, I didn't. There wasn't time. I was angry. I was hurt and I just exploded. I did offer her a way to save the marriage."

"Really, what was that?"

"I gave my word that I'd forgive her. All she had to do was confess and apologize."

She remembered how they had spoiled him with enough material things and not enough common sense. She began to wonder what else the Fleming men were hiding.

"Seems to me you didn't do enough to prevent this breakup," she said.

"You want to know the truth? She can't admit she's wrong, because all her life she's been Miss Perfect. Why would she admit to her wrongdoing?" Mario squawked.

Mary Lee realized then, it was useless to get through to him. "As usual, you're letting your anger rule you and not your heart. You should get professional counseling. I hear that it can help."

"No way. I don't like the idea of talking about my situation with a stranger. How're you getting along with Cara's mother?"

"Naomi and I are still friends. A friendship like ours is hard to come by. She's a good woman and someone nice to talk to. Your father on the other hand, has cooled his relationship with Cara's parents. Wish I knew why."

Realizing the damage her son has caused, Mary Lee decided to salvage her losses and called Cara. Besides she loved Cara like a daughter. And, now she needed to convince Cara of that.

"Hi Cara, how you?"

"Hi, Mother Fleming. I'm doing fine and you?"

"I'm all right. It's been too long, I couldn't let another day go by without talking to you."

Mary Lee announced she had a new computer and that she was trying to learn how to operate it. From there, the conversation veered to Cara.

"All I need to know is, were you involved with another man?"

"Absolutely not. Not then, and not now."

"Did you mention your birthmark to anyone other than Mario?"

"No, I haven't. Something personal, like that, no," Cara said, voice raised.

"According to Mario, the caller knew about it."

"But how? Who would've told a stranger about her birthmark? Mario is lying. I've come to believe he actually wanted out the marriage."

"I hate *not* to believe my son, but your explanation is a logical one."

"Mario didn't tell me what the caller said. It was like I didn't need to know."

"My dear, know that I'm in your corner. Okay?"

"Thanks, it helps to know that." On the tip of Cara's tongue, was to tell Mary Lee that Mario had ordered her out of the condo. But she couldn't. "In case you don't know, he's filed for a divorce."

"Oh, no. He didn't. I'm so sorry," Mary Lee stammered, and paused. "Call me if you need help, okay?"

"I will, and thank you," Cara said.

* * *

Cara thought about her promise to help the day care mother.

She signed onto AOL and entered Family.Com. She browsed chat rooms and read message boards. She clipped snippets of information on finding biological parents. Then she noticed the icon, Chat Room Host and clicked on it. The first host had done community social work for fifteen years. She had worked with hundreds of people from all over the U.S. and internationally. The second host was the mother of two adopted grown sons whose life experience had run the gamut from single mom to online chat host. Cara became impressed and e-mailed them.

With no social life hardly, Cara knew she had the time. Helping lost children would become her main cyberspace agenda. It was then that she decided to become an advocate for lost children.

Later, she checked the main page on Family.Com and found helpful information for Theresa. She printed addresses and phone numbers for agencies and organizations in Illinois.

Twenty minutes later, she joined a chat room called, Wayward Friends. There were fifteen roomies. The conversation proved interesting. Scrolling up and down she viewed screen names, searched for profiles and to her surprise several had created a personal bio.

Then she heard the Instant Message beep. The small screen magically appeared in the top left corner on her monitor. It was from someone named, *MattIwas.*

"Hi, Current wife, you're awfully quiet. A few minutes ago, I saw you in Lost Children and then you left. Looking for your folks, too?"

"Hi, Matt. No, I'm trying to help a young woman find her birth mother. How about you?"

MattIwas responded: "When I was five years old, a strange man and a woman took me from my mother's car. We parked at a gas station. She went inside to pay for the gas. That's when they took me away. My daddy stayed home with my baby brother. That was thirty years ago. I'm looking for my birth family."

"Why don't we meet in a private room?" Cara typed.

"Why not? I can use some advice," *MattIwas* responded.

"I'll name it "Lost Children00. Give me a minute to set it up. Watch for the small screen inviting you to come in and click, *Enter*."

Within a few seconds, it was done and MattIwas entered.

"Okay, this is better. Can you tell me more?" Cara typed.

"Sure. The man who called himself my father, physically abused me until I ran away at the age of fifteen. I lived on the streets for a few days until I met a former prostitute named, Odessa. She let me live with her. I stayed there, worked after school until I graduated high school. By then, I had saved enough money to leave her abode."

"I'm so sorry. You must be really desperate to see your real parents. Do you remember their names? Where you lived at the time?"

"Vaguely. Mother's name was either Martha or Margaret. Don't have a clue about dad's or my brother's name. That's the thing I've struggled with for so long."

"It must've been awful for you to have blocked out such details."

"Yes. No one could imagine what it was like. At first the people who took me were nice trying to get me to like them. When I realized my folks weren't going to find me, I got angry with them and the world. Most of the time I was depressed and in shock. I took my anger out on the folks who abducted me. I never really accepted them. I could write a movie about my life, it has been just that interesting."

"I'm sure," Cara typed.

"Enough about me, what about the young mother you're helping."

"When she turned twelve, she accidentally discovered her mother gave her up for adoption the same day she was born. At sixteen, she was raped and gave birth to a son. Secretly she tried to find her real mother up until she finished high school. Her life has been difficult. Unable to retain a steady job forced her to live an unsafe life in the projects. In spite of repeated arrests for prostitution, she continued to sell sexual favors in order to pay the bills. The son is in day care and he has developmental and emotional problems."

MattIwas responded: "Gee, what a bomber."

"Tell me about it," Cara typed. Can you imagine what it's like having to sleep around with all sorts of men just to eat and pay a few bills?"

"I suppose. No, I just told you a lie. I know what it's like. I'll tell you the rest. After all, we're talking anonymously," he responded.

"True. It's what I like about chat room talks. You can share your darkest secrets. No one will ever know who you are," Cara typed.

MattIwas responded: "Here's the rest. I had this idea I could get rich quick running a pimp business, not like any other. I secured the clientele, arranged the fees up front and provided the love-nest in my four-bedroom apartment. It kept the girls off the street and out of jail. We split the money 50-50. When one of them had saved enough money to get on their feet and move on to a better life, I allowed it. The girls were runaway teens. I kept no more than three at a time. It wasn't a pretty life. But they were safe and I took good care of them. So you see, I do understand and I hate the day care mother has to suffer like that."

"How long were you in business?" Cara typed, wanting to ask if he had sex with them, too.

"Three years. I got caught. It's a long story, so I'll spare you. Anyway, I went to prison, served my time and while in there, I realized that I wasn't cut out to do that sort of thing. Charge it to family genes handed down to me from a heritage I know nothing about. So I got a job selling cars, was good at it, too. Luckily I stashed some money from the business and worked by day and took college courses at night. I got my degree and new career. Now, I need to find my birth family. It's the only thing left for me to achieve and then I'll be truly happy."

"I'm so proud you turned your life around in spite of the obstacles dealt you," Cara typed.

"Thanks. You seem to like helping folks like me. That's good. I could use your help, too," He responded.

"I'd love too. Where should we begin?"

"The basics. I just bought my computer. I'm still learning how to get around on AOL, let alone the Internet." He responded.

"No problem. I'll e-mail you something soon, maybe tonight."

Cara left their private room and clicked on links to other websites. Compelled by his story, she decided to help him, and she believed he felt her compassion toward him. And, she thought, we've established a secret cyberspace bond. Nothing said would reveal our identity.

CHAPTER 10

On Saturday, Cara looked forward to working out at the gym with Jennifer. As soon as she was dressed in a light blue jogging suit, Jennifer called at 8:20 a.m. and canceled their workout without any explanation. She promised to call back later. Somewhat baffled, Cara decided to make good use of the extra time and took care of her outside errands.

She returned home shortly before 1:00 that afternoon. She read her mail, put away the groceries and folded laundry. Soon her thoughts drifted to Jennifer. She's hiding something. Was it her job or marital problems?

She was reminded about her own situation with Mario. As bad as I hurt today, I remember how good it once felt to be with him and that time apart seemed like an eternity and time together never seemed long enough. I miss that glorious time in our relationship, she thought. How could he not care enough to want to learn the truth?

Putting that aside, she turned on her computer, she checked for e-mail from MattIwas and researched information on marriage and adultery.

Finding nothing from her online buddy, she entered iVillage.com. The article for today appeared in a large blue icon: *How Women Feel About Adultery.* All she had to do was click it on. Once on the page, she moved the mouse down and slowly letting her mind absorb interesting messages: "*The betrayed person feels terribly. But he didn't listen to the distress signs. A relationship is like a fire. You can let it go down, but you can't let it go out. Even though you're in another part of the house, you have to go back every once in a while to stoke the coals.*"

On those words she knew she had been on the right track to rekindle the passion between her and Mario. She remembered his affair, but never understood why he broke his marriage vows and hurt her dearly. She read on: "*Men are actually more likely to have extramarital affairs—because they split sex and affection. There are the nice girls you marry and the wild girls you have sex with. The double standard is alive and well.*"

Then she clicked on the message board to find out what other people thought and had to say about the subject of adultery.

Subject: How can women stay with men who have affairs?

"*They don't want to be alone. Children are involved. They lack the means to make it on their own. To sum it all up, they stay because the price is right.*"

Subject: How Women Feel About Adultery?

(1)"Affairs are often a chance to try out something new."

(2)"*When someone starts confiding things to another woman it creates an emotional intimacy that is greater in the friendship than in the marriage. One quick way to start an affair is when a man confides negative things about his marriage. What they're doing is signaling: I'm vulnerable; I may even be available.*"

Cara found it all interesting and yet disturbing, particularly the last one. She thought, if I live to be a hundred and ten, I'll never get accept the reasons for cheating in a marriage. Color me old-fashioned, color me anything, I just can't stomach sleeping with another man while I'm married.

❧ ❧ ❧

At noontime on Monday, Cara arrived at Human Services.

"Good afternoon, may I help you?" The polite middle age receptionist looked up and asked.

"Hello, I'm Cara Fleming." She gave her the brown envelope containing her updated resume. "This is for Mr. Dunlap. Will you see that he gets it?"

"Sure, Ms. Fleming."

"Thank you very much. Have a good day."

On the elevator down, Cara thought, I've taken a bold step to help myself. Nothing comes to those who sit and wait for a miracle to fall in their lap. I need this job like I need a head on my shoulder.

After she arrived home it was almost 6:00 in the evening. She contacted a divorce lawyer Jennifer had recommended. No sooner than she hung up, the phone rang three times. All were from unknown callers. She wondered if the anonymous calls were from Mario.

CHAPTER 11

Two days later, Cara quietly walked inside the law offices of Jesse Garnell and Associates. She wore a two-piece beige shirt suit she bought at Marshall Fields a year ago. According to Jennifer, the lawyer was the best on the south side and affordable. In her mind, the office looked more like downtown Chicago than a neighborhood law establishment. It was well decorated, combining contemporary with afro-centric themes, and some very fine paintings. His wife had hired a young aspiring black interior decorator recently featured in Ebony Magazine.

"Come in, Ms. Fleming. I'm attorney Garnell." He wore a gray suit, appeared to be forty-something, average height, was slender and he wore sparkling jewelry on his hand.

They shook hands and she sat down in a blue and white striped club chair. Fresh coffee permeated the air.

"It's nice to meet you," she replied and handed him the divorce petition.

"Good, same here." His smiled was comforting.

He offered her coffee while he read the document. Later he pounded her with questions. Tired of reliving the ordeal, she forced herself to tell him what he needed to know. This time she didn't omit the oblivious demand by her husband, *I want your ass out of here.*

"Your husband has put you between a rock and a hard place. Can you prove your whereabouts during that time period?"

"Yes. We're required to maintain Daily Time Records. My secretary can pull the files at your request."

"Oh, good, were you absent much?"

"I took a sick day a few days ago, due to whiplash. Fortunately, I survived a car mishap just a few days ago." She gave him the details.

He presented options for how he could get support for their daughter. He promised to contact Mario's lawyer right away and get the show on the road. Cara signed a bunch of papers and she wrote a check for five hundred dollars to cover one-half of the attorney's costs.

"I'm not sure how this could've happened to you. I'll admit it'll be hard to disprove the adultery allegation. But, I can guarantee you that I'll to get support for your daughter."

"That's a relief. It's all I want from him."

CHAPTER 12

Four days later, Cara was pumped up about her interview with Human Services director, Carl Dunlap. She was dressed to impress in a dark brown, pinned striped, three-piece suit and one inch matching heels. Hair freshly shampooed, full of bounce, and flowing down her back.

At 10:30 a.m. she parked her car at a parking garage four blocks from the building. Any other time, I'd stuff coins in a meter and walk as many as twelve blocks just to save some money. I don't mind it this time. The nine-dollar per hour rate is a sound investment toward the job I need, she thought.

Ten minutes later, she appeared at his office door.

"Come in," Dunlap said. He gave her a professional but impressive smile. His square, light skinned-face handsomely set off with his thick, black curly hair and a matching moustache.

For a moment, she questioned his ethnic origin. Cara moistened her semi-dry lips to get the courage to speak. "Good morning. Thank you for seeing me," she politely spoke and quickly sat down on one of the black and white striped chairs facing his massive oak desk.

Right away, he looked at her carefully and thought she was rather cute. He wondered if she could handle the job.

"So, how're things at Parent's Child Care Center?" Dunlap asked, shifting around in his chair.

"Really good, actually," she replied.

"Talk to me about why I should consider you for the Curriculum Coordinator's position."

"Besides my credentials and work experience, I believe I can make positive changes for preschool children on the south side." She sensed she'd gotten his attention.

"Sounds good. Please continue."

"I view the role of Curriculum Coordinator to be that of a leader, someone who can teach as well as motivate the adults: managers, teaching staff and parents. In less than a year, I've been able to make a lot of progress in that area."

"Yes, I'm aware. Word gets around you know and you're to be congratulated. I'm curious, how would you achieve such a goal here?"

She thought for a quick moment. "During the past five years I've learned that employee attitude makes a difference in job performance. They need to know they're appreciated. If they do, they'll work harder," she expounded, taking a moment to gather her breath. "What seems to work well for me is a philosophy I brought from the south."

"Oh yeah, what's that?" He asked, shifting his body around in his chair.

"To be fair, firm and friendly; and not necessarily in that order." Dunlap almost choked on his cigar smoke. He sat erect, facing Cara.

"Cara, I must say, your philosophy is definitely one to model. Don't believe I've heard anyone, man or woman put it so simply."

"Thank you," she replied.

"So tell me, how has it worked for you?"

"Well, for one thing, it helped to win the respect of the people I work with. Actually, they trust me and they know, among all other things, I'll be fair."

"What has been your greatest reward?"

"The achievement of a true team spirit. We hardly ever hear people saying things like, "That's my job, you do it, or I've done my part, now you do yours."

"I see," he said, looking down at his notes. "However, this job involves working with more people than you're accustomed. Why do you believe you can change varying institutional habits and attitudes of people in decision-making roles?"

"Mr. Dunlap, with all due respect," she said, and with a smile and gleam in her eyes, "I can be elastic like a rubber band when it comes to dealing with people. But on the other hand, I can be a fierce fighter when it comes to a worthwhile cause," she told him. "Children, particularly, the younger ones are definitely worth the effort."

"And I agree with you, Ms. Fleming. Somehow that cause seems to always get pushed aside. I see it all the time, even in this department," Dunlap replied, as the intensity in his voice lowered.

"Adults are the most important educators in a child's life," she continued.

"Good point! Is there more?"

"You bet, Mr. Dunlap. When the community-at-large is successful, the department looks good and so will you," she pointed out. At that moment, she didn't know if she won him over or turned him off completely.

"Amazing, just amazing," he replied. "There's one last question, are you aware that working for the city means having to sometimes deal with things that require more than your ability to motivate and inspire?"

Think positive, she thought. He might be trying to ruffle your feathers just to see what you're made of. "If you're referring to the game of politics, yes! I'm aware of that element of the job." That was not a question she expected, hoping she had scored. "Such an influence can be a barrier, but it's not one that would stop me. Besides I love a challenge. It'll just make me work harder," she added.

She's done her homework, Dunlap thought. "You sound pretty sure of yourself," he said, with a trace of laughter in his voice.

Taking the expression on his face as a compliment, Cara smiled and waited for him to speak. He didn't move an inch and suddenly offered her coffee. Perhaps, my answers exhausted him. After a few minutes of chatting more about the department's goals, people relation issues, he thanked her and promised to give her application a thoughtful review.

She drove home less than an hour later thinking she couldn't ever remember having a single job interview exhaust her as much as the one with Earl Dunlap. He shot questions at me faster than the speed of a bullet. Maybe he will or maybe he won't consider me for the job. Without political support, I doubt it, she thought.

She decided not to fret much. She'd given her best to impress him.

CHAPTER 13

Three days later, Cara's eyes shined as bright as the sun had shined through the kitchen window that morning. She poured a glass of orange juice and thought about how her life, and how far she'd come, hoping her situation would change for the better.

At 8:45 a.m. she walked in her office. On her desk was a message from Earl Dunlap. She rushed to pick up the phone to dial his number, knocking over the cup of hot coffee onto the floor. "Doggone it. What a mess!" she jested while she waited for him to answer.

"Dunlap speaking."

"Hello, Mr. Dunlap. This is Cara Fleming returning your call," she spoke in a tone that was as professional as she could manage.

"Oh, yes. How are you Ms. Fleming?"

"I'm fine, thank you. How're you?"

"Terrific," he said and paused. "How does forty-one thousand a year sound?"

"Oh, my God," she paused for a moment. I got the job?"

"Yes, you got it."

"I'm so thrilled, thank you Mr. Dunlap." She could barely get it all out trying not to sound like a bumbling idiot. That means, I'll make fifteen thousand more per year, she thought.

"Well, it wasn't easy. There were two other strong contenders, with a great deal more experience," he admitted. "But, that's all they had over you. What they lacked was something you got, and a whole lot more besides."

"That being?"

"Having strength and vision. You can hold your own young lady. You can see ten thousand miles down the road, while some people I know can only see as far as they can spit."

"I'm overwhelmed but especially so pleased to be thought of like that," Cara said, thinking he was one who spoke his mind without hesitation. And, for the first time in her life, she was almost speechless, filled with a tremendous sense of accomplishment. "If you'll excuse me, Mr. Dunlap, I feel the urge to shout for joy."

He laughed and she started to laugh, too.

"I can see this means a lot to you."

"Yes, more than you'll ever know. And, Mr. Dunlap, I promise to work hard to get the job done."

"That I believe. Can you start in two weeks?"

"Absolutely."

Dunlap advised her to keep the orientation appointment.

"Ms. Fleming?"

"Yes?"

"Welcome aboard. You're in the tough lanes now!"

Around noontime, the cadence of his words still rang in her head like a nonstop drumbeat. She could picture herself standing before a large audience of teachers and administrators saying: "I'm Cara Fleming, Curriculum Coordinator for the south side. I want to take you on a new journey. I invite you to join me."

She put the In-Conference sign on the outside of her office door, locked the door and fell down on her mahogany, executive style chair and closed her eyes. She prayed and cried tears of joy undisturbed for a few minutes.

Then she thought about her parents and dialed the number.

"Hello," Frank answered.

"Hi, Daddy. I've something good to tell you."

"My Lord! Tell me before I burst open."

"I've been hired by a major city department earning a hell of a lot more money."

"You're kidding, for real?"

"It's true," she exclaimed.

"I'm proud of you. Congratulations."

"How's my little girl? I miss her, daddy." Cara quickly asked.

"I know you do. She's doing fine. Right now she's taking a nap."

"Is mom home?"

"She's out to lunch with Mary Lee."

"Okay, tell her my good news. I'll call her later this evening. And, Daddy, tell Ashley I love her."

"I will. But before you go, remember to be careful. Work hard and get your life in order. Ashley will be just fine down here with us," he said, and hesitated. "Another thing, don't forget to check your gas meter often. Never let your car get past a half tank of gas. In case I haven't already mentioned it, carry a can of mace in your purse. I don't want to think about you running out of gas on a street somewhere all alone."

"Oh, daddy. I promise to do all the things you've taught me."

Cara breezed through two brief staff meetings, ordered supplies, and completed two reports by 5:30 p.m.

At 6:00 p.m., she drove home and as she turned onto Columbus Drive, a black Infinity darted over in her lane. The driver followed her.

It was not until she'd reached 57th and Lake Shore Drive that she knew he was stalking her. By then, another vehicle had merged between them distracting a closer view of his face and license plate. The lanes were jammed with rush hour traffic. Even if she had tried, she couldn't have escaped him.

Why would someone do this? Mario, she concluded. Does he actually believe I'm seeing someone else and need to get more evidence? It would help his case against me, she pondered. She further thought, Mario took away my joy and damn near ruined my life trying to be free of me. But he won't take away my spirit.

Thirty minutes later Cara reached the Seventy-First Street and South Shore Drive juncture. The driver turned left on South Shore Drive. Relieved, she remained on course and drove home. She had started to watch everyone. Daddy will be proud, she thought.

When she parked her car at the apartment a few minutes later, Cara checked and didn't see the black Infinity. She quickly entered her apartment, tossed the mail on the sofa, opened a can of tuna, made a tossed salad and decided to get on-line. She had thought all day about her newfound buddy, MattIwas, wondering who he might be, what he looked like, where he actually lived, and what type of person he was. Questions, she knew could never be answered. "One thing I do know, MattIwas is a man," she said.

After she finished eating, she left e-mail messages for Mary Lee and Jennifer telling them about her new job. She didn't tell them how much she would earn.

Then, she read Matt's e-mail: "Hi, Current Wife. I've been busy following through on your suggestions. Got booted offline a few times. Back to square one. Meet me in our private room at 9:00 tonight".

Cara checked her watch. She had three hours to kill. After she fixed a peanut butter and jelly sandwich for lunch the next day, rolled her hair, she soaked in a hot tub of fragrant bubbles. Listening to slow jams on V103 FM, helped the time to past quickly. Too bad, she thought, I can't share this moment with someone special.

At 9:00 a.m., she waited for MattIwas in their private room and thought, I will tell him my secret. It'll be okay.

Suddenly, he entered the private room.

"Hi, C'Wife. How was your day?"

"Fine. I've something to share with you." Cara typed.

"Lay it on me." He responded.

"It's complicated, so, I'll be brief. I've left my husband. Someone told my husband I was having an affair. It's possible he created this lie. I believe he's in love with another woman. He refuses to pay child support for our daughter, claiming she's not his child. He's filed for a divorce." Cara noticed *MattIwas* didn't type a response while she poured out her troubles. "That's my story. What do you think? Any suggestions for how I can find out who did this?" She typed.

"I'm so sorry this happened to you. <Sobbing> Life can be a bitch at times. Where are you?" He responded.

"Chicago. "Where are you?" Cara typed.

"Small world, isn't it? I'm in Chicago, too. I got to run, see you tomorrow. Same time?"

"Sure, in the meantime, good luck finding your family!" She typed.

Cara thoughts about their chat bothered her. Why didn't he say more? Did he care about my problem? Oh boy, I told him too much too soon. But then she thought, all he knows is that we both live in Chicago. He doesn't know my name.

Cara left the room and noticed MattIwas had signed offline. Curious, she checked and learned he didn't have a profile.

CHAPTER 14

Cara dazzled over how beautiful Chicago was in August. A city filled with tourists from all over the world to see the fabulous attractions in the windy city. People covered miles of beaches along the shores of Lake Michigan. Love and romance filled the air.

But she had more important things on her mind.

On Thursday, she waited in the conference room for her orientation session. Clearly, an interior decorator had worked miracles. She glanced the satiny parquet floors, partially covered with beautiful Persian carpet, and antique tables and lamps. Also appealing were live plants trailing from hand painted pots. She had a flair for that sort of thing, having once considered studying interior decoration in college. Instead she chose primary education and now she was glad she did.

Minutes later, a young woman of Hispanic origin, attractive, nicely dressed lady, wearing a department ID badge walked in the room and greeted her.

"Hello, I'm Karen Baker. It's good to finally meet you."

"The pleasure is all mine, Ms. Baker," Cara responded with a smile and a handshake.

"Good, then let's get started, shall we?"

Cara followed her to a small, private room.

Within an hour, Cara had completed and signed a stack of forms and posed for her job I.D. badge. Later she reviewed her job description, work schedule, agency assignments, and protocol procedures. She was given several brochures, recent department memos, and the operational manual to take home.

"Excited?"

"Yes, and you've been a great help, Ms. Baker."

"Just doing my job, dear. Is there anything else you'd like to ask me?"

"No, I don't believe so." Cara stood and smiled. "Well, thanks again. I'll see you on August 1st." She waved goodbye.

Cara approached the elevator a few minutes later. The door opened. Two men hurried off. The tall muscular man with a thick moustache was Duncan Tate.

"Hi, Duncan." She greeted him warmly.

"Hello," he replied, returning her smile. She'd met Duncan right after she and Jennifer became friends. "Cara Fleming, right?"

"Yes, it's me. How are you?"

"I'm okay. Surprised to see you. What're doing here?"

"Would you believe I just got hired?" Cara announced.

"Good for you. Congratulations."

"Thanks," she replied and forced herself to look at the other man who seemed familiar. He had a face too cute for a man and his hair was slicked back on his head. She shuddered, wondering if she was losing her touch. Duncan hadn't introduced him, so, she smiled and turned her attention back to Duncan.

"It was good seeing you. Tell Jennifer I'll call her."

Later as she fought the traffic on Michigan Avenue, somehow she didn't mind the crawly lines of cars bumper to bumper, or hundreds of pedestrians trying to cross Michigan Avenue. From Cara's research about Chicago, she remembered at least a million people piled the downtown area leaving work this time of day. She'd never been able to imagine it, but today she understood.

Her mind started to drift back to Duncan Tate and the guy whose image she couldn't shake. Frustrated that she couldn't remember where she'd seen him, she decided to concentrate on his eyes and mouth. Nothing, not a clue popped into her mind. Maybe, there was something about his hair that was different from before. She'd always been able to put two and two together and get ten. It'll come one day, Cara, she thought.

An hour later she arrived home and glanced at Mrs. Walker watering the potted marigolds in the yard. They chatted a few minutes and then Cara got her mail and went inside to chill.

After a long stimulating shower, she ate the leftover tuna salad, freshly made salad and a can of pineapple for desert. Feeling grateful she'd have nearly six hundred dollars once the bills were paid, she developed a new budget. Some of it would go to her parents to help with Ashley and the rest to her savings account.

Later, she signed online and checked her buddy screen. MattIwas did not appear in her buddy list. Scrolling through her e-mail messages, she was disappointed to find nothing from him.

Since Bradley had fallen asleep earlier than usual, Mary Lee decided to call Cara around 7:30 p.m.

"Hi, how're things going with the care parent? Were you able to help her?" Mary Lee prodded.

"I'm happy to say, that I was. Oh, that one was easy," she replied. "Would you believe, I'm helping someone over the Internet find his birth family? What's strange is, I don't know this person's identity."

Suddenly Mary Lee thought about her older son who died in a tragic fire not long after he was abducted. She knew all too well how it felt to lose someone special. "Really? I'm impressed," she said and hesitated. "I'm curious, what else did this person tell you?"

Cara reached for the printed sheets from her chats with MattIwas. "Okay, I'm referring to my notes: Abducted at the age of five__."

"That's sad, to be taken away from your parents like that. "How old is he now?"

"Thirty-five."

"Does he remember where he was abducted?"

"Yes, according to him, that's one thing he's always remembered. He was with his mother one day. She stopped to get some gas. She left him in the car while she went inside the station to pay for the gas. A man and woman approached the car, claiming his mother had taken ill. He never saw his family again."

"Oh my goodness, what's this man's screen name?

"MattIwas," Cara said.

"What kind of name is that?"

"That's the way it is in cyberspace," Cara replied. "People can call themselves whatever, as long as the screen name is not already in use," Cara said.

Mary Lee coughed uncontrollably and her breathing seemed irregular.

"Are you okay, Mother Fleming?"

"Yes, I think so," she said, continuing to sound as though she wasn't. "Where do I go to learn more about screen names?"

Once Cara was sure her mother-in-law had AOL 6.0, she told her how to create a screen name. "You are allowed up to seven different names __.

"Thanks for your help. I'm still new at this."

By the end of their talk, Cara felt strange about Mary Lee's intentions. Does she think I'm lying about my online buddy? Or, is she playing amateur detective, thinking this guy might be my lover?

CHAPTER 15

No sooner than Mary Lee had hung up, she remembered her promise to Bradley. She remembered the devastation; shame and guilt, she and Bradley felt when they learned their oldest son, died in a tragic house fire along with his abductors. Bradley had refused to take a lie-down and die attitude. Within a month after the abduction, he hired a black investigator to locate Matthew. That effort failed. Heartbroken, feeling helpless and ultimate despair, they sold their home in Greenwood, Mississippi and moved to Memphis. Memory that the older son existed was permanently removed. Mary Lee was sworn to a lifelong secrecy. Not even Mario knew he had a brother. But no one felt more blame than did Mary Lee. He was taken while in her care. This man has got to be my son, she thought.

An hour later, she created a new screen name, Leewoman44. Cara would never be the wiser. Then, she placed MattIwas on her Buddy List, and entered Family.Com. Seconds later, she noticed he was online, too. Realizing she needed answers, she send him an instant message.

MattIwas browsed around the main page for a few minutes. Just as he joined a chat room discussion, the instant message screen sound beeped. Instantly, he figured it was Current Wife, but as he took a peek, he saw the unfamiliar screen name.

"Hello," *Leewoman44* greeted him.

"Hello. Who are you?" *MattIwas* typed. He'd only chatted with Current Wife. Then he thought, after my last chat with her, I believe I know her true identity. It can't be anyone but Cara Fleming. Her words still rang in his head: *I was framed as an adulteress. My marriage was ruined. I live in Chicago.* Out of curiosity, he decided to confirm it.

"Possibly, someone you're looking for," *Leewoman44* responded.

"Oh, yeah," *MattIwas* typed. Still looking at the instant message screen, he thought Leewoman44 could be an innocent bystander he missed seeing in the chat rooms. "Okay, Leewoman, what's up?" He typed.

"Hope you don't think I'm crazy. I'm looking for my son. His name was Matthew. "It's been so long. Haven't seen him in thirty years. Losing him almost destroyed us."

"Hold on, I'll be right back." He stood up from the computer, paced the floor for a few minutes, poured a straight shot of gin and returned to read what Leewoman44 had said again. He thought he was dreaming. Who else would know my exact situation? What should I say? I need time to think.

A minute later, he typed, "Your story is similar to mine. But I need to know a few things like: Where do you live, how did you find me on-line? Are you willing to meet me?"

"Sure, I can do that. My name is Mary Lee Fleming. I need answers too. Just think about it. If you must know, I got your name from Current Wife. She's my daughter-in-law. I live with my husband, Bradley, in Memphis. When you're ready, e-mail me." She responded.

"I just might do that. I'll get back to you later, okay?" He typed.

Alderman Bennett signed offline, his body rocked, mixed feelings bombarded his heart, insecurity about the future and his new life in

Chicago, thrust through his mind. Suddenly it hit him. Current Wife was without a doubt, Cara Fleming. Could it be that her mother-in-law was his real mother?

CHAPTER 16

Mary Lee thought about how she would tell Bradley she needed to go to Chicago, alone. But now, I've done a terrible thing to Cara. MattIwas knows more than he should about her, she thought. Finally, she concluded it unimportant, especially if he turned out to be her son.

The next day the e-mail she hoped for arrived: "If you want to know if I'm your son, meet me in Chicago on Monday morning, 9:15 at the Hampton Inn. It's near Midway Airport. Remember, come alone."

She had never traveled anywhere without Bradley, and somehow, she had to find a way to go to Chicago without him. It's now or never, she thought.

Bradley came home from work, at exactly 5:15 p.m. He seemed exhausted, telling her he'd had a rough day in the sun and that he needed to lie down for a few minutes. She brought him a glass of water and left him alone to relax before dinner was ready.

Forty minutes later, he woke up and came to dinner. His favorite meal was on the table: baked chicken, southern-style succotash, string beans, buttered homemade rolls, ice tea; for dessert, she served fruit laced-Jell-O topped with fresh mint leaves. He seemed fresh from his nap. She mostly listened to Bradley talk about his schedule for the next week: A meeting with the Memphis Businessmen Association, a hundred and ten lawns to cut, and a landscape to build for two new construction homes.

After dinner, they finished their second glass of ice tea laced with fresh lemon slices. They sat in the white, two-seater near several red and yellow Rose bushes.

"Would you mind if I go Chicago for a couple of days?"

"What're you up to now? When were you planning to leave?"

"Monday morning, early."

"That's two days away, what's the rush? Is it Mario?"

"Yes and I'm concerned about him. What mother wouldn't be?"

"Did it ever occur to you that I would want to go, too? Wait until next weekend? I'll join you." She didn't respond. Bradley rattled on and on letting her know he suspected she wasn't being truthful.

She folded her hands and started to worry. She knew she had an obligation to be honest with Bradley. During their thirty-seven year marriage, lying to him was a no-no. She trusted him and he trusted her.

"Mary Lee, what on earth is the matter with you?"

"Oh, you won't believe what has happened."

"What did Mario do now? Is he hurt?"

"No, it's not about that son."

A probing query came into his eyes. "We have but one son."

Right away, she knew that Bradley couldn't mention Matthew's name, not even to her. I've been punished long enough and need to be strong for a change, she thought. "What if I told you it's possible Matthew didn't die?"

Bradley turned abruptly to look at her. "I don't believe you said his name. You promised never to mention that name again. Didn't we suffer enough over his loss?" he sniffed, holding onto his chair.

"If I go to Chicago, I can verify whether or not he's our son. Don't you think I deserve to do that, after all, I lost him?" She told him about Cara's involvement and how she'd talked with the man through e-mail and instant messages.

"Does Cara know this man?"

"No, of course not. Anyway, the man described exactly where and how he was abducted, whom he was with, and the age he was at the time. That's too much of a coincidence for me," she added.

"So Cara's been a regular busy body. That's probably how she ruined her marriage. Poor Mario!"

"Why are you so down on your daughter-in-law? I've talked with her. What she had to say convinced me she was framed, Bradley. Anyway, she's a woman with strong convictions and she's nobody's pushover. Just watch, she's going to be an important leader someday."

"That'll be the day. She needs to get her own life in order before she attempts to lead others." His shoulders slumped. "Look, I'm so tired. First, it was your crusade for Cara. Now you're on our dead son's bandwagon. Who's it going to be next? Shouldn't it be the son who's alive and trying to move on with his life?" He gestured with his hands and hit the flowerpot on the table between them.

With her face distracting him, the words took a second to sink in. But when they did, the enormity of her decision __hope of finding her son alive, hope for her family, clicked in her mind. Without a word, she stood and walked inside the house leaving Bradley, high and dry.

CHAPTER 17

❀

By now, Cara felt important and was pleased. Worry about how she'd survived, gone with the wind. She leaned back on the sofa and reflected for about her first day on the job: flowers from the staff, refreshments and a brief tour over the vast office space, warmed her heart. Dexter Grady, her supervisor, seemed more than friendly, too much so in her opinion. His words still rang in her ear. "Care to join me for lunch today?"

"Thanks, but not today, Mr. Grady," she'd told him as polite and as professional as she could under the circumstances. "There's so much to read and learn, perhaps another time?"

"Sure, I'll hold you to that." He threw her a smile and quietly walked away.

Then she remembered Shirley Carr, 37 and divorced, was the West Side coordinator who worked in the next cubicle. The first thing out of Shirley's mouth was, "You're a fresh face around here. Count on me to help you through the rough spots." Cara really appreciated knowing she could count on someone. She got a brief history about office politics, games the workers played, who to watch out for, and who not to trust. Shirley had explained the pitfalls dealing with program directors and teachers and how to cover your behind.

Cara knew all too well what she meant, having just left a director's position. She'd always managed to work well with Human Services staff and had garnered a reputation as such. As overwhelming as it seemed, she was eager and primed to perform beyond expectations.

By eight that evening, she wrote a time management plan. Taking an hour for lunch at a restaurant was not in her plan. And, neither would she consider having lunch with Mr. Grady. A packed lunch from home to save money and time was more like it. Mondays and Fridays would be devoted to completing and filing reports and making minor schedule changes for the next week.

Then she signed on AOL, hoping to join MattIWas in their private room. It had been four days since she got a message from him. She had found it odd that two days ago, his screen name appeared in her Buddy List. He didn't instant message her, something he always did immediately after she signed on.

After an hour of browsing Family.Com and Ancestry.com for more resources, she deleted junk mail and checked her horoscope. She sensed MattIwas no longer cared to chat with her. Perhaps, he was busy following through on her suggestions.

So, she wrote him a message.

Dear Matt: "Are you okay? Where are you? I've located some information that might interest you. Please respond."

Around 9:15 p.m. the phone rang. She almost didn't answer, but when the caller's name and number appeared on her machine, she decided to answer.

"Hello."

"Hi, this is Dexter."

"Hi, Mr. Grady," she replied.

"Hope it's okay that I called so late. Your line was busy," he explained. "By the way, everyone at the office calls me Dexter."

"I'll try to remember that. Don't get mad if I forget occasionally."

Then she paused for a moment, waiting for him to say more before she would end the conversation.

CHAPTER 18

Mario arrived at Due Drop Inn and quickly pulled into the parking lot around 12:15 that morning. Freddie Sanders was at his usual post, energetically pacing from one end of the bar to the other keeping his regulars happy.

Mario ordered a double shot of Wild Turkey and then he thought about Cara and the divorce. His lawyer had informed him yesterday about her counter petition. She wanted monthly child support and one-half of Ashley's college education when she turned eighteen. It was just one more thing that bothered him as his thoughts were directed to his lackluster social and sex life.

When the bartender delivered his drink, he took a few sips and started to wonder how he could locate Paula Coles. It had been a year ago since he ended their affair. Was she still attractive? Would she want him again? Running his fingers around his glass, he thought, we were like animals from the time we met. We were good together. Memphis would be a great place to start.

The next day, Mario's plane landed at 9:50 a.m. An hour later, he'd checked into his room at the Comfort Inn East. Even the liquor he'd consumed last night hadn't dulled his body to a peaceful sleep. He needed it awake, alert, so he could think and certainly, look his best. Quickly, he unpacked, showered long in steaming sudsy water and put on fresh clothes.

He searched the white pages in hopes to find Paula's number. He remembered that she was going to Italy after their affair ended. But he had his doubts.

Within two minutes he found two listings. The first number was disconnected. He tried the second one. Bingo, the lady's voice on the answering machine was familiar. His hands were shaking. "Paula", he hesitated, "This is your long lost friend, Mario. I'm in town for the weekend. I'd love to see you. Staying at the Comfort Inn East on Poplar Avenue, Room 614. Please call me."

He hung up the phone and hoped she would return his call.

Ten minutes past lunchtime, he heard the phone ring.

"Hello."

"Mario? Is that you?" Paula said, in a silky voice.

"Yes, this is the one."

"I, I don't know what to say, except that __".

"It's good to hear your voice too." He interrupted her. "I figured you'd be out of the country. What happened?"

"Well," she paused. "It didn't work out with Howard."

"I'm sorry to hear that." His voice was low and purposefully seductive.

"Yeah, and now I'm starting all over again. We tried to make it work, seems I stayed away from him too long," she said.

"That must've been rough on you. However, on another note, I've got something to tell you."

"Really? Where're you and the wife living now? Heard you guys left here a year ago."

"Chicago."

"Really? How nice. You like it?"

"Yep, it's a cool place to live."

"Are you sure it's safe for you and I to get together? I don't want another mishap with your wife." She spoke in a broken whisper.

"Trust me, this time, it's safe."

"What does that mean?" Paula asked.

"I missed you. Can you come to the hotel and meet me today?" There was a clingy desperation in his voice.

"I'm on my way."

He ordered a bottle of her favorite wine, chilled it and relaxed.

❧ ❧ ❧

When Paula had arrived and parked her car, excitement bounced like tiny red-tipped sparks on her face. She ate like a bird and walked every day to maintain her sexy, five-seven, small framed, slim body. She rubbed a light coating of raspberry-flavor blush on her full lips, sprayed on a lightly scented fragrance, one that Mario always liked on her in all the right places.

Minutes later, she walked up to the hotel like a woman who knew how to get where she wanted to go.

A few minutes later, she tapped on his door once, and right away, she saw Mario, dressed in a Louis Vuitton V-neck beige silk shirt and sleek brown pants. The gold chain around his neck made him look hip. He captured her heart all over again.

"Hello you," she said, smiling. She took three steps and was inside his room.

"Hi, Paula. It's good to see you again." Mario saw strength to her face, but she looked better than before, more mature. It was her eyes that drew his attention. They were dark, intelligent and unflinching. Her tinted brown and blond streaked hair cut in a just above-chin length wedge set off the shape of her round face. Still, as sexy as before.

They held each other in a long embrace.

"Thanks for coming to see me," he whispered while still holding her. "I've missed you so much."

"Missed you too. I __. "The simple sentence she'd started told him what he wanted to know. She still wanted him. She managed to pull away and sat on the loveseat.

He filled two glasses with chilled wine and looked at her admiringly. "I need a friend." A grin flashed across his face.

"What led you back to me?"

"Cara and I are getting divorced," he said, and sat down without looking at her. He began by telling her the important things about his marriage, including the birth of Ashley, and the reason they left Memphis.

"She cheated on me," Mario blurted out, unable to hold it any longer.

"I'm shocked, in fact I don't believe you, Mario."

"Believe me, it's true." He told her all the sordid details.

Paula folded her hands in disbelief. "Not the woman I met as your wife, preaching to me about morality, exposing her open wounds to me in verbal terms you wouldn't believe," she blurted out and fumbled her hands. "Mario", she said, eyeing him quizzically, "do you really want me in your life?"

"Yes, why not?"

"What exactly does it mean? We ended our relationship just to save your marriage. It was difficult, but I did it, she said."

Holding her close, "All that's behind us now. All I know is that I need you in my life. Let's take it from there and see what happens."

She looked at him, feeling recharged, "Well, my darling on those words, all I can say is welcome back, Mario."

CHAPTER 19

❀

Cara rushed past the worshippers, clad in their Sunday best. Only a few hours ago, she worried over what she should wear. A festive red would've suited Cara's celebratory mood, but she thought it was too flashy. Instead, she chose an ankle-length, jade suit. It was a birthday gift from Mario a year ago. She felt right in step with everyone on the dress code.

Not far away, she glimpsed Barbara Rhodes helping an elderly lady walk down the aisle. She waited for the right moment to share her good news.

"I couldn't be happier for you. When do you start?"

"Two weeks from now. Imagine that. The big guy called to give me the word. Thanks, for the tip," Cara said.

"You're welcome. Remember, you put forth the effort. Congratulations."

Cara smiled. "True, but it was your call that led me there. I'll forever be grateful that God blessed me through you, Barbara."

Suddenly, Cara remembered the pastor's upcoming anniversary, a formal attire gala in early December.

"How're the ticket sales going?"

"Like hot cakes. We're expecting a huge turnout," Barbara replied, looking away momentarily. Barbara waved at Alderman Bennett.

"Let me know if there's anything I can do to help with the reception," Cara said.

"Just come and have fun. I've got everything under control," Barbara told her.

"Alright. Enjoy your Sunday." Cara smiled and waved her goodbye.

❧ ❧ ❧

Cara had scarcely found the time to pull her life together. In a few months, the trees would be stripped bare of their bright fall foliage and the windy city's chill would be nipping at her nose. And, once hibernation and the holidays set in, there would be little chance for her to venture out.

After leaving church, she dreaded going right back to her lonely apartment. She decided to take a long drive on Lake Shore Drive and enjoy the beautiful scenery of Chicago's lakefront. She needed air to fill her lungs with the pungent scent of autumn, as she passed through the little dramas that took place in her life.

Ashley crossed her mind and she thought about the fun she'd have playing outdoors with her granddaddy. She remembered how it was when she was a little girl, throwing balls, playing hiding and go seek, taking neighborhood walks, and even coloring pictures at the kitchen table. He'd always let Cara win, letting her believe she was better than he was.

When Cara reached 48th and Lake Shore Drive, she glanced for a moment at the high rise she and Mario once lived in and couldn't help but let memories haunt her again. Leaping down two and three steps at a time, like a bat escaping hell. She remembered some more. *I can't let him catch me. What if I don't make it?*

It had all come back, only more profound than before. Her face was drenched in wetness, her heart thumped heavy in her chest. Suddenly, she was about to drive straight into the cement wall that protected the outer drive from violent waves off Lake Michigan. She quickly steered her car to the left and luckily, she slowed down just enough to keep from hitting the vehicle in front of her. Her hands shook so badly that she had to pull over to the side of the road twice. Cars whizzed by her and she didn't see them.

Gathering her strength ten minutes later, she pulled back onto the Drive. She had started to feel at ease when she approached the Museum of Science and Industry, the largest museum in the world. It was then that she realized then, that somehow she had to launch a search for the culprit who framed her. But before that, she had to try and put that night far out of her mind or else she'd have an accident for sure.

She soon approached Soldier's Field, home of the Chicago Bears, and the museums where she'd gone on field trips with the preschoolers: The Aquarium, the Adler Planetarium, and the Field Museum. It wasn't long before she had arrived in the heart of the city known as the Loop, home to the financial district and tall skyscrapers. The Sears Tower was more than impressive. She glanced over at the lake. People were sailing off in their private yachts, while some lazily sprawled around those still docked. She wondered what life must be like for the people who could afford to own one.

As she swerved around the curve past Randolph Street, she saw the tall magnificent structure to her right. That's where Oprah Winfrey and other mega rich people lived, she thought. She continued to drive north to the North Avenue Exit and then turned around to go back to the south side, wondering how she'd spend the rest of her Sunday.

It was almost 3:00 that afternoon when Cara walked inside her apartment. It was just as she had left it. Cleaned, plants watered and sufficient light flowed from the windows. She pulled from the refrigerator her dinner cooked the night before, baked chicken breasts, lima beans and cornbread. All there was left to do was toss a salad and cut a slice of watermelon for dessert.

Later, she booked a flight home for Thanksgiving, scheduled an appointment with her doctor and dentist, and set a date to treat Jennifer to lunch. She made a notation to check with the day care parent. She planned her meals for the entire week.

Then she phoned her folks. Naomi answered.

"Hello."

"Mom, it's me. How you doing today? How's Ashley?"

"We're fine. How're things with you?"

Gleefully, she told Naomi about her trip home for Thanksgiving. Yet, it seemed like forever when she'd see her daughter again.

"I'll make the sweet potato pies." Cara said.

Naomi yelled out to Frank who was sitting in his big chair watching the Saints football game. "Cara is coming home. It'll be like old times."

He took the phone with a smile on his face. "Hi, Baby Girl. I'm glad you're coming home. Just so long, you leave Ashley here with us," he chuckled.

Cara loved it when her father called her that. It made her feel snug and tight like a cuddled teddy bear. "Oh, daddy, you worry too much. I do want my daughter with me. But only for a little while longer, she stays with you and Mom."

Cara ended the call on a happy note thinking her day had gone well.

Then the phone rang.

"Hello, Hello," she said. The caller slammed the phone without saying a word. Cara hung up, thinking the anonymous calls had started to wear on her mind like an over rung dishrag.

She figured it was time to do something to fight back.

She recorded a new voice mail announcement: *Hello, since you've decided to hide your name and your number, I won't answer this call. However, if you choose to leave your name, your number and the nature of your call, I'll get back to you as soon as I can. In case you're not an anonymous caller and I'm unable to view my caller ID, I don't want to miss your call. So leave me a message. Thank you.*

CHAPTER 20

As a man trained to observe, Alderman Bennett recognized the woman who stepped inside the lobby at the Hampton Inn. She seemed overly friendly and warm, a memory he'd clung to over the years. She had his eyes, facial shape and unblemished skin, colored like a pecan. Her hair was blended with gray and black hues, and styled in a neatly cut Afro. She was overweight, but not by more than ten pounds. She looked smashing for a woman her age in an emerald laced, two-piece blue-jean suit. It had all come back to him. She was still a good-looking woman, but aged like a good bottle of wine.

He was anxious and nervous as he eased toward her. "Hello, I'm Matthew. You must be my mother."

"Yes, it's me," she beamed, looking him over from head to toe. Her voice gave him a thrill deep in the pit of his stomach. Everything about her fit together, everything in his world was all right. There were no pieces misplaced, mismatched or mistaken. Tears streamed down his face and he couldn't imagine what the viewers walking in and out thought as he grabbed and hug her.

Bennett gently pulled her from the middle of the lobby to the side and they embraced, holding each other and unable to fight the tears.

After a few minutes, she pulled away slightly. "Thank you Jesus," she said looking up momentarily. "You're really Matthew. You're here in the flesh. There's so much I want to say, if I could only stop crying." She hugged him some more.

"It's okay, Mother. You know, we have every right to let it all out."

From her purse, she pulled out enough tissue to share with him and they both dried their faces.

"Let go inside. I'll order breakfast. We can talk all day if you want." He led her inside pulling her carry-on behind him.

The restaurant was half filled mostly with people in between flights and he had chosen it on purpose. Hardly anyone would recognize him. Soft music played in the background. The polished floors and sandy striped-papered walls, chandeliers beautifully spaced apart from the ceiling, and rows of live tropical plants staged a lovely scene. They were seated at a corner booth that offered a clear view of the sprawling traffic on Cicero Avenue.

Mary Lee looked away long enough to gather from her purse a few mementos from his past: His kindergarten class picture, a mini family photo album and his birth certificate. She'd managed to stash them in a private safe deposit box until now. He looked at each one and smiled.

"Fancy that, it's little o' me," he exclaimed, holding the picture in his hands. His face was rounder and he showed a happy smile.

"It was all I had left of you."

The waiter appeared with a pot of coffee and took their food order. They ordered the same: Pancakes, scrambled eggs, sausage, juice and coffee. Bennett poured their coffee. She preferred two packs of Equal sugar and he poured sugar from the glass container. He took a long sip of his coffee and looked at the pictures. "Do you mind if I hold onto these just until you're ready to leave?"

"All of it is yours to keep. I no longer need them, son." She couldn't help notice how well he looked. Except that he had Bradley's body shape and a receding hairline, he looked the spitting image of her. She wondered what he was like otherwise. What type of work did he do, was he married, single or divorced, were there children and what was his life like. Still overwhelmed by the experience of seeing him, all she could think of at the moment was how she'd been robbed of the opportunity to raise and love her own child herself. She wanted to tell him how she felt about the people who took him away, but she didn't. That warm look in his eyes might disappear. Mostly she felt grateful he came through the ordeal seemingly all right.

"You've grown into such a fine looking man. Your dad would be so proud."

"How is he?"

"He's all right. He's skeptical that you'll turn out to be our son."

"I'm sure. It bothered me that I didn't remember his name."

"You were so young. He won't hold that against you. What happened to you was not your doing, son."

"It was rough growing up with strangers. Although I never gave up hope I'd find you someday, my knowledge of my past seemed to fade with time," Alderman Bennett said.

The waiter returned and placed their steaming food on the table. Afterwards, Mary Lee and Matthew hurriedly covered the pancakes with maple syrup and ate in silence for a few moments. She wondered why he asked her to e-mail him under a different screen name. Why didn't he want Cara to know it? Obviously he had his reasons and she decided it was best to leave that one alone too. Perhaps at another time they could talk more openly about everything that mattered.

"I can't wait to see your father's face when I tell him you're alive," she said, savoring small portions of pancakes and eggs.

"I can't wait to see him."

"Now that we're together again, I want to know all about you," Mary Lee said, and sipped her coffee.

Taking his time to draw in a deep breath, he was prepared to tell only what she really needed to know at this point. He checked his watch. It was 10:30 a.m. There were appointments he'd planned to keep thinking that Mary Lee would turn out to be a hoax. Everything and everyone would have to wait for later, he thought.

"Mother, I guess if there's anyone I can tell the truth to, it's you. How good are you at keeping secrets?"

"You're looking at someone who deserves an Oscar for having kept a lifelong secret."

"What on earth could that have been?"

"The secret was you. No one knew you existed except your father and me. Your father couldn't handle the publicity surrounding your abduction, neither could he handle losing you and knowing he'd never see you again. He swore me to secrecy. We moved away from where you were born and started a new life in Memphis. Mario, your brother, thinks he's our only son."

He looked at her, jaws slightly clenched, taking another long deep breath. "Wow, that's heavy. I remember, he was so tiny, lying in the crib. In a way I guess I can understand my father's decision. But to never tell my brother about me, I, I want to know his reasoning."

"Your father is a wonderful, hardworking, courageous man, but inside can't deal with the hurt and pain. His decisions are rash and he's quick to make judgment. Mario is just like him. Losing you almost took him off this earth. I think it was the only way he could survive and make something of himself. He owns a lucrative landscape business and has taken good care of us."

In dazed exasperation, he hesitated with bewilderment. "It must've been awful for you to pretend all these years."

He opened the photo album searching for another glimpse of the man he thought might be Mario. She stopped him before he turned to the next page. She pointed to the man wearing a graduation cap and gown.

"This is Mario? He resembles dad a lot," thinking he only had Cara's picture and nothing of his brother. He wondered what Mario looked like today.

"He's slightly taller than you, good-looking, loves sports and he keeps himself in good shape. He and Cara have a little girl named Ashley." Her pleasant smile quickly faded. "But now, his family has been disrupted. She left Mario. He's angry most of the time."

A muscle flicked angrily at his jaw and he grew uneasy. He could sense her pain.. "I'm sorry to hear that."

"I know you are son. You were going to tell me something earlier, something you could only tell me."

"Yes, I remember. I go by a different name, and a new identity. Because of my shaky past, I'm Giles Bennett."

"Oh," she stammered. "Giles. How interesting, is that the name they gave you?"

"Yes. A woman named, Loretta and Kirk Bennett raised me. I hated living with them, but then I got used to it." He smiled blandly. "That's not all, Mother. I wear the title, Alderman. You can't tell anyone about me, except daddy."

"My God, so my big boy has a new name and he's a Chicago politician. This will knock Bradley off his rocker. Matthew, I mean Giles. I'll keep your secret. But can you tell me why I should do that?"

"It's a long story, maybe someday, I'll tell you why."

After they finished eating they left the restaurant and walked to the hotel entrance. Alderman Bennett reserved a suite at the Hampton Inn for Mary Lee. He used his cellular to reschedule his appointments. He would spend the rest of the day getting re-acquainted with his birth mom, treating her to lunch and dinner. He would show his *real* mom some of Chicago's fabulous attractions.

After she had checked at the hotel, the limo driver took them for a ride on Chicago's south side. From there, sightseeing in the Loop and along North Lake Shore Drive.

They had lunch at Mike Ditka's restaurant at 12:30 p.m. She couldn't wait to tell Bradley about her entrée, Da Pork Chop, thick juicy and served with green peppercorns and roasted garlic jus.

Alderman Bennett had a hefty aged New York Strip Steak with sautéed mushrooms.

Breathing a sigh of relief, Alderman Bennett was happy and content, if only for the moment. The thing that had mattered the most to him was finding his birth family. That he'd done. Since he turned his life around to become a good guy, he knew he could risk everything he'd accomplished if his secret were to be revealed, not even to a brother that doesn't know he exist.

CHAPTER 21

❦

Rushing back to her desk from the ladies room, Cara thought about the paperwork on her desk and knew that she had a lot to do before the day ended.

The phone rang. "Hello."

"Cara, it's me," Shirley replied. "I was about to leave the building. How's it going?"

"Really well. I think I'm going to like it here." Cara was glad to hear from a friendly soul."

"That I like to hear. Don't forget we have a staff meeting tomorrow."

"Thanks for the reminder. Our supervisor came by to tell me. He can be a real *bull in the collar* at times." Cara whispered.

"Don't let him hear you say that. But you're right." Shirley's voice lulled and then she laughed. "Just don't step on his toes and you'll be all right. He's a perfectionist and you can't bitch about it. He drives himself even harder than he drives the rest of us."

"I appreciate the warning. Sounds like someone to stay away from," Cara said. Her reply lacked a ring of finality. She almost told Shirley that Dexter Grady had called to put the moves on her early that morning while she used the copier machine. But she shrugged him off, seemingly without any repercussions. I wonder if she knows about his other side, she thought.

"That, my dear is up to you. He's had some kind of chip on his shoulder for years," Shirley added. "And, now I've got to run. I'm off to visit two of my agencies on the west side."

"Well, hope the rest of your day is a good one."

Halfway through the first report, Cara remembered the encounter that morning with Dexter Grady:

"Cara," he said. "How was your weekend?" His rugged good looks and toughness reminded Cara of Richard Roundtree. His eyes would look at you and take hold, and then on the other hand, squeeze you for a moment and then drop you when you least expected it. As though life on the job were a game.

"Peaceful. I went to church Sunday. How about yours?"

He had told her his weekend would've been better had she been with him. "Oh, pay me no mind, I guess I find you so damn attractive. What's a man supposed to do?" He said.

Cara remembered thinking, you could leave me alone and let me do my job. Instead, she told him she would take what he'd said as a compliment and started to walk back to her desk. He wouldn't give up. He followed along and asked if she had a few minutes. "A few, but then I must get those reports done for you." She told him.

She didn't find it difficult at all deciding if he was serious or joking. There was an edge of sarcasm to certain things he said, except for this time.

"So, how's the job so far?"

"Pretty good, actually. I plan to visit the agency on 45th Street tomorrow to review their operations."

"Oh, by the way, been meaning to ask you something."

"Really, what?" She sensed it wasn't about the job and started to feel uneasy around him.

"I've got this cocktail party tomorrow night. I'd love it if you could come with me," he asked, brushing against her arm. "It's a party for a police detective, Lester Miller."

Quickly she thought, I won't turn this one down, Lester is someone I need to talk to. Maybe I can pick his brains. Optimism is the best step toward real progress. And, it's a chance I'll take.

"You know I hate to say no __," she said, wondering what he must think of her now.

"I refuse to take no for an answer," Dexter interrupted.

"Why me? I'm sure you know a bunch of ladies you could take," Cara said jokingly, but cautiously. "It's not my style to mix business with pleasure, but this time ___, all right, I'll make an exception." Her voice was uncompromising, yet oddly gentle.

He seemed pleased by her answer and he finally walked away.

Cara rushed to finish everything on her list for that day, thinking she must be out of her mind to go out with a supervisor. She couldn't let that slip in judgment bother her now. I can't believe how things are going my way for a change, she thought.

CHAPTER 22

Cara drove to work on Tuesday morning, dressed in a three-piece cherry suit just right for the office and yet stylish enough for the party. Her hair was neatly coiffed in a rolled ball, and she wore a mild touch of make-up and soft blush on her lips. She brought along matching heels, a makeup kit, 14-carat gold matching earrings and necklace, a beaded crème purse and toiletries.

As she turned to enter the outer drive, she noticed that the black late model car that had followed her since she left home was still with her. Am I being paranoid or what this time? She wondered.

She slowed enough to read the license plate, *AGIA*, but couldn't get a good look at the driver's face. He was medium brown skin, wore sunglasses, suit, and tie. He looked somewhat familiar.

She figured it was time to call in the big boys, something she could use from Detective Lester Miller. By the time she'd reached Michigan Avenue, the stalker suddenly disappeared.

Later, she parked her car and entered the building.

Quickly, she stepped inside her cubicle, hoping for a small amount of privacy.

A few minutes later, there he stood smiling.

"Good morning, Ms. Fleming. Did I see you come in earlier?"

"Hello, Mr. Grady. I'm not sure, if you did or not."

"You look very nice," he said.

Cara smiled, thinking he couldn't decide what he wanted to call her. "Thanks," she murmured while starting to read the memo on her desk.

"I don't know how I did it, but I'm glad I changed your mind."

She smiled. "What time shall we leave?"

"6:00 p.m. I should let you get to work," Grady uttered.

"Good idea. I'll be ready."

Cara reviewed job procedures, department memos and typed reports. Happily, she finished her work 11:15 a.m.

Then she thought about MattIwas, checked her e-mail on the office computer. To her surprise he had sent her a message. Opening it, she read: "I'm out of town for a few days, don't know when I'll return. I'll get back to you later. Hope life is treating you well. In the meantime, here's something to keep on your mind: There's hope when something has died. There's hope when you think you're down and out and have nowhere to turn. There's hope when you've been lied on and had to give up your happiness and peace of mind. Best regards, Matt."

She thought after she'd read his message over and over again, at least he didn't fall off the face of the earth. He cared enough to give her inspiration. She was impressed.

While she ate her lunch at her desk, she thought some more about Matt: Why did he stop sending me e-mails? I want to help him find his birth mother only he doesn't seem to care anymore.

The rest of the afternoon went perfectly. No interruptions from Grady. No phone calls. Before touching up her appearance, she checked on Jennifer. She let the phone ring more than enough.

Exactly at 6:00 p.m., Dexter Grady waited on the first floor near the main entrance. She copped a friendlier-than-thou attitude for a few seconds, wondering what she'd talk about with Dexter. I hate doing this. For sure, it's the last time, she thought.

Dexter stepped forward neatly clad in a dark blue and tie. "Well, hello again. Ready?"

"Hi, ready as ever. I'll follow you there." Cara replied.

"It's better that you ride with me. I'll see to it that you get back to your car safely."

"Oh, I don't know. I think I'll follow you."

"Okay," he said, shrugging his shoulders. "If you insist. It's only a few blocks away."

Dexter had deemed Cara an enigma. No matter how hard he tried, he couldn't figure her out. Why would a woman built like she was and with a face like hers pursue a career in education, of all things? She could have made a fortune modeling at a New York fashion agency.

A few minutes later, he pulled into the entranceway of the John Hancock building, spiraling up and around several times until he found a parking space. Cara was right behind him. They parked and got out of their cars.

"Well, I see you made it without any problems," he cackled.

"Yep, it was a little scary at first."

Moments later, they boarded the elevator.

"Brace yourself lady. The ride to the 96th Floor takes about three minutes."

"Oh. Sounds a little scary if you ask me." She felt the push upward, and watched the numbers increase on the display. She held her hands together tight. Cara felt pain in her ears. It reminded her of the way her ears felt during takeoff on a flight.

They both walked inside the semi-quiet elegant *Signature Lounge*. Soft music played perfectly. Men dressed in police uniform and women clad in dressy attire were busy chatting, strolling about and seemingly enjoying themselves.

Right behind them came Renita Dates, an attractive yet more than a casual friend of Dexter's. Her spoon-shaped body was clad in a blue pin striped suit. With her was a short petite lady wearing a dressy sleeveless black jumpsuit and heavily clad in sparking gold necklace and earrings.

"I see you made it, Dexter," Renita greeted them.

"Hi," he replied, "Nice to see you. Meet Cara Fleming."

"Hello, it's nice to meet you," Cara said, in her usual friendly manner.

"Likewise," Renita replied. "Dexter and Cara, this is Keisha Hayes, wife of Commander Stanley Hayes from Area 2." Keisha and Stanley had been happily married for ten years. She was his stronghold, the woman behind a successful black man who had made it near the top on the Chicago police force. Neither of them slept around. Stanley had been Lester's mentor and boss. He took Lester under his wings like a brother, guiding his career from a rookie cop to Detective in less than six years. The cocktail party for Lester had been Stanley and Keisha's idea. Lester had been awarded a medal of honor for his investigative work on a high profile case. He ingeniously cracked a case involving the mysterious disappearance of a young girl, linking the crime to the perpetrator.

"Hi, it's nice to meet you and thanks for coming. We're expecting a nice turn out for Lester," Keisha said, and smiled.

"When is the guest of honor due to arrive?" Grady probed.

"7:30," Keisha replied, checking her watch.

"It's a surprise party, but you know how word can get around. We think he's aware," Renita said.

"What a lovely thing to do," Cara said.

Keisha looked at Dexter and Cara and said, "Hope you guys enjoy the party. There's plenty of food and the drinks are on the house."

Just as the two ladies started to walk away, Dexter glanced at Renita, "Check you later," he said, eying her guardedly. He knew he'd have some explaining to do later, but on the other hand he didn't relish the thought that this was payback on Renita, even though it hadn't been his original plan. For a year or so, Dexter and Renita, a two-year rookie cop assigned to domestic violence had dated each other purely for sexual relief outside their marriage. It was understood, when in public, they would behave professionally, regardless.

While leading Cara to a window table, Dexter was forced to get his mission right. He recalled a phone conversation with Joe Michaels two days ago: "Grady?"

"Yeah, speaking. How can I help you?"

"I need some information about a new employee, Cara Fleming."

"What do you want to know about her?"

"I'll take whatever you can get."

"The dirty low down, under the rug stuff you can't get on your own, being the clean guy you are. Right?"

"It's very important, Grady. I need it ASAP."

"In that case, I'll get right on it."

Since that day, Dexter Grady had to work fast to put his plan in action. Cara hadn't been an easy subject to know. Phone calls, constant attention to her on the job, lunch invitations, nothing seemed to work until now. Although he was glad that he'd found something that appealed to her, he wondered why.

Dexter threw Cara a coy smile as he got up to go to the bar.

A few minutes later, he returned to their table near the large windows holding two glasses of white wine.

Dexter sipped his wine and watched her for a minute. "Are you having fun?"

"Yeah. I must admit, it feels good to get out of the house."

The wine had started to warm his insides, his spirits. But she'd seemed preoccupied. Her mind focused, seemingly, in no-man's land.

"You wouldn't object to a question or two, would you?" he asked, and she turned to look directly in his eyes.

"Ask away."

"The word at the office is that you're the loner type. You keep to yourself."

Cara grinned. "It's true. I'm not there to socialize."

Mostly they talked at first about the job, how she was getting along with the staff, and her prior experiences as a teacher in the south.

"I am curious about something. Are you married or single?

"For the moment, I'm separated from my husband."

"Too bad. How did he ever let you leave him?"

"Sorry, but I don't care to answer that one. How about you? What's your marital status?" Cara asked.

"I'm hitched. Been like that for fifteen years."

"I thought as much. It's good that this party isn't a date situation," she said.

"Why'd you say that?"

"I respect the sanctity of marriage. It's as simple as that."

Dexter smiled. So the lady has spoken. That being the case, he wondered, why is she out with me tonight? The fact of the matter was that he thought he had her all figured out. Although prim, proper, he figured she'd eventually come around.

"What if you met and fell in love with a married man? What would you do?" He asked.

"Stick to my guns, sir."

"Ever heard the old saying, there's always a first time for everything?" He asked.

By now she was bordering on boredom. It's no wonder why she felt the need to put a stop to his interrogation. "Dexter, so that you know, I'm different. I loved my husband very much, was faithful to him from the day we met and fell in love. For some reason, I'm still faithful. How does that grab you?"

Shrugging his shoulders. "You're definitely not like most women. That's for sure. Seems to me your husband let a good woman get away."

"Thanks, I appreciate that."

"Do you have children?"

"A daughter. She's three, more like going on twenty-three."

Dexter stepped away to chat with a few people.

Instantly, she got up and walked to the window. She looked at the vast blue water. Browsing the Internet, she remembered noting important facts about Chicago's John Hancock building. A few floors from being the tallest building in Chicago, second only to the Sears Tower. It housed everything from ground floor shops and restaurants, to corporate offices and residential apartments. As breathtaking as it was, her view from the 96th floor was like a child gazing at a miniscule toy play arena. The people and the cars that moved on the street, seemed like ants, tiny and crawly.

She started to think about Lester, and remembered that before the split, Mario never introduced her. He promised to do so at the annual Police Ball in December.

At 7:35 p.m. everyone stood and rendered applause, as the tall, lean and extremely handsome guy stepped in the lounge, alone. Her heart tripped into overdrive. His true age hidden by his unblemished light tanned face reminded her of someone famous. He wore a dark brown suit that translated instantly into sex.

Mario had surely played down Lester's looks, she thought.

Dexter Grady returned to their table. He'd rubbed Renita the wrong way. Unable to tell her the truth about why he was with Cara, he needed to regroup.

"Hi, I'm back, missed me?"

She slowly spoke to him, thinking, *no-way, Hosea.*

Then she focused her attention back on Lester. He strolled about the room, shaking hands with the guests. He moved toward Cara and Dexter's table.

"Dexter, my man, how's it going? Lester said.

"Just great, Lester. Congratulations on your award."

Lester glanced at Cara. "Hello." His gaze fixed on her.

"Hello," she said.

"Oh, excuse my manners," Dexter stammered. He quickly introduced them. For a moment, he noticed that Lester seemed to want to say more, but instead, Lester just nodded his head and excused himself to the next table.

Dexter took Cara's arm in a possessive fashion.

"Would you care to dance?"

"I suppose it would be all right."

They danced not too close to a tune by Anita Baker. But all Cara could think about was how she was going to get Lester alone, just for a few minutes. It was now or never, she thought.

When the song ended, Dexter left to get more wine, and Cara returned to their table. Alone again, she started to feel awkward. By chance, she looked up seconds later. Lester had had returned. Was it her imagination, or did their eyes lock every time they looked at each other? For a moment, they only gazed at each other, both of them obviously thinking about something different.

"Ah, you're alone, finally," Lester said. "Mind, if I ask you a personal question?"

"No, not at all," she replied, noticing the faint light that twinkled in the depths of his light brown eyes.

"I have a friend, his name is Mario. Are you __?"

"Yes, I'm the one, Detective Miller." Feeling more at ease.

"Really!" He said, blushing. "Please, call me Lester. As they say, it's a small world at times." He folded his hands together. "So, how're you doing?" He sat down across from her.

"I'm okay," she said and smiled. "Actually, the main reason I'm here with Mr Grady, of all people is because I need your help. Only I couldn't tell him that."

"Is that right?"

"He's my supervisor. For some reason, after several attempts to take me to lunch, he approached me yesterday about a cocktail party. He said it was a surprise party for you. Of course, I accepted his offer."

"Well, on that note, I'm glad we finally met. So, how can I help you?"

"It occurred to me," she said, moving around in her seat, that as Mario's friend, you could possibly answer some questions for me," she said.

As he studied Cara more intently, Lester realized that Cara was more beautiful than he imagined. With a gentleness that surprised even him, and considering the fact that she was his best friend's wife, Lester merely touched her hand with sure, but careful fingers. He figured for her to go to such lengths to meet him, it had to be important.

"I hate what happened to you guys, and if there's anything I can do," he said, gently but timely pulling away.

"I was hoping you'd say that," she said, politely.

"So, how're you doing otherwise?"

"Mostly okay now, but lately, I have reason to believe I'm being stalked."

"Really, what happened?

After she explained her reasons, Lester pulled a business card from his jacket pocket. "Take this and call me soon. We'll talk." He took out another card and asked her to write her phone number and address on the reverse side.

"I don't know what to say," she said, feeling relieved. "You're a nice guy, just like Mario said you were."

He threw her a reassuring smile. Just then Dexter walked to the table and she got quiet.

"Hey man, take care of this lady," Lester said, seemingly without reservations. "She's precious cargo."

CHAPTER 23

❁

As Lester drove home from the party, he soon realized that Cara could be in danger. In any case, learning the truth about the Fleming marital situation had piqued his interest.

He walked inside his condo at 10:45 p.m. and called her.

"Hi, this is Lester."

"Well, hello," she said, sounding a bit surprised.

"I noticed you and Grady left the party early. Did you get home okay?"

"Yes, it was his idea to leave, actually. It couldn't have come at a better time for me."

"Good, you got rid of him and you're home safe and sound. We need to talk about this stalking matter. The sooner the better."

"I agree. When did you have in mind?"

"Tomorrow. 7:00 p.m., at my apartment. I'll whip up a gourmet dinner. We'll have that talk then."

Without hesitation, she gingerly blurted, "Dinner? That isn't necessary. The most I'd hoped for was a chat over the phone or __."

"Or, what?" he gently interrupted her. "For my friend's wife, that just won't do."

"Okay, then dinner it is."

"Terrific. Looking at the address you gave me, I'm only a few blocks away from you. Is seven o'clock okay?"

"Really? How close are you?" She asked.

"7447 South Shore Drive."

How interesting, she thought, remembering Joe Michaels lived in the same building. "I see. Okay, I'll be waiting."

Cara hung up feeling as her life had changed, for better or worse. She'd taken on two interesting men, *not out of greed but need*. She figured Dexter and Lester were out of her league and off limits. She analyzed her evening with her supervisor. She hoped the standoff wouldn't affect her probationary evaluation two months from now.

Just when she thought about her dinner tomorrow night with Lester, her phone rang at 11:00 p.m. It startled Cara. It was Jennifer and as much as Cara loved talking to her, she hated getting late calls. It turned out that Jennifer only wanted to find out about her date. Cara told her it went well and that to her surprise, she met Mario's detective friend.

When Cara tried to get Jennifer to share things about her own situation, Jennifer merely said that things had gotten better between her and Duncan.

CHAPTER 24

Bradley had become emotionally traumatized since he learned Matthew was alive. But in one sense, he was relieved and happy. The son he'd buried out of his mind and his heart was back. His son was a man with a new identity, and a sense of purpose guiding him. Irrespective of the misfortunes thrown his way, he had somehow become a powerful political figure in Chicago, of all places.

As Bradley sat on the patio he stared at the surroundings and tried to sort his feelings. He remembered during the drive from the airport, Mary Lee filled him in on the details: "Matthew has your strength and determination to succeed, but he looks the spitting image of me, Bradley." Her words made him feel like his world was about to disintegrate all over again. Like the world he once knew when Matthew was abducted.

As Bradley moped around the house, he wondered, how he would explain Matthew's emergence, especially to Mario? He cared what others would think, too. His reputation for truth and integrity, a devoted husband and father, a church going man, and a respected member of his community was about to crumble out of control.

He'd also lost face with his wife, the woman who delivered the same son twice: *in birth and from death*. Even his command over her had seemingly weakened.

Around 3:00 on Monday afternoon, Mary Lee prepared lunch for them: tequila chicken wings, black-eyed peas and bacon risotto and rolls. She knew Bradley hadn't eaten anything all day.

"Come and eat, Bradley. You need to keep your strength up," she said, watching him in a chair on the patio.

Without a word, he got up, walked to the kitchen and sat in his favorite chair.

"What're we going to do about this?" Mary Lee asked.

"I'm all out of answers," he finally spoke up and lifted a wing to his mouth.

"Do what I did, go and see your son. Talk with him," she pleaded.

"You think Matthew would come to Memphis?"

"Just call him, Bradley, you might be surprised."

They ate the rest of the meal mostly in silence. Mary Lee noticed how quickly he cleaned his plate.

"Feeling better?"

"Yeah, somewhat." He got up and walked back to the patio. She followed. "As I see it, you haven't committed any crime. My God, losing Matthew like we did was too much to handle back then. You did what you thought was best for us. I'm just as much to blame. Remember, I agreed to go along with the plan, keeping his existence a secret," she expounded.

"Now it's come back to haunt us," he bleated.

Mary Lee suddenly thought about Cara and Mario's situation. She figured the failure to communicate had prevented an amicable solution between them. Wasn't it enough that marriages failed for ordinary reasons? And, to be framed as an adulteress was a crime, unwritten in society's law books. Yet, she knew it was her son's unwillingness to trust and believe in his wife that ruined their chance at happiness.

"Isn't it time we tell the truth?" she asked, looking at him intently. "Haven't we let guilt shadow our lives long enough? Explain why we did it and let the chips fall where they may."

"You're always right about such things. As my wife, you've always been the conscience for wisdom and for doing the right thing. You never wanted to keep him a secret, but you did, in honor of our vows. I'll always be grateful to you for that," he said."

At that moment, Mary Lee put her arms around him and held him tight. "I love you, too, Bradley. Everything is going to be all right," she whispered, remembering that he always showed her that he loved her, but had over the years found it difficult to say the words.

"You've always been there for me, and have suffered enough. Now I'm compelled to be honest with you, first," he said.

"Oh, about what?" Mary sat looking at him afraid of what he'd say.

"Mario is seeing another woman. Her name is Paula Coles."

"No, really! Did you meet her?"

"Yep," he replied softly. "And, there's something else. I acted like a fool with Cara over the telephone. I'm too ashamed to face her again. I can't believe I did that."

"None of this has been easy for you, has it, dear? We'll get through this together, Lord willing," she offered.

Mary Lee had left their phone number with Matthew. She believed Matthew was afraid to make the first step. Just as she was about to go inside the house, she stopped and looked back at her husband.

"When you're ready, call your eldest son in Chicago. Talk to him before it's too late."

On those words, Bradley got up and walked inside the house and dialed Alderman Bennett's cellular, thinking it's now or never. There was no answer after four rings. Then Bradley heard Matthew's voice on the answering service, "This is Alderman Bennett, leave your name and number. I'll get back to you as soon as I can."

"Matthew, this is your father, Bradley Fleming. Call me back, son!"

❧ ❧ ❧

By the time Alderman Bennett returned to his office late Tuesday, he'd decided not to contact Current Wife again. He counted on his mother keeping her word. All he cared about was seeing his father and getting to know him. Nothing else and no one else seemed to matter to him now.

Somehow, he felt he would meet Mario. Someday, they'd become friends. The problem was that he didn't know how to do that just yet. "I'd love him like a brother, only he wouldn't know I was his brother," he whispered softly behind closed doors.

Then he decided to check his voice mail messages. He had several. When he got to the one from Bradley, he stop listening, picked up the phone and dialed the number Mary Lee gave him.

"Hello, Bradley residence," the faint male voice answered.

"This, this is Matthew," Alderman Bennett said, trying to sound impressive.

"Oh, my God. My son, it's really you!" There was silence for a moment. Seems neither men could think of what to say next.

Finally Alderman Bennett spoke, "It's good to hear your voice, Dad."

"Likewise, son," Bradley coughed. "Matthew?"

"Yes, it's really me, Dad. How you doing?"

"Fine, now. I just wanted to say," Bradley panted, "this is the greatest thing to happen since man landed on the moon. I missed you son. My life was never the same after they took you away."

"I can't wait to finally see you again, Dad."

"Why don't you get on a plane and come home. Me and your mom will be glad to have you."

"Okay, I'll leave tomorrow morning," Alderman Bennett promised, expecting a response. When there was none, he wondered whether his father was overcome with emotions, or if he'd stepped away to get his mother to the phone. What he didn't know was that she had walked outside to water the flowers.

"Dad, Dad, are you there?"

CHAPTER 25

At 6:00 p.m. on Tuesday, Cara was home. She thought that her day had gone exceedingly well, considering that Dexter didn't come to work. The rumor at the office was he took a sick day. She'd been prepared to thank him and make sure he understood it was the last time she'd go out with him.

Before she would shower and get dressed, she checked the kitchen calendar and noticed she had a hair appointment on Friday. There was a notation to mail the electric and phone bill by the end of that week, and on Saturday, she'd have lunch with Jennifer. Then she quickly remembered she hadn't called her parents in over a week. She planned to call them after her dinner date with detective Miller.

An hour later, she crossed the living room and pulled back the shade. Cara saw a shiny dark blue sedan pull up. At the mirror, she quickly checked her appearance. She wore an off white silk skirt, and a deep pink embroidered blouse that set off her face. Her long dark brown hair had been brushed, and swept out behind her in a healthy mane. Her nails were perfectly manicured and polished a deep pink, just like her toes. She had on low-heeled off white sandals exposing her smooth feet.

She grabbed her purse and locked her door.

Lester got out of the car and opened the door for her.

"Hi," he said, throwing her an admiring smile. "You look nice."

"Thank you." She smiled the feline smile that was so perfect for her voice. She slid her body into the squeaky-clean air-conditioned car.

When Lester got in and closed his door, he looked at her and smiled once more. She noticed that he was even more handsome than the night before. His warmth surrounded her as he reached over her to get a CD from the glove compartment. He smells good, she thought.

"Shall we proceed?" Lester asked, giving her a warm smile.

"Yes, I can't wait to taste your cooking." She breathed it all in, feeling comfortable around him and she realized what kind of person he appeared to be. For starters, a normal one who had normal feelings and one who cared about others. He appeared to possess a gentle spirit uncommon for a man and he spoke with kind words, smiling often. And, he seemed to give full attention to what would please her, making sure she felt safe and comfortable around him. So far, so good, she thought.

Lester's building was twenty floors or more tall with a security guard, lobby and two elevators. Walking down the hallway on the eighteenth floor, she felt as if she were in an office tower or hotel. He turned the lights on and held the door opened, letting her enter ahead of him.

"Here we are, make yourself comfortable. I'll get the wine," he said and sauntered off to the kitchen.

Cara noticed the buff colored trousers and a black Pierre Cardin shirt he wore. She sat and gazed around his tastefully decorated living room. Everything, especially the papered walls in soft earth tones, the vertical blinds to the off-white carpet, impressed her.

He returned holding a decorative glass of white wine and left her alone.

"Hope you like it," he said, handing one of the glasses to Cara. They sat facing each other, Cara on the couch, Lester in an armchair to the side.

She took a couple of sips. “Umm, I like it.” She gazed the surroundings again. She admired the blooming Peace Lilly in the corner of the room. “Your apartment looks really nice. Did you have help?”

“No. It was a matter of putting what I liked with what worked well together.”

“Well, you’ve done a terrific job for an amateur.”

“Thanks,” he said and smiled.

“I’m curious, what’s for dinner?” Cara decided to speak.

“Steak, double-baked potato, and veggies of course.”

“Hmmm, sounds terrific.”

“Good, now while I get dinner on the road, make yourself at home. Select a CD and set off some music for us,” he said.

“Sure, I think I can do that.”

He left the room and she put the wine glass down on the black and gold coaster and stepped to the music center. She chose a Lionel Hampton CD. The system at first seemed a bit complicated. She scanned the features: a five disk CD player, tape decks, with Dolby and Pro-Logic settings.

Soon, smells of onions and garlic wafted from the kitchen. She looked toward the kitchen and saw Lester looking at her, holding his wine glass. She wondered for how long. Somehow she had to remember their reason for being together. It wasn’t because she was lonely, or, because he was lonely. The reason was to pick his brains, Cara reminded herself. He knew more than she did about the reasons for her marital mess.

Suddenly, she glanced toward the kitchen door and noticed Lester watching her.

“Lionel was a good choice. Is jazz a favorite of yours?”

“Yes it is. Is it for you too?” she asked.

“Oh, sure. Jazz and RB are my favorites. Care to join me while I finished the steaks?”

Cara settled at the dining room table. She admired the table centerpiece: flaming candles in brass holders, over a soft metallic gray tablecloth.

"How do you like your steak?"

"Well-done," she answered, thinking the last time she ordered a steak that way it came back burnt.

While watching Lester skillfully handle the steaks, she recalled that Mario never talked much about the Lester's personal life. Was he dating someone, was he ever married? Did he have children? She wondered.

A few minutes later, he plated the meal and delivered it to the table. Then he took the salad bowls from the refrigerator and placed them on the table, poured more wine and sat down across from her.

Before taking a taste of her food, she quickly bowed her head and blessed the food.

Afterward, Lester opened his eyes and lifted his wine glass in a toast.

"Cheers."

She sipped her wine and cut a small piece of her steak. He doused his steak with A-1 sauce, sprinkled some salt, cut a portion in cubes.

"Um, you're quite a chef."

"I'm glad you'd like it," he said.

"According to Mario, you're terrific in the kitchen." She smiled and left it that. The wounds were still too deep for her to comment. She did talk openly with him about other things during the meal.

Twenty minutes later, he wiped his mouth. "The guest bath is down the hall. Make yourself at home. Oh, feel free to check out the place, do whatever ladies do while I clean up." Lester chuckled.

"Thanks."

Inside the bathroom, Cara noticed the round wicker basket that sat in the middle of the aqua ceramic covered vanity. Colorful towels, an unopened toothbrush, breath mints and cologne spray were neatly arranged. She had to smile at the tidiness. Did he have a housekeeper? She wondered.

She stepped softly toward his bedroom. It was furnished in much the same way as the rest of the apartment: pearl white walls and muted gold-carpeted floors. The oversized master bedroom had a king size bed, a matching nightstand and armoire. The massive roll out windows revealed a full view of Lake Michigan. The evening sunset spilled straight over blue water and through the floor-to-ceiling windows, tinting the room with gold and orange colors on one side of the room. The walls showcased professionally done landscapes.

A few minutes later she entered the kitchen. Lester was putting the last item in the dishwasher. He washed his hands, while keeping his gaze on her. He thought about what he knew about her. Cara had always been a major part of their conversation. Images of her had well-taken shape in his mind, her beauty inside and out. Now, he figured he knew why his friend hadn't wanted his lovely wife exposed, anymore than necessary to other men. But now, he'd decided he wouldn't let that bother him. If nothing else, he would get to know her and let her interrogate him.

"Did you find everything okay?"

"Yes, I did. The view is simply breathtaking. It must be nice," she said.

"It's my haven away from the world of robbers, murders and drug dealers."

She smiled and walked back to the living room and sat down.

Lester soon joined her and sat in the chair. He realized that Cara was remarkably able at tossing the conversational ball. They talked about everything but Mario, until he could stand it no longer.

"Not that you want to know, I saw Mario on the courts two weeks ago," he said with his detective face on.

"Really, how is he?" She asked feeling like the air in her balloon had been released.

"Okay, I suppose. I can't seem to ever beat him at tennis," he joked.

"That's your friend, always the competitor." Cara exhaled a couple of deep breaths and looked away for a few moments. "In case you don't already know, we haven't spoken a word to each other since we parted."

Lester arched his eyebrows mischievously. "You miss him?"

She gathered her thoughts. "There're times I can't help it. But then that's expected, don't you think?"

"He wouldn't admit it, but I know he missed you, too. Perhaps he couldn't bring himself to tell me that. He was heartbroken that night we talked."

"Well, so was I, Lester. Does anyone ever stop to think how this thing affected me? Honestly, I've been to hell and back a million times over."

He studied her for a moment and slowed the interrogation. Then he touched her hand gently. "I care. You can talk to me. Sometimes, the temptation to pass judgment is just that. However, you can trust me."

Cara's temperament cooled down a bit. "In my defense, I innocent. Someone framed me!" She pleaded.

"Did he tell you what the caller said?"

"Nothing that explained why he felt the evidence was so convincing. Can you imagine that? I asked how he could believe an anonymous caller. His crazy answer was and I quote, "Because what he said, told me he wasn't lying."

"I don't mean to upset you, but do you have a peculiar birthmark anywhere on your body?" Lester asked.

"Unfortunately, I do. Why?"

"The caller described it in detail. He also said the two of you had plans to get married. Oh, yes, there were photos of you and this guy," he said, watching her reaction. "He didn't mention that either?"

"Pictures? __. He told me absolutely nothing. I wouldn't confess to a lie, not even to save the marriage. So, he got mad again and ordered me out of the condo."

"No, he didn't. What was he thinking?"

"If I knew, I'd tell you that too.

"Well, I thought running after you with a gun, was a stupid thing to do and I told him so."

"When did he talk to you?" she asked.

"Two days later. We met at Due Drop Inn. I advised Mario to work things out with you. I believed he would."

"Want to know the truth? He was hell bent to believe my guilt."

"I see what you mean."

"Lately, I've started to doubt whether the anonymous call was real. Maybe, Mario needed a reason to end our marriage. As I see it, no one other than him, my parents and my doctor knew about the birthmark." She added.

Lester shook his head. "So the guy ordered you to leave. "Wow, I'm so sorry."

Suddenly she was driven to tell him more. "Three weeks later I moved out." She finished her wine. "He's disowned our three-year old daughter."

He stared in complete surprise. "Why?"

She raised her eyes to find him watching her. "Oh, Lester," she blushed awkwardly, "it's too embarrassing to repeat."

"I'm a professional prodder. Don't feel like you have to tell me if you don't want to."

Then she got quiet and she seemed miles away. It gave Lester pause to wonder whether there was another man in her life.

"Are you dating anyone?"

"No. I'm still a married woman."

"I'm impressed," Lester said. He stood up, smiling with satisfaction, thinking she was a good woman just as he'd imagined. "I'll be back, hold that thought," and eased his way to the bathroom.

A few minutes later, he returned. "For purely selfish reasons, I'm glad it's taken this long to meet you Cara."

She wanted to smile at that, but in her state of mind, the memory and the pain controlled her mind. "Would you believe he's already filed for a divorce?"

"I'm so sorry," Lester said.

He got up and sat beside her. He wanted to put his arms around her, to comfort her, but it would have taken some major adjustment. Instead, he took her hand in his and held it for a few minutes.

"For what it's worth, I believe you. Charge it to my gut instinct, but know that I do."

"You sure?" She asked.

"Yes, and that's my final answer about this matter."

"Thanks, now why do I want to believe you?" Cara replied.

"Umm, blame it on your instincts. You've got some good ones. So, what's this about someone stalking you?

She told him everything. "I got the license number. Can you find out who the plate is registered to?"

"You bet. First thing tomorrow, I'll take care of it."

After one more glass of wine, she checked her watch. It was nine-thirty.

"Dinner was just superb! Tomorrow is a work day," she said."

On that, Lester escorted her out of the apartment and locked the door.

Ten minutes later he parked and walked her to the apartment door. They stood there for a moment.

"Maybe, I'm treading dangerous waters here, but I hope we can get together again. I could use a good friend, too," he said staring at her.

"That would be nice, Lester. It might be nice to have a male friend."

"Great. I'll call you tomorrow, okay?"

"Sure. Goodnight, and thanks for everything," she said and smiled.

Cara turned the key to open the door and walked in her apartment. She decided to check her caller ID. Two unknown calls, and one from her parent's home registered on the display. She had to laugh wondering what the unknown caller must've thought listening to her tough words. Thinking it uncommon for her parents to phone after 9 p.m., she returned the call.

"Hello," Naomi answered.

"Mom, I just came home from a dinner outing. Is everything okay?"

"Mario's father had a heart attack two days ago. He's in the intensive care unit at Memorial Baptist."

CHAPTER 26

❀

Somehow it was times like these that encouraged loving, spiritual thoughts. Although Bradley's maltreatment toward Cara broke her heart it was not the time to feel uncaring. Her thoughts filtered back to that night: "*You've ruined his life. I promise you, that I'll see to it that you lose custody of my granddaughter. You're not fit to raise that child.*"

She prayed for her ailing father-in-law.

Just before she left work, Lester called. He told her that the license plate belonged to Alderman Giles Bennett.

"Are you serious? Why do you suppose he'd want to follow me?"

"Cara, is there something you haven't told me?"

She brought him up to speed about the accident and how she learned Joe Michael's relationship to Alderman Bennett. "My girlfriend's husband confirmed it."

"Can I come to your place this evening? We need to talk some more."

"Yes, of course. I can whip up something quick to eat."

"Lovely, but since this is last minute, don't put yourself out for me," he said, pausing. "I'm not a fussy guy, okay."

At 6:45 p.m., he ranged her doorbell and she let him.

"You have a neat and charming place," he said.

"Thanks."

She filled him in on the remaining details __.

"What a story. Seems to me, you have an anonymous benefactor. Course, that sort of thing is commonplace here." His brows set in a straight line. What's the church member name?"

"Barbara Rhodes. She's the administrative assistant to the pastor."

"What church do you belong to?"

"Turner Chapel A.M.E. Church. Why?"

"Oh, just asking." A warning voice whispered in his head. The thought of having to question Barbara left his face clouded with uneasiness. She's the last person I need to face, especially in such a delicate matter as this, he thought. "The pieces all seem to fit."

"Can you explain what you mean by that?" Cara asked, hesitating.

"That all indications point to Alderman Bennett. That he probably helped you get the job. That he's been keeping tabs on your whereabouts. Do I need to say more?"

She took a frank and admiring look from him and smiled. "As strange as it seems, you could be right. If it's true, I want to know why," Cara replied.

"So do I. Politicians don't do favors without expecting something in return. But guess what, as far as they're concerned, you're in the dark—in the shadow of someone's brilliance."

They exchanged a subtle look of amusement.

Cara brought up the accident again __.

"I don't like the sound of that," he replied.

"I wouldn't given it a second thought if Jennifer hadn't told me that Michaels was a top member on Bennett's staff. "Oh, I just remembered something," she said, all excited. "He lives in your building."

"Michaels?"

"Yes. He was kind enough to hand me a business card.

"I'm grateful for his stupidity." Lester promised to give priority to her situation. He would leave no stones unturned. He'd made the arrangement over the phone before he left his apartment.

"Starting tomorrow, you'll have twenty-four hour surveillance. A group of police officers will take turns during off duty hours to protect you. Don't be alarmed. Just do your regular routine, and keep your cellular charged."

"No kidding, you'd do that for me?"

He lifted her chin, and managed to pierce her uneasiness. "I'll help you get to the bottom of this mess," he said firmly.

"You're a good friend, Lester."

He helped her make the kitchen tidy again.

"Oh, thanks for the meal," he said afterward.

Then she started to think some more about the alderman. If Alderman Bennett is the culprit, what's his motive?

Then Lester got her to talk about her supervisor. "You said some things that night at my party, that left me puzzled. Be careful around him. He can make trouble for you."

"Hope I don't live to regret my standoff with him."

"If there's trouble for you on the job, tell me right away."

"I will."

Lester stood up and walked to the door. She followed him.

"Don't forget, someone legitimate will be following you for about a week. The officers will be dressed in plain clothes."

CHAPTER 27

Lester pulled out of the garage at 8:00 a.m. and stared through the car windows at the gray clouds hanging low over the south side. It looked like it would rain today.

Later, he bought coffee and Danish at McDonalds. He parked and called Barbara at home on his cellular. After three rings he got her voice mail. He left her a message to call him at his office.

Lost in his thoughts about Cara, he continued on in the morning rush hour traffic on Stony Island Avenue. He couldn't shake the romantic attractions he felt for her. She was without question, the most extraordinary woman he'd ever met. No woman had reached inside him and held his attention the way Cara had. Certainly he'd met women as beautiful as she was. He'd dated and made love to women who were just as intelligent and articulate. Yet, none of them came close to rousing up inside him the things that Cara had stirred up. Without a doubt he cared about his friendship with Mario, but not to the point of denying himself a close friendship with someone he was unquestionably attracted to.

Thirty minutes later at the office, a knock at the door revived him from his thoughts. I'll have to walk that bridge if I should have to, he thought.

"Come in," he said, and got up to close the windows. Outside, it had begun to rain again. Thunder rumbled and Lester saw flashes of late summer lightning through the window.

Carl Jerome, a tall medium-light skinned guy, hair shaved closed to his head, entered Lester's office. He was twenty-nine and a third year uniform officer, single, never married. He had a three-year old son by the woman he was living with. Because of his dedication to protecting women against crime, Lester chose Jerome to coordinate the surveillance team.

"Good morning, Detective Miller. Got a minute?"

"Sure, come on in and pull up a seat."

Jerome sat down. "We're ready to get this show on the road," he said, handing Lester the schedule.

Lester read plan: Officer names, dates and times.

Officer Jerome leaned back in his chair. "As you can see fifteen men will work four hour shifts, including the weekend. Some can do more than others. They'll keep in contact using their cellular phone as the shift change. I'm the point man to contact if there's a problem. They'll keep a detailed diary of where the subject goes, date and time."

Lester supplied name, address, phone numbers and a complete physical description of Cara and the car she drove.

"Occasionally, she has to travel the south side on job assignments. She rarely goes anywhere in the evening and weekends, except to make personal errands on Saturday. She goes to church on Sunday. She'll keep me posted if and when her schedule change."

"Okay, I believe I got it all down," the officer said and closed his note pad.

"I can't thank you enough," Lester said, standing up and smiling with satisfaction. Lester further emphasized that they pay close attention to anyone who seemed to be following her. Get the license plate and a description of the person, if possible.

"Call me when you have something to report. Doesn't matter what it is or how late the hour. Oh, and make sure she stays safe," Lester said.

"We'll do. Now if you'll excuse me, I'll get busy."

No sooner than the officer left, Lester reviewed his notes about a murder case: Black prostitutes found strangled in the Wentworth area. Then the shrill sound of the phone perked his attention. He started to feel a bit uneasy thinking it was Barbara. Yet he was comfortable with her decision to end their relationship a month ago.

"Detective Miller speaking."

"Hi, this is Barbara. I'm returning your call."

"Hello, how are you?"

"I'm doing fine. What can I do for you?"

"I have reason to believe you're in a position to help me." He was courteous and yet patronizing.

"For the life of me, I don't have a clue how I can do that, but ask anyway."

"Remember Cara Fleming?"

She muttered hastily. "Yes. Someone who wanted to remain anonymous asked me to tell her about a city job. Am I on the right track?"

"Yes," he replied, solemnly.

"How did you know that?" Barbara asked.

"It would take too long to explain. What I can tell you is that it involves her safety."

"How so?"

"I've reason to believe someone is stalking her."

"I see," she replied. "Is she in any trouble?"

"No," Lester replied.

"Is she still with her husband?"

"They're separated," he answered, trying hard to remain cordial. "From what she's told me, it's not due to any fault of her own."

"How did you get involved, Lester?"

"She came to me for help, and so, I agreed. I understand she's a member of your church. Won't you do this for her, if not for me?"

She cleared her throat. "All right. A guy named Joe Michaels came to see me. His boss, Alderman Bennett was just doing a good deed to help a fellow citizen of the community. I didn't give it much thought. It's common knowledge that Bennett helped people, with no strings attached. He's a member of our church. He seems like a good guy. We look out for our church members.

"Yeah, I know. You did a good thing helping Cara. I honestly believe without this job, she wouldn't survive on her own."

"It's nice that you care. Does she know you're talking to me about this?" Barbara asked.

"No," he said, clearing his throat. "Oh, one more thing my friend, the transaction between you and Michaels is strictly off the record."

"I'm counting on it. Trouble from a politician is the last thing I need."

"Thanks, I owe you one," Lester said.

Afterwards, he locked his door to think and reflect some more about Cara. He didn't know where it all would end with Cara. One thing for sure, he was going to determine Bennett's interest in her.

CHAPTER 28

On Saturday, Cara had a long talk with Ashley. Afterwards, she discovered that Bradley's condition had not changed. Frank was off on his twice a month fishing trip with a neighbor, while Naomi stayed home with Ashley.

Looking ahead, Cara figured going home would be sooner than Thanksgiving, if Bradley passed. Suddenly the thought, MattIwas should've returned from his trip. What's with that guy? For some reason, I can't let go that easy, she thought.

Checking her watch, she turned off the computer, locked the windows, and grabbed her handbag. She locked the door and walked out of her apartment at 11:30 a.m.

She got in her car as though she didn't have a worry in the world. She pulled off looking through the rear view mirror. A few seconds later, she noticed a white vehicle pull out behind her. She smiled as she drove toward Seventy-Fifth Street. The cellular rang and she answered.

"Ms. Fleming, this is Officer Jerome. I'll be your watch guard for the next eight hours."

"Good morning, Officer, thanks for letting me know that. I'm going to the *Wok-n-Roll* restaurant in Hyde Park to meet a girlfriend."

"How nice. I'll go along too, just for the ride," he said, jokingly.

Around noontime, Cara and Jennifer surprisingly arrived at the restaurant entrance the same time.

"Hi girlfriend," Cara said, giving her a hug.

"Hey, Cara, it's good to see you. How are you?" There was a slight gentleness in her voice.

"I'm doing okay, and you?"

"Wish I could say the same," Jennifer replied.

Then they walked inside. Other than a few people arriving to pick up orders, the restaurant was empty and quiet. They walked to the counter and Jennifer ordered an egg roll, shrimp fried rice and the sweet and sour chicken. Cara opted for an egg roll, a small beef fried rice and a small Chicken Bok Choy.

They sat down at a window table. It was a lovely sunny day. People strolled along the sidewalk, cars passed by on the busy street. Jennifer's face was set, mouth clamped and eyes fixed as she sat down. She seemed far away in thought, as the sunlight streamed through the windows.

"How're things at home?" Cara asked.

She turned to face Cara. "With what, me and Duncan?"

"Yeah, what else?"

"We live under the same roof, but sleep in separate bedrooms and we come and go as we please. Most of the time we're cold and distant toward each other," Jennifer answered.

Ten minutes later, their order was ready. They returned to sit down at their table.

"Are you sure you're happy with the way things are between you and Duncan?" Cara asked, taking out the egg roll.

"I don't know. I'm not leaving him if that's what you're thinking. Before I do that, I'll do something else."

"What's that?" Cara asked.

"Would you believe, have an affair, too! After all, I got needs too. It's the only thing I can think to do."

"Are you serious?" Cara replied, sipping on her diet coke. "As long as Duncan doesn't catch you. It could be a reason for him to divorce you? Think about it. You'd defeat your purpose of staying with him."

"Why the hell would he care? Based on what I know, he'd welcome it. I just want to get even and at the same time, get on with my life," she replied, in a quick, firm voice. "But, I be damned if I'm going to walk away and lose what I've worked hard for all these years."

Cara grinned. "You don't fear catching a sexually transmitted disease, or worst, AIDS?"

"That's why they make condoms. Yesterday I checked out a shop in the Loop called *Bedroom Stuff*. I've always been embarrassed by dirty bookstores and sex shops. This place is different. You won't believe how relax you feel when you walk in."

"Interesting. Did you buy anything?"

"No, just looked around," Jennifer replied. "I guess I needed something to do that do. On my way out the place, a guy hanging around the discreet entrance told me he was waiting for his girlfriend, like I needed to know. But guess what he said after that?"

"What pray tell?" Cara asked, laughing.

"He said there ought to be a tasteful place next door for guys. That it's not just women who find porno stores disgusting."

Then Jennifer hesitated for a moment longer, not sure she could say the words aloud. But then she couldn't hold it any longer. "Maybe, I ought to go back and get me a few play toys including a plastic man to make it totally real. The only thing I'll get then is *Plastic Aids*."

Cara laughed hard. "I suppose your fantasies can be as good as reality. Of course, I've never heard anyone say something so private, so downright funny."

After they'd finished joking around, she told Cara about her growing alcohol problem and how it was about to threaten her job. A few days ago, another teacher found Jennifer napping during lunchtime. A half empty vodka bottle was nearly concealed inside her purse. The teacher obviously pretended not to see and didn't say anything, except to nudge Jennifer awake and tell her the bell had sounded.

Stunned, Cara said, "I hope you'll forgive me. But I need to throw out some food for thought. You can let the words go in one ear and come straight out the other, but please hear me out," she pleaded with an air of tenderness.

Jennifer exhaled some and put her fork on the plate to listen.

"A woman, just like a man, has the right to be happy. You need to find courage to be strong and determined. Consider all your options before you decide to stay in a marriage that could ultimately destroy your health."

Jennifer turned away at times, hands clenched stiffly at her sides.

Cara knew it was time to change the subject. "I've got something to unload. Mario told me, and I quote, "I want your ass out of here. So there it is, I said it. Sorry I kept that from you."

"So that's what happened," she finally spoke. "To be honest, I thought you left him in a moment of rage.

"Whatever," Cara said, politely.

"But a grave injustice was done to you and I'm still mad as hell about it."

"True, but I'm not going to let it erode me into oblivion," she boasted. "Where there's a will, there's a way. I believe that with all my heart and soul."

"I hear you preacher woman." Jennifer straightened her shoulders and cleared her throat. "Anything else?"

"Yeah, feel up to coming to church with me next Sunday?" Cara asked.

"Oh, boy. I'm too messed up to go there."

"Come on now. Where is it written that you've got to be a saint free of sin to go to church? Life is all about living and learning. It's the best place I know to learn God's Word to help guide you along the way."

"I hear you," Jennifer remarked jokingly. Then she paused for a moment and said, "I don't know. Maybe I feel that way because I have a problem with hypocrites, the pretenders and the want-to-be Christians."

Cara nodded and smiled. "Okay, think about this one. Each of us has to answer to God someday. You're responsible for saving your own soul, just like everyone else. If it makes you feel any better, I admit I'm no saint either. It's okay to fall by the way sometimes. What's important is that we get up and try again. That's what matters. Now, my friend, I'm through preaching. Remember, I love you, but God loves you more."

CHAPTER 29

Mary Lee had kept a constant vigil by Bradley's bedside. Fearful that she'd lose Bradley, she cried often. Flashbacks flurried her mind for when Alderman Bennett flew to Memphis to be by Bradley's side the day before. He'd hope his father would regain consciousness. It was a hush-hush trip and he wore ordinary looking clothing, sunglasses and a white-bibbed cap. She had introduced him to the nursing staff as a friend of the family from Mississippi.

She remembered asking him, "Won't you please change your mind about meeting Mario? He'd never forgive us if he should learn the truth," Mary Lee whispered, unable to decide what to call him.

"That's a chance I must take. You're a champion of keeping a lid on. If you don't, I won't. The chance of Mario finding out are a zillion to one," he whispered back, and at the same time watching Bradley. "I believe that the past is the past and that's that! Considering how everything that I've done to start a new life to become a respectable citizen, I could ruin it all. It's one secret that will have to stay buried forever."

Somehow, that didn't make any sense to Mary Lee. Cooling her temper, she could only hope her son would change his mind.

Before he left Bradley's side, she remembered that Bennett hugged and kissed his father's cheek. She always carried a disposable camera in her purse. As Bradley slept, she took a snapshot of them cheek to cheek.

The secret was more than she could handle. Matthew had turned out to be like Bradley and Mario, stubborn. She couldn't help to wonder, what was wrong with her Fleming men and their pride.

CHAPTER 30

Lester had launched a secret investigation into Bennett's life. A routine check about his life in Chicago revealed a clean record. Not even a traffic ticket. Single. No claims against him for child support.

Using his police connections, Lester found Bennett's social security number. Using the Internet, he performed a credit and criminal background check. He found nothing alarming, except that Bennett had earned wages using a Detroit address dating back only to 1993. What did the guy do before then? It was like he didn't exist before then.

He decided there had to be more and he wasn't going to stop until he found it. He called a detective friend in Detroit to get him everything they had on a Giles Bennett.

By 12:30 p.m. on Monday, a four-page report came across his office fax. Three people with the name, *Giles Bennett* located. One was incarcerated in Michigan State penitentiary, another was deceased, and the third one had served two years for prostitution and released four years ago.

Lester called his detective friend back and asked for all the information they had on the third Giles Bennett. Within two hours he got the results, a phone listing for Loretta Bennett.

Immediately, he dialed the number.

"Hello, my name is Lester Miller. I'm calling from Chicago. May I speak to Mrs. Loretta Bennett?"

"This is Mrs. Bennett, how may I help you?"

"I'm calling about someone very important to you."

"Just who might that be?" Lester sensed her hesitancy."

"It's about your son, Giles. I was wondering if you'd agree to talk with me. I can fly to Detroit tomorrow morning. Just name the place and time."

"How is he? I haven't seen Giles since he was fifteen."

"He's doing quite well."

"Thank God," she said. Then she told Lester where to meet her.

"Thanks, ma'am. I'll see you tomorrow around noontime."

✦ ✦ ✦

Dexter Grady took a call from Joe Michaels at the office. He gave Michaels a glorified report about Cara Fleming and it seemed to satisfy Michaels. Further information on Cara was no longer needed. He was left wondering about Michaels' interest in Cara.

He decided to push his luck with her. Before she clocked out that day, he fell in step with her as she walked to the water fountain. She clutched a stack of papers in her hand.

"Hi. I've got two tickets to see Gladys Knight and Denise Williams in concert this Sunday. Do me the honor and come with me, please?" He asked, smiling.

There was a long pause as she studied him. She had been rehearsing the words in her head all afternoon, just in case he approached her.

"Mr. Grady, I hate to be rude, but I simply won't go out with you again. Perhaps at another time or another place in my life, it wouldn't be a problem."

"I see," he sighed deeply. "It's Lester Miller, isn't it?"

She noticed his smile had completely vanished. "Detective Miller and my husband are good friends. I needed his help with something you couldn't begin to understand. That's all there is to it," she said.

Cara waited for a staff member to pass by before it was safe to continue. "But then, why should I have to explain that to you?" She spaced the words evenly.

"Just wondering, 'cause women somehow fall for that guy right off the bat. Actually, if it means anything, I envy the him," he said, contradicting her with a smile that set her teeth on edge. He stared at her for a few moments. "Ms. Fleming, believe it or not, you're so transparent. Even Ray Charles can see that," he remarked, and walked away.

Hope this is the end of you, she thought.

CHAPTER 31

Lester called Cara soon after he arrived home. She told him about what happened at work.

"It's time to watch this guy," he said and got quiet. "Oh, I'm happy to report that I found the alderman's mother. She's in Detroit."

"Wow, great work, Lester. "This is the break we needed."

"Thanks, I'm flying to Detroit tomorrow. I'll call you after I get back."

* * *

Lester arrived at Bennigans on Brush Street in a taxi at 10:30 a.m. the next morning. Walking past several booths filled with people, he approached a middle age lady sitting alone. She wore a red blazer and black skirt. She looked ordinary, as she stared blankly through the window and she wore too much make-up.

"Mrs. Bennett?"

"Yes, and you are?"

"Lester Miller. How do you do?" He held his hand out for a handshake. "Thanks for seeing me like this."

"Please, sit down," she said, in a polite voice. A waiter arrived and took his order for a cup of coffee.

"Is he in trouble again? What is it you want to know about my boy?"

"Whatever you can tell me, ma'am." Lester said and sipped his coffee.

"Giles was a good kid turned bad. He ran away from home when he turned fifteen. To this day he never called us. After he turned 18, he was arrested, served time for his crimes.

"Would you like to see what he looks like now?" Lester asked, and pulled out a newspaper clipping.

"Sure."

She scanned the picture with three men posed in suits at a groundbreaking ceremony. Eyes filled with tears, she continued to read. "This is Giles," she said, pointing at the second man from the right. "I can't believe he's a Chicago alderman," she beamed. "I would've never dreamed it."

"I can see you're proud of him."

"At least something good came out of it."

"Care to explain that?"

"It's a long story, Mr. Miller. All I care to say is, poor Giles had a rough time growing up. It's a wonder he's alive today. I suppose it's okay to talk about it now that my husband is no longer living. God rest his soul."

"I'm sorry to hear that. When did he pass on?"

"Two years ago. He died from colon cancer."

"So, Giles and his old man didn't get along?"

"Right. He beat the boy a lot; sometimes he went too far. All I could do was try to comfort him afterwards. Guess as time went on, Giles just got tired of the beatings. I couldn't stop him, I didn't dare to," she bleated holding her head down.

"If it helps any, your husband reminds me of someone, my stepfather. I guess now I know how my mother must've felt. The sad thing is that the child repeats the same cycle of abuse with his children. Even today, the problem is widespread and there seems to be no end to it. Men and women abusing children, wife abuse, you name it, the subject has gotten national attention."

"It's just awful if you ask me. What has all this got to do with your coming here to talk to me?"

"For some reason, your son is stalking a young woman friend of mine. Someone mysteriously framed this lady as an adulteress. Her marriage was ruined. Then out of the blue and using his political power, your son gets her a job with the city making almost twice what she was making before. Recently he's been following her to and from the job."

"You sure he's the one who framed this woman?

"That's my problem. The dots don't connect."

"I don't see how I can help you. Whoever this woman is, I wouldn't know her from Adam or Eve."

"Cara Fleming is her name. She's from Memphis, Tennessee. She and her husband moved to Chicago a year ago." He noticed her facial expression change.

She pulled a photo of Alderman Bennett from her purse and passed it to Lester. This is what he looked like when I last saw him. Have you met my son?"

"Not personally. Mind if I ask where was your son born?"

"Detroit," she blurted out nervously.

"What about his relatives, namely, brothers or sisters, cousins? Perhaps they can help me."

"He's an only child. My dead brother had a son, but he was killed in the Desert Storm war."

"What's your son's birth date?"

"March 10, 1963."

Lester calculated that he was thirty-six. He figured he had something concrete to work with. "Now that you know where he is, do you want to see him again?"

"Yes, but only if he wants to see me. If he were to walk through the door right this minute, I'd welcome him with open arms."

"That's good to know," Lester said.

"I pray Giles is not involved in this young woman's troubles."

Lester grinned and leaned back in his seat. "If you do decide to contact your son, don't mention our meeting." He gave her one of his business cards. "You see the alderman isn't aware I know these things about him. It might make him nervous."

Quickly she glanced at the card and exhaled a deep breath. "You're with the Chicago police. What's really going on here, detective?"

"Just a routine check to make sure the alderman is not in any trouble. Honestly, the Chicago public thinks he's a good politician."

"That's a relief."

"So, as I said, if you can think of anything that would connect him to the Fleming name, call me. This might be your last chance to help him."

He laid a fifty-dollar bill on the table. "This should more than take care of our tab, and thanks. You've been more help than you realize," he said, and smiled.

* * *

Less than thirty minutes later Lester arrived at walked into the main police headquarters. He would run a complete search on Kirk and Loretta Bennett. It was clear to him that Mrs. Bennett was hiding something. He had doubts about the alderman's birthday. It was worth it to prove his suspicions right. At best, he could secure a copy of the birth certificate.

An hour later, the results came back. From the three-page report, Lester read:

Kirk Bennett and Loretta Bennett—owned a black cosmetic retail and women's hair salon in Meridian, MS for fifteen years, Both were sold in 1961 for three hundred thousand dollars<end of field>; no dependents <end of field>;own a home in Detroit, MI since 1969. <End of field>; Kirk, deceased 1997, arrested for spousal abuse 1970, charges *dropped; <End of field>; Loretta, living, unemployed homemaker, SS recipient. <End of record>*

Finally, he looked at the last page hoping that the alderman's birthday would be confirmed. The words stood out like a blinking neon sign: Search results for male, Giles Bennett Detroit, MI born on March 10, 1963: "*O results found.*"

"Damn, that can't be," Lester whispered. He asked his police buddy to search police records for Meridian, MS.

Less than thirty minutes later, Lester leaned back in his chair and hands folded behind his head. He studied the second report. Search results for male, Giles Bennett, Meridian, MS: "*Found (1) record: Giles L. Bennett, born February 23, 1964 to Kirk and Loretta Bennett, subject died on November 18, 1965, Cause of death, third degree burns, child abuse*".

What the hell is going on here? Lester thought.

CHAPTER 32

Bradley passed away at 3:45 p.m. Mary Lee felt like her whole world had come tumbling down around her. After the body was removed, she managed to pull herself together and drove home.

Sitting in her living room an hour later, she called Mario. Understandably upset, he promised to come home right away. Scarcely able to do anything else, she rested on the sofa flat on her back and cried some more. Suddenly she thought about her son who preferred the name, Giles Bennett, to his given name. Then she called him.

"Hello Giles. How're you doing?"

"Okay," Alderman Bennett said. "I was thinking about my father before you called. How is he by the way?"

"He's gone. Your father just passed," she said.

"Oh, no." There was a long silence. "I'm so sorry," he said frantically. In a choked voice, "Are you okay, Mother?"

"I'm holding up okay for now."

"I wish I could be there with you." He said.

"I know. Don't suppose you'll come for the funeral?"

"No, I can't." Email me the arrangements. I promise to call you later that evening."

"Is that all? Please son, we can't lose you again."

"You won't." He paused for a moment. "I just realized you didn't call me Matthew."

"I'm playing it your way. Only because you asked."

"Thanks, for understanding. But it doesn't mean I'm not proud to be a Fleming or that I don't love you, and daddy or my brother."

"Good, I needed to hear that. But you know, a mother's love is like a rubber band, stretchable as far as possible until it snaps," she whimpered.

Then she called to tell Naomi and Frank the news. Both were sad and expressed their sorrow. "My friend, I'm here for you, no matter what you need, just call me, okay?"

"I'll need it. When this is all over, I need to have a private talk with you," Mary Lee said.

After she hung up, she took the family Bible and walked to the kitchen. It was where she sensed Bradley's presence the most. She spoke to his spirit: *"I'm alone now. I've got two sons living as strangers in Chicago. I can't live with the way things are, not by myself. Oh, Bradley," she started to cry. You've been my life partner so many years. What am I going to do without you?"*

CHAPTER 33

Lester arrived in Chicago around 5:45 p.m. He showered and changed into comfortable attire, and grabbed a cold beer from the refrigerator. Sitting on the sofa, he opened his beat up attaché case, and pulled out the manila folder labeled Alderman Bennett. He read his notes and print outs of the massive computer search. Three things stuck out in his mind as puzzling: Other than a criminal conviction, a car salesman job for four years, and no record of his birth origin, Bennett didn't have much of a past. According to the Bureau of Vital Statistics in Mississippi, the real Giles Bennett died when he was almost two years old. More than likely, the father was responsible. So who is this guy, Lester wondered. Where did he come from? How did he come into this family? Lester realized he was dealing with a man who had a blemished past, not to mention an illegitimate one.

Of course, the conviction record would've posed problems for him getting elected and somehow no one cared enough to do a thorough check into his background.

However, a deeper question was nagging at Lester: Could it be that Bennett wanted Cara for himself? *Frame, ruin and rescue, and claim, would make sense.* Nothing else had up to this point, he thought.

At 5:00 p.m. the phone rang, interrupting his thoughts.

"Hi, this is Cecil."

"Hey. What you got for me?" Lester asked.

"It took a little digging, but I found out how Ms. Fleming got hired." My boss, Alderman Tucker twisted some arms. Just between me and you, I believe he did that as a favor for his friend, Alderman Bennett."

"Is that right? Okay, thanks, Cecil. I owe you one. Maybe I'll see you on the courts this weekend."

"I'll be there. Hate to cut this short. I got another stop before I go home."

"Sure, you've been a big help."

Hanging up the phone, Lester realized that Bennett had good reason to maintain his anonymity. He finished the beer, checked his watch and saw it was fifteen minutes to six. He needed another excuse to see Cara and decided to ask her to dinner. Surely, she'd want to know what he learned in Detroit, he thought.

He dialed her number and let the phone ring three times and he heard her soft faint voice say, "Hi Lester."

"Hello, are you okay? Sounds like you got a cold or something?"

"I'm fine. It's Bradley Fleming. He died today." She let out a sigh.

"Gee, I'm sorry. How did you learn about it?"

"My mother. They're all torn up over it. Bradley was a good friend to my family."

He thought about Mario and how much he loved his father. It had been over a month since he hit a few balls on the court with Mario. Several attempts to reach him by phone just to see how he was doing had been unsuccessful. Lester had taken that to mean his buddy had hit pay dirt finding a new love.

"How was your trip?" Cara asked.

"Glad you asked. Feel up to grabbing a bite to eat?

"Sure, it'll be good to get out for a change. I'll meet you there."

"You sure, I can come by to get you."

"Someone could be watching me. For both our protection, we shouldn't be seen leaving the apartment together again. At least until my divorce."

"Right. Okay, meet me at the Medici on 57th around 7:00 p.m."

An hour later, Lester waited at a table facing the main entrance. The place buzzed with voices of semi-casually dressed men and women dining out for the evening. The high ceilings and cheerful Italian décor gave the place a nice setting, though the atmosphere could at times get a bit loud for in-depth conversations. A cavernous, but packed restaurant in the heart of the diverse Hyde Park area, the restaurant was wildly popular with University of Chicago students. The food ran the gamut from American to Italian to Mexican, with hearty breakfasts that seemed to ease the effects of a hard night of partying.

Lester noticed Cara as soon as she entered. He gestured her in his direction. She looked lovely in a solid gold blazer and black fitted skirt.

"Hi, aren't you a sight for sore eyes," he said and hugged her casually.

"Hi Lester, I needed that." They both sat down.

"It's good to see you." She tossed her head and gave a gentle tug at her sleeve.

A friendly, string bean waitress soon appeared, poured some sparkling water into each glass and took their order and pranced off.

"Are you going to attend the funeral?" He asked lifting the menu from the table.

"Yes, of course. I'm taking a flight to Memphis on Friday," she replied, anxious to hear about his trip.

"Loretta Bennett was as mysterious as her son."

"Meaning?"

"She lied about his birth date and where he was born." He opened the folder, pulled out the reports on Bennett and asked her to read them.

When she finished, the salads arrived. “I don’t know about you, but I’m famished,” Lester said, digging into his salad. “I hear you have the mind of a Sherlock Holmes. What do you think?”

“I don’t know.” She quickly scanned through the documents again. “According to this, Kirk and Loretta’s five-year old biological son died due to child abuse. His name was Giles. Oh my goodness,” she said, reading further. “Then came another child, around the same age and with the same name. He’s the Giles Bennett we know.”

“It’s puzzling, to say the least, Lester said. You want to know what I believe? Alderman Bennett is interested in you.” All the signs are there. Since you left Mario, he’s made it possible for you to make more money. He followed you around the city and he was probably behind the strange phone calls.”

She didn’t want to go there just yet. She tasted some of her salad while thinking about Loretta Bennett. “The more I think about it, Loretta Bennett lied to you. It’s like the second Giles Bennett appeared out of thin air.”

“Yeah, more than she care to,” Lester said.

“On the other hand, the alderman is wasting his time. I want nothing to do with him.”

“Glad to hear that. Some women are attracted to powerful men who can offer them security. Maybe he figured you’re one of them. He laid the foundation, and now it’s pay back time. When he makes his move, you’ll know. And, I’ll be watching.”

“I feel better already. I don’t need any more battles to fight. Alderman Bennett won’t win this one,” Cara said.

CHAPTER 34

Early the next morning, Jennifer overheard a conversation between Duncan and his male friend:

"I need to talk about something in confidence. Promise you won't tell a soul?" Cecil said.

"Sure go ahead," Duncan replied.

"Remember the lady we saw at Human Services?"

"Sure, she's Jennifer's best friend."

Cecil explained his involvement with framing Cara. "I told her husband we were having an affair. At the time, none of it made any sense."

"I think we should talk in private. Jennifer's other habit is listening to my phone conversations," Duncan said.

"Say no more. Meet me at Gladys Restaurant."

Thirty minutes later, the door slammed shut. The car pulled out of the driveway.

Jennifer hurriedly phoned Cara.

"Good morning. You got a few minutes?" Jennifer asked, in a voice that was fragile and unsteady.

"Hi, what's up?"

"I got something important to tell you," she said. "Hope you're sitting down."

"I am, go on," Cara replied.

"I know who framed you __."

"Oh my God, I remember now."

Mario had played tennis that day and she went alone. Cecil Hawkins was the guy with the pretty face, and curly hair. Cecil promised she could easily get a modeling job. They took pictures together and some of her alone. Cara considered the matter fun and frolic and pushed the thought out of her mind.

"Cecil was the guy I saw with Duncan. His hair is different now," Cara said and realized she finally had the proof.

"Oh, okay. I'm glad I thought to call you," Jennifer said.

"Can you tell me more about this man?"

"You don't want to know. They're all crooks."

"Why, do you know something I don't?"

"Trust me, someone got him to pull it off," Jennifer assured her.

CHAPTER 35

The sun shined brightly on the pavement when Duncan arrived at the restaurant. Cecil was seated at a table near the window. The breakfast crowd was buzzing with conversation and smells of sausage and coffee permeated the air.

"Hi," Cecil said, glancing up from the menu. "How was traffic?"

Duncan sat down. "Slow. There was a major accident on the southbound Ryan. What're you having?"

"The usual." The waitress came and took their order and placed a large pot of coffee on the table.

For a moment Cecil stared into space, sipping his coffee.

"I hate I'm involved."

"You're sure it's the same woman?" Duncan asked.

Cecil leaned forward, "Yeah, I'm sure."

The food arrived. Two plates with the same order: Biscuits, Sausage and Eggs. Duncan sprinkled salt and spread ketchup on his eggs.

"What else did you tell her husband?" Duncan asked.

"That she had a birthmark on her butt that looked like a strawberry."

"You got to be kidding."

"No, I wish I were. I had to convince her husband that I was her lover. Anyway, I dropped a package with the pictures at the security desk. I gave him details about where she worked, the time she got to work and left each day."

"Why didn't you tell me you recognized Cara?"

"Guess I wanted to forget. A guy I play tennis with sometimes, asked me to find out who sponsored Cara Fleming's job."

Suddenly Duncan shook his head and laughed.

"Don't laugh." Cecil's voice was tender. "I did what I was told."

"I don't believe this. Thanks to your shenanigans, they're separated."

"I had a feeling that would happen." Cecil continued to spill his guts. "A month ago, Joe Michaels asked me to follow her around."

"This is getting crazier by the minute. I'm concerned that Mario can finger you as the caller. Can he?"

"Dammed if I know." Then Cecil pointed to his head. "Now you know why I changed my hairdo. "Anyway, Mario has probably trashed the pictures by now."

"You don't suspect anything criminal going on, do you?" Duncan asked.

"I don't know. Doing what I did couldn't have been as innocent as Michaels made it sound, but if something criminal went down, I'm f__."

CHAPTER 36

On Thursday, Lester had worked late at his office, preparing a testimony for a double murder case. Exhausted, he piled the papers in a folder, turned out the lights and clocked out. Later, he bought a whopper meal from Burger King.

Arriving home at 10:00 p.m., he checked the mail first. He noticed a mysterious letter postmarked in Detroit. Mysterious because it was missing several important details: a return address, date, and the sender's name. His heart escalated like an airplane pushing back from a runway. After he opened it, the words typed on a sheet of ruled paper startled him:

~

"I hope this helps the young woman you spoke of. I've got cancer. I need to clear my conscious. The man in the photo is not our biological child. We took him and raised him as our own. My late husband did it to please me. Because of our situation, it was easier than adoption. We had sold our business and were headed north to start over. During a three-day stop in a small Mississippi town, I saw a woman at the mall. She had a small boy I believed could pass for our own child. My husband used the woman's license plate to trace her name and address. They had a young infant, too. So we took the older child. The next day we followed the mother until she stopped at a gas station. She left him in the car. While paying for her gas, we seized the moment and told the boy his mother was ill. We convinced the boy we would take care of him until the ambulance came for her. We fled with him and never looked back. I loved the boy as my very own. In his own crazy way, my

husband loved him too. That's why the boy away. The child often cried for his real parents. He ran away from us when he turned fifteen. Try not to be too hard on him. He's a good man. I just know it.

Floundering in shock, Lester flopped his body back on the sofa staring at the letter. Wow, thank you for small miracles, lady, he thought. Tossing Cara's name out in their conversation did the trick. He knew Mario's family live in Memphis and Mario was an only child. The holes were closing in, but there're still too many loose ends.

❧ ❧ ❧

The next day, Cara had boarded her flight to Memphis. Once airborne, she remembered her departure from O'Hare: Lester had insisted on driving her to the airport and she let him. He focused mostly on her and not their secret investigation this time. She sensed he wanted to come with her.

Almost two hours later, she entered terminal one at Memphis International airport and her thoughts drifted to her parents and Ashley. It was the end of September and the weather was a perfect sunny 80 degrees. There were long embraces and tears. Glad to be home, she relaxed.

❧ ❧ ❧

Naomi served hot tea and southern-style teacakes. Holding Ashley close to her, Cara talked about the job, her apartment, Mrs. Walker and how glad she was to have Jennifer for a friend. And, she talked about the day care parent searching for her birth mother.

Ashley added the dessert to the conversation when it was her time to get a few words out before bedtime. "Mommy, buy me a 'puter for Christmas, please, please__. I want to be like you."

"In that case, yes. Santa will put a computer under the tree," Cara said, barely able to control herself. Like mother, like daughter, she thought and laughed some more. She gave Ashley a bath and put her bed.

Later, when Cara said goodnight to her parents, she tiptoed into her bedroom, pulled back the covers and positioned herself close to her daughter.

"Hi mommy, I fooled you. I wasn't sleep," Ashley said, putting her arms Cara. "I love you mommy, glad you came back home."

"I love you too, honey."

"Can I bring my friend Tee-Tee over to play tomorrow?"

"Sure. I can't wait to meet her. Go to sleep now." Cara continued to rock her quietly hummed Ashley's favorite lullaby, *Rock-a-bye Baby.*

So glad we've got each other, Cara thought, watching Ashley fall asleep. She was grateful, and yet so lucky to have a beautiful child who loved her no matter what. She wondered how long could she continue to let her stay hundreds of miles from her. It wasn't long before her thoughts turned to Mario and how she would react seeing him at the funeral. The only thing to do was to be kind, sympathetic and as friendly as possible, she figured.

The Slater family had arrived at the church at 11:30 a.m., dressed in black and looking somber. Flowers encircled the casket. Soft music played while droves of people filled the church.

Alderman Bennett sat a few rows from the back of the sanctuary, disguised as an older gentleman with gray hair and a beard. He wore dark tinted sunglasses and a black suit. He'd glimpsed Cara walked past holding hands with a little girl. He figured she was his niece.

He opened the obituary again. Bradley's oldest survivor was omitted. My name should be there too, he thought.

Less than two hours later, the pallbearers moved the casket down the aisle and the family followed. He realized that Mario looked more like their father. As Alderman Bennett gazed his family, he wished he could've reached out and touched his brother. Share the grief. Yell and scream out loud for his dead father. He wanted what he had missed for thirty years. The family he wasn't allowed to know, the history, the family traditions he had not been part of, simply because his identity had been staked on false information. He wanted what Mario had been given throughout his growing up years: *Love, support and family togetherness.* The strangers he grew up calling his parents were like a distant memory to him. He wanted to unravel his fake appearance, announce that he was alive and well. But he couldn't because someone knew too much, too much for his own good.

Suddenly he recalled that day in his office nine months ago when an acquaintance from his past called:

"Hi, remember me?" Paula asked.

"Vaguely, it's been quite awhile. Who are you?"

"We met when you lived with my sister, Odessa Grant."

He paused to think. "Oh, yeah. How are you?"

"Good. I recognized you on a WGN news clip recently," she said. "How does it feel to be a Chicago alderman?"

"To tell you the truth, it feels good. Why?"

Then she asked him to do the unthinkable.

Thinking about that episode in his life almost shattered his thoughts about his father. He knew Bradley had been successful and he started to wonder. Was he a fraud? Was he a mean man? Miraculously, he'd found his real family. The pretense he never existed started to wear heavily on his mind. He'd been careful not to leave a trail connecting him to the frame-up.

Once the family had proceeded down the aisle, he joined the crowd exiting the church. Moments later, he saw Paula. She stood outside alone gazing at the family. She looked slightly older. He thought she'd taken good care of herself, but then that's what the Grant sisters did. Only he couldn't remember if she worked the trade like Odessa.

At the gravesite Alderman Bennett's mind riddled with more sadness and guilt. He stood in the back of the large crowd and listened as the crowd sang, *Jesus Keep Me Near The Cross.*

Slowly he walked to his rented car. Tears flowed down his face as he heard the words, Ashes to ashes, dust to dust. He thought, I lost him years ago and I've lost him all over again. Unlike every great tradition, my father had to die before I could understand how much I miss him and what he means to me. The only way I will know my father is to try to understand the world he left behind. But given my past and the new life I've created, I could never be anything but an outsider, he decided.

Meanwhile, Mario watched Cara talking to his mother while he was reunited with Ashley and Naomi. As soon as Cara was alone, he walked up to her

"Hi, Thanks for coming."

"Hello," she responded and paused for a moment. "I'm so sorry about Bradley. How're you holding up?"

"Okay, I suppose. I still can't believe he's gone."

"Neither can I. I'm sure he's in a better place now."

"How've you been?" He asked.

"Oh, okay. How about you?"

"The same," Mario replied, and fumbled with his tie. "I've got to go. Thanks again for coming."

She turned away to walk toward her family and noticed Paula Coles talking with another woman. Cara felt as violated and cheated as she had after their encounter a year ago. She couldn't believe Paula had come from Italy to attend Bradley's funeral. Did she leave her husband? Where was she living? Did she know that Mario was about to be a free man? All at once, she was swept with anger, and loneliness so fierce, that she couldn't bear to stand there any longer.

Paula looked at Cara and waved with a smirk-like smile on her face.

Cara waved back. She swung her purse over her shoulder, trying her best to shake the unpleasant thoughts. She walked along with Frank and Naomi and Ashley to the car.

Ashley whispered to Naomi, “Why didn’t my mommy and daddy sit together in church, grandma?”

CHAPTER 37

Cara got inside her father's car and realized how alone she felt. She had imagined she would feel relieved, free to feel unattached from Mario. Instead she felt abandoned and at risk for more heartbreak. From a distance she took one more look at the gravesite and she heard Naomi's voice.

"How was talking to Mario?"

"Pleasant, but brief," she said.

"Have you heard from your l-a-w-y-e-r?" Naomi winked at Cara.

"What's that grandma?" Ashley blurted out.

Cara had to smile. Frank remained quiet and listened. She sensed Naomi wanted to hear more about the divorce proceedings but she lacked the energy to talk about the matter.

The short ride back to her parent's home was mostly quiet. Shortly after they got out and went inside, Frank changed and got busy raking leaves from a neighbor's backyard. Naomi went grocery shopping.

Cara took Ashley on a shopping spree at the mall. She bought presents for all of them. She even bumped into a few old teacher buddies. She waved and they exchanged meaningless friendly chat. Following a light snack on McDonald's burgers in the park she played with Ashley in the park.

Cara returned home at 4:35 p.m. with several new outfits for Ashley and gifts for her parents. Then she watched Ashley play with her friend, Tee-Tee.

Around eight that evening, Naomi prepared dinner: Fried catfish, homemade rolls, meatless spaghetti tossed salad and ice cream for dessert.

At the table, all heads were bowed and hands held around the table while Frank offered the blessing: "Thou are great. Thou are good. We thank thee for this food, our daily bread, Lord. And, we thank you for bringing Cara home safe to us. Amen."

During the meal, Cara thought, I really miss being here. The easy laid back lifestyle, fresh air, and the food certainly taste better. But, I don't miss the lack of privacy.

After they'd finished, Frank and Ashley went into the living room to watch a rerun of *Good Times*. Cara helped Naomi clean the kitchen, and later she presented them with the gifts. Opening them, they didn't whoop and send the wrapping paper flying the way they used to in the old days. Her parents took their time, preserving the lilac and lavender paper and the gigantic ribbons.

Frank pulled out the green robe and matching slippers, his face showed a pleasing look. "Baby Girl, how did you know this was what I needed? Thanks," he said, giving her a hug.

Naomi seemed more than overjoyed as she sat looking at all nine pieces of a new cookware set. "Out goes the set I've had for the past six years. I'll cook breakfast in these tomorrow," she said, laughing and hugging Cara.

Cara spent some quiet time with Ashley. When her daughter was in bed, she joined her parents in the living room. Frank mentioned to Cara that teacher salaries had improved in Memphis and that she should consider returning home to live.

An hour later, she went to bed thinking she wasn't really sleepy. So she read a bestseller about a perfect, faithful wife and mother who'd discovered that her husband had cheated on her. She couldn't help to relive some of her own experiences from Mario's affair and how she'd reacted when she learned the truth. The heroine in the novel had been jilted and left alone, but in the end, she found true love and happiness with another man.

Cara considered the story in contrast to her own life. She had a second chance with her husband after his affair. Yet, only a year later, to have it blow up in her face over a bald-faced lie. She knew how she was framed. Once she connected the dots, then she could move on with her life.

Finally, she thought about Bradley and was glad she'd forgiven him. It's good to say what need to be said, mend fences while you're still breathing. When you're gone, it's all over. Nothing can be said or done then, she thought.

The next morning, Naomi yelled, "Get up sleepy heads, breakfast is just about ready." Cara had been awake a few minutes before she heard her mother's voice and had sneaked in and out of the shower and was almost dressed. She happily washed Ashley's face and watched as she brushed her baby teeth.

Later at the table, they all sat down to sausage, pancakes, hot syrup, and scrambled eggs cooked to perfection. Cara cut Ashley's pancakes and generously poured pure maple syrup. They ate in silence for a few minutes.

"I don't want to come to Chicago." Ashley said and laid her fork on the table. "Mommy, when you coming back home to live?"

That did it, Cara thought. She glanced at Frank and then Naomi, her eyes searching for an explanation. Then she watched the playful emotions on Ashley's face, thinking and feeling it was all of them against her.

Cara just smiled and scooped the rest of her eggs in her mouth. After she cleared her throat, "That's a good question, Ashley," she answered and looked again at her parents. Feeling helpless to do anything about it now, she had been moved by her daughter's statement. "I'll think about it, darling."

"Good answer," Frank spoke, sipping a big gulp of his coffee.

Naomi shrugged her shoulders and whispered, "That was her idea, Cara."

"Yes and keep what Ashley said in mind," Frank said.

When breakfast was over, Cara finished packing and Frank put her small carry-on in the car.

They arrived at the airport an hour later and with time to spare. They talked some more. Cara always agonized over leaving them, and it wasn't any easier this time. Frank brought the camera for picture taking.

An hour later, Cara got up to take her place in the boarding line, Naomi hugged her tightly and said, "I love you. I'm so proud of you. Whatever you decide will be okay with me."

"Love you too, mom. Thanks. You're the best. I'll call you." She felt a clutch in her heart as the words stuck. Yet, she had to put a good face on for her mom.

Then she picked up Ashley and held her close. Feeling lucky to have her too, Cara told her how much she was going to miss her. She seemed so adjusted living with her grandparents. Cara started to worry about the day she'd break their hearts.

Ashley was coming to Chicago regardless, she thought.

CHAPTER 38

Safely tucked on the plane, Cara felt like she was suspended in a cocoon between her past and the future; a special place to be alone amid total strangers and think. Propelled into a metamorphosis that she wasn't prepared for. As the plane soared high over Memphis, her heart tugged painfully as she looked down to the rapidly shrinking places. It once meant everything to me. Growing up as a child, getting my education, my marriage and the birth of Ashley. Memphis will always hold a special place in my heart. But now it seems as though I'm sliding from one fantasy into another, she thought.

An hour and forty-five minutes later, she breathed excitement. The vast Chicago skyline: towering skyscrapers, the endless flow of water, and millions of homes and buildings, were breathtaking. She exhaled a sigh of relief thinking, this is home to me now. I'm still in control of my destiny. I've got to make the best of it, whatever that means.

Safe on the ground, she used her cellular to notify her parents. Then she rushed through the connecting tunnel and she saw Lester. And she lit up inside. They looked into each other's eyes, and all was right with the world.

She took a step toward him. "Hi."

Lester hugged her. "I'm glad you're back."

"Good to be back. Seems we're forever hugging and welcoming each other back from somewhere."

"Yeah, it does." They slowly pulled apart and shortly afterwards, made their way through busy O'Hare on the escalator and up to the next level to board the People Mover Train to the remote parking lot. The temperature roared in the low nineties and it looked like it might rain.

They chatted back and forth during the five-minute ride. He took her baggage and they piled into his car and from there to the check-out booth where he paid the parking fee. In no time he was driving full speed on the Kennedy expressway.

Feeling sure of herself more than ever around Lester, she took the lead.

"I know how I was framed."

"My God," he replied, sounding enthralled. "How did you find that out?"

"There just wasn't the time to tell you before I left." She said it before she thought about her promise to Jennifer. "Can you keep my source anonymous?

"Of course," he said, voice resigned, wondering how many more times he would have to make such a promise.

"It was Jennifer who told me. She overheard a phone conversation between Duncan and a guy named, Cecil." She told him what she knew.

"What the hell?" Lester nearly choked on his words.

"You said that like you know him," Cara said, staring at him.

Lester let out a long, audible breath. "Yep, I know him."

Lester and Cecil enjoyed an occasional drink when their paths crossed after a game of tennis. "As a favor to me, he checked around at Human Services. It seems Alderman Tucker got you hired as a favor to Bennett."

"Holy cow, you're kidding. So, that's why I got hired so quickly." She turned her head away and pushed her hair off her clammy forehead.

"There's more. Loretta Bennett sent me an anonymous letter confessing how they kidnapped the alderman from his mother."

"It's starting to come together, don't you think?" She commented.

Lester felt his head swirl around like a kid would feel on a fast moving merry-go-round. He knew he'd stepped into a messy situation that had begun to reek with more intrigue by the minute. What must Cecil be thinking?

"I've missed you. How did things go for you in Memphis?"

"They want me to come back there to live, can you believe that? My daughter will come here before I go back."

Lester smiled and shot a quick look at Cara. "I left Mario a voice mail but he never returned my call. I figured he'd already left for Memphis."

"Probably. He seemed sad but he's holding up okay. He talked to me for a hot minute after the burial. Thanked me for being there. Then he was off to attend to his mother."

"You might've thought it odd that I don't mention his name anymore," Lester said.

"Yes, I have. Why?"

"Mario has put some distance between us. I've not seen him on the courts in over a month.

"You want to know what I think?" Cara blurted. "I believe he's seeing his old flame, Paula Coles. For some reason, she's returned from Europe and she was at the funeral."

And then like a tremor that started in her head and moved through her body, it came to her. Could it be possible? She wondered.

She closed her eyes, deciding to think about Paula later.

"Talking about being bold. Did you see them together?" Lester asked.

"No. Perhaps this time around, they're being careful."

Lester picked up speed, veered into the right lane and merged cautiously on southbound Lake Shore Drive.

Thirty minutes later, he approached her street and drove on.

"Where're you taking me?"

"Don't worry, I'll get you home. But first there's something I want you to see."

Soon Lester parked his car in the ground level.

"I won't be long," he said and got out to go inside.

While she waited, Cara thought long about Lester's subtle advances. Should I give in or tell him to get lost?

Fifteen minutes later, Lester opened the door, startling her.

"Here it is," he said putting the opened envelope in her hands. While he drove, she read the letter over twice.

Five minutes later, he parked in front of her apartment.

"Do you have a few minutes?" She asked.

"Sure I do," Lester said.

"Come with me. I have something to show you, too." He grabbed her bag and followed her up the steps.

Once inside her apartment, Cara pulled open the blinds and turned on the air conditioner.

"Help yourself to something cold to drink." Then she eased to the computer room and grabbed the Chat Room file.

Lester probed the refrigerator. There was bottled water, orange and cranberry juice, skim milk, and half bottle of wine to choose from. He chose the water and he returned to the living room holding the bottle. Still alone, he turned the radio on to station FM95.

Cara returned with the folder labeled MattIwas and sat down beside him on the sofa. She watched him read the printed sheets. Then she told him about her online ventures and how she came to meet the anonymous character online.

When she finished bringing him up to speed, she asked, "What you want to bet this screen name belongs to none other than Alderman Bennett?"

Lester leaned back on the sofa. "I don't know. That's a long shot, Cara."

"Take another look at the one where I told him I lived in Chicago. For a while I wondered why he stopped communicating with me online. Foolishly, I told him where I lived and about the frame-up. Who knows, perhaps it scared him off. Why else would he fear keeping in touch with me? Think about it, his screen name is MattIwas and his license plate reads, AGIA. It has to represent, *AldermanGilesIAm*." What do you think now?"

"I see what you mean, Lester said, and stared at her.

"Now read what he had to say two weeks after I told him my story." Cara had carefully highlighted Matt's words of encouragement.

"Cara," he interrupted, lowering his head before her. "When I meet a master, I bow." He stood and lowered his head and smiled.

"Stop kidding me. If only I could figure the rest."

"No, you're good. I can see how important it is to you to learn the truth."

"Absolutely, and it has nothing to do with getting Mario back. I want to restore my innocence and bring order to my life once and for all. I can't move forward unless that happens."

Abruptly she got up and went to her bedroom. She returned seconds later carrying the engraved briefcase she'd bought while shopping at the mall.

"This is a little something for you from the south," she said, and handed it to him.

"You shouldn't have," he said, noticing the engraved initials, *D.L.M*. "It's just what I needed. Thanks."

"You're welcome. You've been too kind and I thank you," she said. She went to the kitchen for a glass of water.

A few minutes later, Lester followed her. She turned and there he stood a few feet away, eyes brimming with tenderness and passion.

"We make a great team. And, I'll help you through this ordeal. He paused and walked close to her. "Cara, "I'm falling in love with you. I guess I just wanted you to know that."

"Really." Cara offered a smile, feeling like she should say something.

"Did I shock you?"

"No." She smiled sweetly."

"That's an honest answer, one that I'd expect from you. I don't want to scare you off or anything, just wanted to tell you how I felt."

"I see." She hesitated, her brow dimpled. "I care about you, too, but that's __." She stammered, not willing to say more and she walked past him to the living room.

"Cara, wait!" He caught up with her and took hold of her arm. She refused to look at him and he wondered if he said too much too soon. "I'm sorry, I guess I couldn't help myself."

Before she could open her mouth to respond, he took her into his arms. She was powerless to resist him. His mouth searched for hers, and she didn't turn her head. She opened her mouth to him, and he kissed her long, slow and deep.

"Lester," she murmured, breathing deeply, and with a giddy sense of pleasure. "What about your friendship with Mario?"

"Should I care about that now?"

Although she'd been surprised to hear his answer, she wasn't quite ready to embark on another relationship. She'd learned the hard way to take things slow when it came to matters of the heart.

"I'm afraid, and although the past is the past, I need you to be patient with me."

He looked stricken. "For you, I can do that. I've got nothing but time."

Lester seemed reluctant to let go, but he slowly pulled himself away and she walked him to the door.

He turned to face her. "I would like nothing better than to spend next weekend showing you the city. Please say you'll let me."

"Sounds exciting," she said, and hesitated. "I'd like that."

"Great. Now, as much as I hate to, I better leave while I can. I'll call you later?"

"I'm not going anywhere."

He blew her a kiss on his way out. A few minutes later, before he got in his car, he glanced up toward her living room window. She waved and he waved back at her.

She couldn't believe what had just happened. Revived to a legitimate state of deep caring, passion and romance for another man, he'd left a burning mark on her. Everything I thought I knew has changed me into something different today, and it isn't necessarily a bad thing, she thought.

CHAPTER 39

❦

Cara put her thoughts about Lester in the left corner of her mind. She considered important matters left on her plate: *the divorce hearing, and the adultery allegation.* Had the lawyer gotten the judge to grant a court date? Her perfect attendance record at work surely would disprove the anonymous caller's claims. However, it was the bit about her birthmark that bothered her the most. No one other than Mario, her parents and her doctor knew. Her problem was figuring how Bennett could've known about her birthmark.

Then she thought, I've got to thread the needle left floating around in this haystack and maybe then I'll find my way out of this horrible nightmare. Then she searched her memory further about why Bennett would've gone to such trouble. According to Lester's theory, Bennett wanted her for himself. But then, since he got me the job, not once has Bennett made a move on me. Even so, she continued to think, why would someone with his public standing, notwithstanding his shady past, go to such lengths risking his political career? Where's the motive?

Thinking long and hard got Cara nowhere. She had a mountain of circumstantial evidence, proof that he'd done these things, but no motive. She felt like she was sitting on a roller coaster at Great America, moving up and down and all around in a one-dimensional sphere unable to see clearly.

She opened the folder and over the desk, she laid out every document she had saved from computer printouts: e-mail, instant message and private room chats, Lester's police investigation, and Loretta Bennett's anonymous confession letter.

She let her eyes focus closely on the opening words of Loretta's letter: "I hope this helps the young woman you spoke of. I've got cancer and I need to clear my conscious."

It was enough to cause Cara to want to know more. Fumbling through Lester's notes, she found Loretta's phone number and address.

CHAPTER 40

The next day, Cara's flight had landed in Detroit. She remembered reading her horoscope: *With the moon in its current sign, your secret is made of nothing more than lucky connections and a good memory.* I'm ready to jump into something different with both feet, she'd decided.

Less than an hour later, she arrived in a yellow cab. The driver parked directly in front of Loretta Bennett's home. She quickly paid the driver and then she stared at the dimly lit two-story brick house, quickly easing her way up the steps.

She rang the doorbell once. A tall middle-age lady dressed in a yellow robe slowly opened the door. She had a sour expression on her face.

"Yes, may I help you?"

"I hope so. Are you Mrs. Bennett?"

"Yes, and you are?"

"I'm Cara Fleming. May I have a few minutes of your time?"

"I wasn't expecting you, Ms. Fleming. What is this about?"

"It's about me. My innocence. My future. I have reason to believe you can help me connect a few dots."

"Well, you people don't give up, do you? Come on in. I'll give you a few minutes. I'm usually in bed around nine every night."

The living room was amply decorated, somewhat appealing, lit only by a brass floor lamp and minus a flow of cooled air.

"Thanks, Mrs. Bennett. I won't take much of your time. My flight back to Chicago leaves at 10:00 tonight."

Cara sat down in a tall leather chair near the lamp facing Mrs. Bennett. She embraced her mission with dynamic vitality. She explained how she met a character named, MattIwas. Mrs. Bennett crossed her legs and moved her body forward in her chair. Cara figured she'd made it to first base and was encouraged.

"It's not his real name, just a screen name. Everyone who uses the Internet has one. It protects your privacy.

"Please go on."

"Okay, I will," Cara eagerly replied. The man and I were in the same chat room. The conversation was about adoptions and children lost from their biological families. I told him why I was there and somehow I guess he thought I might be able to help him. We became online buddies. We sent e-mail messages and chatted often in a private room. One day he told me what happened to him thirty years ago. So, when Detective Miller showed me your letter, I couldn't believe the similarity of the two situations."

"What exactly are you trying to say?"

Cara pulled out a copy of a chat room printout and the letter she sent to Lester. "Please read both sheets and then tell me what you think."

When Mrs. Bennett had finished, she was momentarily speechless. "I'd hope writing that letter to your detective friend would be the end of this. I see it wasn't," she said. Then she stared at Cara and paused a few moments. "I hear you have a young daughter?"

"That's correct."

"Then you know what it's like for a mother to want to protect her child. It's true, I didn't give birth to Giles. Right or wrong, I considered him my child. Our own son died. We gave the new son his name, *Giles*."

"If it makes you feel better about this, Giles has a good reputation, a good heart and, he's doing well for himself in Chicago. You'd be proud."

"Really, what has he done to make you believe that?"

"Besides everything he does for the people in his ward, he made sure I found a prestigious job with the city. Without it, I wouldn't be able to make it alone. And he did it under cover. He hasn't asked for anything in return. More interesting than that, we're total strangers."

"I'm glad he helped you. Women have a hard time as it is in this world."

There was a long silence. "All I want to do is to prove my innocence. You're the only person who can help me. You wouldn't be hurting your son. I won't let that happen," Cara promised.

"How can you sit there and say that? Once the truth comes out, somebody is bound to be hurt."

"You'll have to trust me. In your letter, you stated you needed to clear your conscience. Well, I need to clear my name. Please, won't you help me?"

Cara fumbled around in her large handbag and found a business card. "Please, take my card. Call me anytime."

"What is it you want to know?" Mrs. Bennett asked, turning to look at the clock on the wall.

"I believe Giles' last name was once, *Fleming*," Cara said, leaning forward, "I base my theory on what you said in the letter. Were did the family live? Do you remember his parent's name?"

"Bradley and Mary Lee," she uttered, without blinking. At the time they lived in Greenwood, Mississippi."

Cara looked at her in surprise. A soft gasp escaped her. "Is Giles his real name?"

"No, it was Matthew. My husband thought it best to change it. Kirk Bennett hated leaving loose ends."

Cara felt like an atomic bomb had exploded insider her. She felt weak and clammy. She quickly thought, *MattIwas, I got you now!*

"You know anything about these people, Ms. Fleming?"

"Yes, as a matter of fact I do. I am married to the younger brother, Mario."

CHAPTER 41

Cara spent the fifty-five minute flight time back to Chicago in a state of disbelief. She got what she hadn't expected, an earth shattering bombshell. Holding the truth in the palm of her hands. What she hadn't expected was that it would change the lives of the Fleming family forever, including her own.

Sipping on bottled water, she wondered about Alderman Bennett's motive for ruining her marriage. Revenge is the likely choice. He felt cheated out of a life that was rightfully his. Maybe, he blamed the entire family for his misfortune in life. Why else would he have wrecked havoc on his own brother? She thought.

Then she remembered the strange way Mary Lee asked for her buddy's screen name. In her mind, it explained why MattIwas ended their cyberspace relationship. In that case, Mary Lee had reunited with her other son and he knew Bradley had died. Did the alderman attend his father's funeral? Perhaps, he came and was perfectly disguised, she concluded.

The plane landed on time and she boarded the half crowded shuttle bus. In parking lot F, she located her car. She checked to see if anyone had followed her. She quickly got in and drove off, stopping to pay the parking fee.

As Cara turned left on Cicero Avenue, she detected someone following her. The man stayed with her as she turned onto the Stevenson Expressway. She wondered if it could be one of Lester's watchmen. Weeks had passed since he'd stopped the round the clock surveillance. Maybe he lied. "Didn't he trust me?" She asked out loud. She drove like a bat out of hell.

Calming her nerves, she called Jennifer on her cellular.

Once again Cara was reminded how much Jennifer relied on her caller ID. "Hello, Cara. Where are you girlfriend?"

"Hi, I finally caught you home," Cara replied.

"Whatever do you mean?" Jennifer replied laughing louder than usual. "Where are you? You don't seem to be at home," she said, and laughed.

"Ah, ha, I fooled you didn't I?" Cara explained that using the cell phone cut household expenses. "Anyway, I've tried more than enough to reach you since I got back from Memphis. How you doing?"

"I'm all right. How was your trip?"

"Oh, everything went well. The funeral was sad of course. Mostly I enjoyed being with my family. I took my daughter shopping. She's so amazing. Don't be surprised to see her living with me one day soon."

"Knowing you, I can believe that. What're you doing with yourself these days?" Jennifer asked.

"Busy doing the usual. But I'm managing to get on with my life. How's your situation at home?"

"Glad you asked. Duncan is acting really weird. Lately, I'm getting strange feelings about my safety."

"Uh oh!" Cara knew all too well how such thoughts could wear on your mind. "Let's get together and talk. Something interesting is happening to me. I need to talk about it.

"All you got to say is where. Lord knows I need an excuse to get out of here," Jennifer said.

Cara suggested that they grab a burger after work the next day. Protecting her alibi for using the cellular, she told Jennifer she was going to take a bath and go to bed.

When Cara reached the King Drive exit she couldn't really determine if she was being followed or not. Whoever it was, Cara knew she was playing in the major leagues for sure. There was no turning back. Talking to Jennifer had calmed her nerves.

Once Cara parked in front of her building, she hurriedly went inside and locked the door. The first thing she did was to check her caller ID. There were only three calls: Two from Lester, and just as she suspected, a call from Jennifer. She called Jennifer back.

"Hi, I saw where you called. You wouldn't by any chance be checking up on me, would you?"

Jennifer explained that she remembered her doctor's appointment tomorrow at five o'clock. They decided to meet at seven instead.

After Cara hung up she frantically dialed Lester's number. Checking the apartment over, she waited for him to answer.

"I called you earlier. Where were you?" Lester probed.

"Hi, I'm all right. But, you won't believe where I've been."

"Don't make me wait." There was a long pause. "Come on, you can tell me. By the way, your line is safe. I had it checked today as a precaution," he stated.

"Detroit." It was then that she realized he took watching over her seriously.

"You didn't. Why didn't you tell me? I would've gone with you!"

"I'm sorry. There wasn't time to discuss it with you. Besides, I had a hunch that the name, *Fleming*, meant something to Loretta Bennett. Guess what, it paid off."

"Fascinating. How did you get her to talk?"

"I was very direct and to the point. I showed her the information. From there one thing led to another. She told me everything. She admitted to stealing Giles from Bradley and Mary Fleming. Can you believe his real name is Matthew Fleming?"

"Get out of here. Mario's brother?"

"Yes, they're brothers," she replied, sounding upbeat for a change.

"What led you probe in that direction?"

"They never claimed him as a dependent on their tax returns. I figured they took him illegally."

He paused taking a deep breath. "Yes it's all making sense now. Your sleuth abilities surpass my wildest expectations."

Suddenly she remembered Lester's two phone calls earlier. "Was there a reason why you called this evening?"

"Yes. You know too much. I've seen too many cases where the guilty party decides to silence the one who know too much. This one screams danger, Cara."

"Should I be shaking in my boots?"

"At the risk of repeating myself, yes ma'am. You know too much."

Lester asked her to give him a minute or so to think about a plan. "For starters, don't talk about this matter with anyone including Jennifer or your parents over your home phone. Use your cell phone. Tomorrow, your line may not be safe to talk."

CHAPTER 42

Mario took off during his lunch hour to get the paternity test results. He planned to surprise Mary Lee with the news later. Before he entered the main lobby at Jackson Park Hospital, he put out his unfinished cigarette in the large cement ashtray.

A few minutes later he entered the reception area and introduced himself to the cheery faced middle-age lady who greeted him. He was on time for a change and she told him the doctor was waiting. He slowly eased into the small, bright and neatly furnished room and sat down in one of the chairs facing the doctor's desk. He rubbed his head and moved around in the chair more than once.

"Good afternoon, Mr. Fleming. Calm down or you might go into cardiac arrest." Dr. Orzette was a gentle giant with sparsely gray hair and moustache. He had aged well and his mild mannered personality garnered a huge clientele.

"I didn't sleep well last night, Doc. Just buried my father a few days ago. My nerves are just about shot," he said and sat down."

"Oh, I'm sorry to hear that. I can understand what it must be like for you, but try to take it easy." The doctor offered Mario a glass of water. "You should try it sometimes. It's a good remedy for settling the nerves, when there's nothing else to grab."

Mario thanked him and got up to help himself to a cup of sparkling water from the corner dispenser. He gulped it all down faster than he'd ever drunk a can of beer.

"So, am I going to live or die?" Mario asked and sat down.

"According to the results of your annual physical, you'll live. Do you have any health concerns I don't know about?"

"No, absolutely not. I feel fine."

"Good. Then the only recommendation I have is for you to lighten up on the smoking, better yet, stop!"

"I'll try, as you know, old habits are hard to break."

Dr. Orzette shook his head and closed Mario's medical folder. Then he opened the file labeled, M. Fleming's Paternity Test. "Now, about the paternity test. We've carefully examined both your and the child's blood tests. There's a 99.9% probability that you are the child's biological father. In fact she has your blood type."

"I am?" Mario settled back in his chair, his eyes gleamed like a glassy volcanic rock.

"Absolutely, there's no question in my mind. I hope this is good news for you."

Mario felt like a fool but at the same time, relieved to know the truth. He shook hands with his doctor, thanked him and quietly walked out of the office thinking how he'd wasted precious time as far as Ashley was concerned. He knew he had no one to blame but himself.

As he scurried out of the hospital, his thoughts drifted to Cara. The worst obstacle for him now was facing her with the news. He felt glad that something good had come out of their marriage, although he still believed she had been unfaithful to him.

He returned to work just in time for his 1:30 p.m. volleyball class thinking that today, was a new beginning. The first thing he had to do was to pay child support payments, including delinquent payments. And, Paula flashed his mind. He figured she was the one to help him heal his wounded heart, since his marriage to the woman once thought to be his lifelong love was about to end.

❧ ❧ ❧

Mary Lee sipped coffee while she sat at the kitchen table reading over Bradley's will. As his sole beneficiary, she had money, plenty of it. Her worth was estimated in cash, savings accounts, stocks and bonds, a large insurance policy and the landscape business, over eight hundred thousand dollars. It was in her plan to honor Bradley's wishes and give Mario the landscape business valued at over two hundred thousand dollars.

But now, as she thought further, there's Matthew to consider. Mario must be told he has an older brother.

Needing to talk to Naomi alone, she called and invited her to dinner. Then she defrosted two steaks, scrubbed two white potatoes, took out a pack of store bought dinner rolls, and made ice tea to refrigerate for later. She planned to serve a tossed salad and steamed vegetables to finish the meal. She would broil the steaks in the oven once Naomi got there.

At exactly 6:05 p.m., Mary Lee put the finishing touches on the table setting and then the doorbell sounded. She greeted Naomi standing on the porch holding a gift bag. Mary Lee smiled and thanked her. After both ladies embraced in a long friendly hug they relaxed on the sofa for a few minutes.

"It's just a little something I've put together for you," Naomi said, as she watched Mary Lee pull out the purple-laced bound photo album. It contained pictures Frank took over the years from when Cara and Mario first met, their first date, graduations, the wedding, reception, birth of Ashley, their first house, parties, picnics and other family gatherings.

"This is so amazing. I had no idea you saved all of this. Oh, and there's the one I took with Bradley at Ashley's first birthday party. This isn't all that you have is it?"

"No, don't be silly. You know Frank. Taking pictures is one of his hobbies. He always bought doubles. Anyway, we thought you'd appreciate this for old times sake."

But it was Naomi who was the keeper of rituals in the family. She put her foot down on turkey dinner for Thanksgiving and Christmas and she taught Cara everything she knew about cooking. She always decorated the tree and made sure her family went to church on Christmas day. And, she was the one who put the photos into albums.

"I do," Mary Lee replied. "I'm so grateful to you and Frank. Those were the good old days, weren't they?"

"Yes. A lot has changed since then, and we're always going to be a family. We won't let nothing change that my friend," Naomi said.

Mary felt a warm glow flow through her and then she jerked to her feet and checked the food. She returned a few minutes later and sat down on the sofa.

"It smells good, whatcha you cooking?"

"Your favorite, filet mignon." Mary Lee leaned back and closed her eyes briefly.

"I can't wait." Naomi sat erect. "Now, what was it you wanted to tell me?"

For a moment Mary Lee thought wistfully of Matthew and his cautious advice. Don't tell anyone about my connection to the Fleming family. It's best to leave things as they are. If only Bradley had been brave enough to tell the truth years ago, this wouldn't be so difficult now, Mary Lee thought.

"I," she began slowly. "I've been keeping a dreadful secret from everyone."

"Oh, what is it?" Naomi reached and grabbed her by the hand.

When Mary Lee had finished, Naomi knew everything. "Oh my God," she whispered softly, her hand folded around her. Tell me about Matthew."

"I might as well __. He is a Chicago alderman and his name is not Matthew anymore."

"You're kidding me, right?" Naomi interrupted. "Did Mathew come to the funeral?"

"No, I'm sorry to say."

By then, dinner was ready. Naomi took her seat while Mary Lee served the food.

"I see," Naomi replied, and blessed the food. "Couldn't he have come anyway? Who in Memphis would've recognized him? "By the way, how is Mario?"

"He's okay. It's like he's gone off into his private world these days. How's Cara?"

"She seems to be doing all right. Frank and I both worry about her, how she's faring by herself and all. Now that she's making a good salary, I suspect she's planning to snatch our granddaughter to live with her."

"Snatch," Mary Lee said. Her eyes turned dark and insolent. "Please don't use that word."

"Right. I can understand your reasons."

Following the meal, Naomi helped Mary Lee clean the kitchen.

Later in a quiet moment in the living room, Mary Lee mentioned about the money Bradley left. She had enough to help both sons. She worried that Mario would blow his inheritance and she feared Matthew would refuse his.

"I won't forget Ashley. She will go to college without money worries. Keep that to yourself, okay?"

"Gee, that's awfully nice of you."

Naomi started to feel like her best friend was beginning to use her newfound power. Money. The root of evil, she thought. More importantly she got the message loud and clear. Keep her mouth shut and Ashley will be taken care of. She hated being used like that.

"Aren't you worried Mario will learn the truth?"

"Yes, and so that you'll know, I'm tired of keeping secrets. It's hard for me to sleep at night. Oh, there's something else you should know."

"What's that?"

"It was Cara who accidentally discovered Matthew in a computer chat room. According to Cara, they talked mostly about adopted and lost children trying to find their birth parents. Cara gave him advice to help him to find his parents. She told me things about this man that didn't seem coincidental. I faked a reason why I wanted his screen name. She gave it to me. The rest is history. Can you believe it?"

"Good gracious a life! Naomi replied. Does Cara know who Mat-tIwas really is?"

"No. Giles stopped sending her e-mails. So much has happened since I talked to Cara. Discovering my son was alive, Bradley's death, the funeral __. Maybe I'm afraid she'll ask the wrong questions."

"Knowing my daughter, she's good for that."

"I'm glad I got this off my chest." Mary Lee said.

"Well, I hate to eat and run, but I need to get home and tuck Ashley in bed. She likes a bedtime story before going to sleep."

Naomi hugged Mary Lee good-bye. She drove home with a lot on her mind. She understood clearly Mary Lee's dilemma but it had become increasingly troubling knowing the truth.

She wondered why Cara hadn't mentioned the bits and pieces she'd come to know. They're no secrets between them, or were there? She thought about Cara sitting at the computer talking to strangers in chat rooms. Aimlessly going about her life, completely in the dark about who framed her and destroyed her marriage. What's going to come of my child? She thought.

Because of a few people living their lives in anonymity and harboring stupid secrets, my daughter's character has been defamed. Now, she's headed for a divorce, Naomi thought.

CHAPTER 43

❀

Cara and Jennifer met after work at *Fuddruckers* in Calumet City, a south suburb of Chicago. Standing in line to place their order, Cara couldn't help to notice Jennifer. Her face was puffy even with makeup heavily applied. Unfortunately, her perfume didn't shield the vodka.

"So, what else is new?" Cara smiled humbly and squeezed Jennifer's hands. "What's got you so afraid living in your own home?"

"He's trying to get rid of me."

"What did you say? I'm really starting to worry about you."

"I'm worried about me too. All I seem to do lately is think the worst about everything. I'm not sure if I should stay there any longer. So much has happened in the past few weeks, you wouldn't believe any of it if I told you."

"Has he threatened or hit you?" Before Jennifer could respond, Cara stepped up and ordered a quarter pound Cheeseburger platter, fries and soda. She mentioned to the cashier to put both orders on her tab. Seconds later, Jennifer placed her order. Cara selected a cozy window table for them.

Jennifer arrived at the table two minutes later and sat down. Among other emotions was a deep sense of shame on her face. "To answer your question, Duncan hasn't hit me yet. I don't know, maybe I'm being paranoid or something. More and more, he's acting cold and testy. And I give him the same," she said.

"Talk to me. God knows you won't have a minute's peace until you do." Cara said firmly.

"Okay, I will. Once I was an asset to him. Someone he obviously valued as a companion, an occasional lover, and someone to help pay the bills to keep us in comfort. Now, I'm a liability to him."

"Do you honestly believe he would harm you in any way? Is he having an affair?"

"Yes, to both. Only, I can't talk about the affair. Duncan purchased two 45-magnums, two automatic rifles, and several small revolvers. He keeps one in his car, unconcealed. I never liked guns and dared not say anything to him about it. Actually, he has more guns than he has shoes."

"Wow, I see your point."

"He's become categorically mean and miserable to be around. He kicked Bagels in the head because he peed all over the house. Two days ago, I broke down and cried over Duncan's decision to have him put to sleep. I convinced him to take the dog to the humane society."

"Jennifer, you can't work things out with a crazy man. It seems that men are protecting their pocketbooks more than ever before. They don't care how they do it. Of course in your case, minus children and child support issues, you have marital property. Surely, you can get half of everything. What I want to know is what happened to make you believe he wants to harm you?"

Jennifer explained how she'd taken a carton of orange juice out the refrigerator. She was going to take the juice upstairs and fill it with vodka. When she discovered it had been opened, she noticed he stopped eating his breakfast and, he turned his head, slightly watching her. She poured some of the orange juice in a glass. It didn't look quite right and she decided to empty both containers down the drain. Duncan shook his head in disappointment that she didn't drink it.

"It's a feeling I can't explain," Jennifer added, acting like she shouldn't say anymore to Cara.

"I don't like it that you have to live like that," Cara said as tears filled her eyes. "What if he decides to create false accusations about you? Considering what happened to me, anything is possible."

A frown flickered across Jennifer's brow.

Just then, Cara's name was announced over the intercom. They picked up their order and walked around the buffet, selecting salad vegetables and toppings for their burger. Stopping at the beverage machine, they both chose diet sodas. Cara returned to the table.

"I'm sorry if I overstepped my boundaries."

"Apologies aren't necessary," Jennifer said. "You can say whatever you want. In the end it's up to me, right?"

"Then come and live with me until you can find a place to stay."

Jennifer leaned her elbow on the table and rested her chin in her hand. "Where would I sleep? There's a lot in the house that belongs to me." Jennifer jostled on the table and bit into her burger.

"For you, I'd make room. The offer is good for as long as you need it."

"Thanks. Now, I want to hear your exciting news."

"Oh, nothing so exciting that it can't wait for a while," Cara replied, with an adventurous toss of her head. She wished like the dickens she could tell Jennifer about her friend, Detective Miller, and all the rest. What good would it do either of them anyway, she thought.

They left the restaurant an hour later and Cara walked Jennifer to her car and hugged her tightly. "I'm counting on you to be good to yourself. I'll call you every day."

She had started to feel close like a sister to Jennifer. In blood, sorrow and strength. But, with all that Cara was facing in her own life, she hadn't realized how brittle her own safety had become and how lonely she was until she saw what Jennifer's life and her unhealthy marriage had done to her. Cara thought, Jennifer needs to see herself as the solution and not the problem. Forget what she might lose by way of assets, and consider that living a healthy, happy life was far more valuable to her. Women do it all the time. They leave and start all over again, only to discover the tradeoffs are worth it.

It took Cara less than thirty minutes to return to the city. She stopped and picked up toiletries, pantyhose, and Centrum vitamins before driving home.

At her apartment, she got the mail, went inside and locked the door and still thinking about Jennifer. Four calls registered on the caller ID and there were several from unknown numbers. Checking her voice mail indicated no one had left messages. She felt as though the nightmare was starting all over again and that the voice message hadn't stopped the unknown calls.

After she undressed and changed into an oversized T-shirt, she looked through the mail, and saw a letter with a return address: Mario Fleming, 5340 South Blackstone.

She unfolded the letter and much to her surprise was a check from him totaling $2,100. She put the check aside and quickly scanned through the words: *Dear Cara: Ashley is my daughter. I'm sorry I doubted that and for how I've behaved towards her. Enclosed is the child support money I owe you. Court ordered or not, the payments will continue." Mario*

❦ ❦ ❦

For a change after getting home, Mario opened his door feeling as though he had everything under control. He was certified as Ashley's father, had reclaimed a woman from his past, and he had more money in his bank account than he'd ever expected.

He remembered his secret affair with Paula and how he'd walk around the house in Cara's presence humming and prancing to the tune, *Me and Mrs. Jones*. With a conscience free of the dead-beat-dad stigma, he found himself trying to sing, *I Believe I Can Fly,* in the shower.

It was time to hook up with Lester for a game of tennis. Lester rarely ever beat Mario. Breaking a two month long silence, he decided to place the call.

"Lester, my man. How's it going?"

"Can't complain. How're you and the family holding up?"

Mario assured Lester that he and his mother were doing well and he thanked Lester for the sympathy card. "I told my mother about you."

"Good, so, how're you doing?"

Mario told Lester that he was seeing an old flame from Memphis and that he was finally caught up with his child support payments to Cara.

"What made you change your mind?"

"Why you say that?" Mario asked.

"Correct me if I'm wrong, but, I seem to remember you talked about it before."

"Probably." Mario lied. He never mentioned Ashley and his paternity concerns.

"Hey man, I'm glad that matter is settled," Lester said.

"Enough about my problems, feel up to hitting a few balls tomorrow morning?"

"Sorry, but I can't. I'm helping someone work through a difficult situation. Maybe, another time."

What is it you aren't saying, Lester? Mario thought.

CHAPTER 44

Five o'clock marked the end of the working day for most people, but plainly not for Cara. Earl Dunlap had requested a meeting to discuss her less-than-satisfactory performance evaluation.

"I don't understand. This evaluation is not correct, Mr. Dunlap," she said, holding the form. He didn't appear to believe her and she was poised to handle whatever he had to say. Right away she knew she had to put up or shut up.

"Are you questioning your supervisor's conclusion?" He asked.

"No, not a question, but a protest! This report is wrong and it doesn't represent the truth about my work."

"Why is that, Ms. Fleming? It's hard to believe someone with Dexter Grady's service record would stoop to such a level. What exactly did you tell him?" Dunlap asked and shrugged his shoulders to hide his confusion.

"That I didn't mix business with pleasure, that I was here to do a job and not to socialize with him or anyone else on the job. It just goes against my grain to mix the two."

"Can you prove your case?"

"I most certainly can."

"Good, bring me the proof. I'll hold off signing the report."

"Thanks, I appreciate that."

She politely excused herself from his office and copied information from her files: Coordinator Reports, memos, names and phone numbers of her contacts at community agencies. She gathered attendance record at meetings, dates and times that he asked her out to lunch. She remembered he called several times at home and decided she'd bring her caller ID. Grady's phone number was stored in memory. She piled her papers measuring a foot high into her brief bag and clocked out at 6:00 p.m.

Just as she was about to pull out of the parking lot, her cellular rang. It was Lester.

"Hi, doll face."

"Hi."

"Are you okay? You sound troubled about something," Lester inquired.

"Perturbed is more like it." She told him about her meeting with Mr. Dunlap.

That __Grady", he thought. "It doesn't sound good. Can I come over? We can talk about it."

"Sure, come around seven-thirty." She pushed the off button, fit to kick somebody.

The drive home took longer than expected and when she arrived, it was 7:05 p.m. She showered, changed and drank a glass of water.

Lester arrived on time and after they reviewed her defense plan, she began to feel hopeful. Then she mentioned the letter and the money Mario sent her.

"I talked to Mario yesterday," Lester announced. "I know about the paternity test. I'm glad for you."

"Really? What do you suppose changed his mind?"

"Beats me. We didn't talk long. He suggested we get together on the court. Seems he can't wait to whip me again. I turned him down, told him I was helping out a friend with a problem. That's the other reason I needed to see you. I've thought about what I said to him, I think I goofed."

"Really, why?"

"It occurred to me that he never talk to me about his daughter's paternity."

"Oh no. If you're right, he will wonder how you knew and will start to get ideas.

"Let's hope not. Lately, it's hard to keep a straight head, especially around you."

She smiled. "Mario had a lot to drink that night. Maybe he can't remember."

At this point, Lester figured for both their sake, it was best to stay away from Mario.

"I want you to think about your happiness," Lester said. "Put aside all the unpleasantness around us. You deserve to be happy for a change." He kissed her on the hand.

"Amen to that," she said and smiled.

"To keep you that way, I've got a plan," he said. The last stop on our date this weekend is a cruise on Lake Michigan. You shouldn't return to your apartment. Bring an overnight bag to the condo around two o'clock tomorrow. I'll arrange guest parking in the underground garage. You can stay in my guest room," he said.

"Really. Can I think about it?" Cara asked.

CHAPTER 45

Lester turned off the stereo, thinking it was time to make a decision. He could either work to get his life in order or return to his old ways. He almost laughed when he realized there wasn't any choice at all. He'd already made his choice. He'd chosen Cara over a life of rambling hopelessly with different women. She would never fit into his old life. But he could fit perfectly into her life.

His spirits lifted suddenly when Cara walked out of the guest room at 5:30 p.m.

"You look stunning," he said and smiled.

"Thanks, and you never look more handsome."

"Are you ready for a night on the town?"

"Yes, I believe so," Cara responded and grabbed her purse.

A few minutes later, Lester escorted her to his car.

Dinner was at *Onesixtyblue* restaurant in downtown Chicago. Michael Jordan's involvement helped it become a people-watcher's paradise. Sport stars, often frequented the elegant eatery converted from a pickle factory, and other celebrities complimented even the self-consciously hipped patrons' expectations of a great evening. The architectural design, the black painted glass walls, thick black columns, wavy ceiling fixtures that look like hard-candy ribbons, was rather masculine. But the warm indirect lighting and elegant table settings softened the blow.

Cara seemed wonderfully surprised at the charm that oozed from the understatedly elegant room. They both dined on a seared salmon fillet crusted with asparagus, expensive wine and chocolate bars with mango sauce. The service had been impeccable so far. The server was polite and friendly, and the food was prepared with a flair for presentation.

"Do you come here often?" Cara asked.

"Actually, no. A police buddy brought his girlfriend here for Sweetest Day. He gave it rave reviews. I figured it was a place fit for you."

"It's the best I've ever been to."

"There's more to see and do before this evening is over, my dear!" He sipped some more wine.

She asked him about his childhood and was surprised when he didn't evade or pass it off with a joke.

"What do you want most out of life?" Cara asked.

"Mostly love, happiness and a sense of security. I've always wanted someone I could like as well as love. And, someone I could agree and disagree without becoming disagreeable."

Hands wrapped around her glass, "From all the above, which is more important?" She asked.

"Let me put it this way, I don't want someone I can live with. I'm looking for someone I can't live without." He laughed.

She returned the laugh with a smile. "I couldn't agree more." She finished her shrimp and wiped her mouth. "Two things I'd wondered about: your astrological sign and your marital history.

"I'm Pisces, and you?" Lester asked.

"Scorpio. I've read that a match between us rates on a scale of one-to-ten, eight for comfort; nine for communication and seven for chemistry."

"Is that right? I'm not up on astrology, but I'm glad we're a perfect match."

At exactly 7:45 Lester ushered Cara out of the restaurant. He took her to Grant Park. Amid a starry sky and an unseasonable 71 degrees in early October, they walked from Michigan Avenue to Columbus Drive. Lester told her it's where Chicago's major events were held: parades, fairs, carnivals, festivals like the Taste of Chicago in July, Venetian Night in October, country and jazz concerts.

A Denzel Washington movie at Navy Pier was next.

Around midnight, he whisked her on the Spirit of Chicago for a moonlight cruise on Lake Michigan. The 3-deck ship accommodated up to six hundred passengers. Featured, were narrated sightseeing of Chicago's skyline, all-you-can-eat buffets or seated dinners prepared by executive chefs, live music, and cocktails galore.

Off in a world of their own, they danced, sipped wine and behaved like newlyweds on the Fiesta Deck in the large crowd.

After the ship docked he took her home with him. It was 2:30 a.m. when they walked inside. Lester secluded himself in the master suite to shower. Cara showered in the guest bath, changed and walked to her room. Just as she was about to enter, Lester appeared in the hallway. He was wrapped in a long robe. He took her breath away momentarily.

"I'm sorry, if I frighten you." His gaze was as soft as a caress and she felt her pulse beat in her throat.

"Don't be silly," she said and smiled. "I should get to bed if I'm going to make it to church in the morning."

The smoldering flame she saw in his eyes radiated a vitality that drew her to him like a magnet. His large hands slipped through her arms, bringing her closer.

"I thought a goodnight kiss might be in order."

As though the words released her, she flung herself against him and suddenly she was lifted into the cradle of his arms. His mouth covered hers hungrily sending new spirals of ecstasy through her."

She could see the pain in his eyes as he thought about what she said. And he seemed to want another one. He kissed her again, followed by a series of slow, shivery kisses.

Then he whispered in her ear, "I want you so much it hurts."

"No, we shouldn't," she said, fighting the urge to push herself away, to get inside and close the door behind her.

"I know I promised I wouldn't do this," he murmured as his grip tightened while his attitude became more serious. "I just want to love you, that's all."

It surprised her that this time she had no desire to back out of his embrace.

Lester gently lifted her body into his arms and carried her inside the guest room __.

After what seemed like hours, Lester had made her a satisfied woman, unable to move at her own will. Settling back to enjoy the feel of his arms around her, she was happy and in that moment she didn't seem to care she'd lowered her morals a bit and slept with a man without the benefit of holy matrimony.

She would let tomorrow take care of the shame, and the self-disgust.

CHAPTER 46

The next morning Cara was fully aware they had slept together.

"Good morning," he said, staring at her.

"Tell me it was all a dream." She felt ashamed. She was still a married woman, how could she? She wondered silently.

"Oh, but it wasn't. It's real time and last night, I made you mine. This morning, I make you breakfast," he stated passionately, wrapping his arms around her like a warm blanket. "Do you realize how beautiful you look when you wake up?"

"No, I haven't noticed."

"Because of you, my luck has changed."

"What do you mean?" she asked.

"Just that you're the type of woman possessed with everything a man needs and wants. Together, we can take on the world."

"Sure, tell me anything. Seriously, as good as it was, and as much as I needed it, this *won't* happen again," she said and shifted her body to look at the ceiling. "I'd like to shower and change, then I'll devour whatever you dish up for breakfast." She watched him get up and throw on his robe. "I was thinking you might consider going to church with me today."

Turning to face her, "For you anything. We can take off after we eat." He bent down and kissed her. Finally he pulled himself away staring deeply into her eyes.

She waited until she was alone to lie there, in only the soft, lingering glow of pleasure and reflect. And, that he was Mario's friend didn't matter either. As good or as bad as it was to give in to Lester, she couldn't think of anything or anyone else at the moment. The rest of the day would be theirs together.

After she showered and dressed, she entered the kitchen and welcomed the smell of onions, green peppers and coffee. He delivered two plates to the table, each with a ham omelet and toast. He poured them a tall glass of orange juice and filled two black mugs with steaming hot coffee. He waited until she blessed the food and they plowed into their omelet.

"How is it?" He asked.

Her smile broadened in approval. "Better than any I've ever eaten. The eggs and seasoning are a perfect blend. I could get used to this."

"Good, I love spoiling you."

Exactly at 10:00 a.m. they were dressed for church. Cara had on a two-piece Liz Claiborne, red jacket and matching long fitted skirt, taupe bag and matching shoes.

Ten minutes later Lester drove away from his South Shore Drive condo. Unexpectedly after he passed Seventy-Fifth and Paxton Avenue, he glimpsed Mario's car trailing a block behind them.

Instantly, he thought, I don't need this. What's with this guy? Whatever happened to moving on with his life? Without alarming Cara, he wondered when and where did the pursuit begin. A likely confrontation with her soon to be ex worried him.

The next day at work Cara fought to keep self-control as she speculated what Dunlap had decided about her evaluation. Everything had been turned in on Friday. Dunlap assured her he would speak to Grady. And, surely, she'd learn her fate before the day was over.

She completed two site visits mingled with teachers and the children. When the day ended, there wasn't a word from Dunlap. "Perhaps tomorrow," she thought as she clocked out.

The phone rang just as she arrived home around six that evening.

She answered and it was her lawyer.

"Cara, I've got some bad news. Mario has thrown a monkey wrench in your divorce settlement. He's claiming you're unfit to raise your daughter. He wants custody."

Her breath quickened, and her cheeks became warm. The words made her feel weak and sinful. She wanted to toss them back in Mario's lap, scream that he was without honor too.

Instead she asked the lawyer, "Why? Can he do that?"

"Prolong the divorce. Are you sure you've told me everything about your situation?" Garnell asked.

"Mario hasn't talked to me since his father's funeral. I haven't a clue."

"Fortunately she masked the tremor in her voice. Then she mentioned Mario's letter and lump sum child support payment. "I'm sorry, should I have called you?"

"Right. I can't help you appropriately if you hold back," Garnell demanded.

"Oh boy, it never ends, does it?"

"Don't jump the gun just yet," he said. "Let me find out what's going on. I'll get back to you as soon I have something to report."

She plopped down on the sofa, thinking that a peaceful split was out of the question.

CHAPTER 47

Two days later Cara stepped onto the elevator trying to feel hopeful. As the crowd began to thin, little knots formed in her stomach. Half worried and half optimistic, she refused to consider her fate.

When the last two people got off ahead of her, she held her head up, fidgeting nervously with the strap on her briefcase and walked toward her cubicle. She couldn't help to pass Dexter Grady's office. As usual his door was open.

"Ms. Fleming?" he called out to her.

She stopped slowly to walk back to his office door. "Good Morning, Mr. Grady." He waved for her to come inside.

"Can I have a word with you?"

"Sure," she replied, and walked inside and sat down.

"It seems that my behavior and action have been inappropriate. I've corrected your evaluation. The new version should be on your desk. It was foolish to rush to judgment." By now, cold sweat coated his forehead. Will you accept my apology?"

"If you are as sincere as you sound, I'm sure I can do that," she said feeling as if a huge weight had been lifted from her shoulders.

"Thank you. I really mean that."

"You're welcome, but also, relieved, she said, wondering if her luck will hold out in the likelihood of another mishap.

"If that's all, I'll get to work now," she said and stood.

He walked her to the door, shook her hand and wished her good luck.

Later, at her desk she opened the brown envelope and found the revised evaluation report signed by Grady. All that was left to do was for her to sign it. She did exactly that and delivered it back to Grady's office.

❦ ❦ ❦

It was lunchtime and it couldn't have come fast enough for Lester. It was his day off and he surprised Cara on her job. In secret, Dexter Grady would have hell to pay if she didn't get the correct evaluation.

He found his way to her office with a little help from the receptionist. She stood staring out the window, looking at the bordering skyscrapers. She had just finished typing reports due that day and had stepped a few feet from her desk to think. And, she lacked an appetite to eat her lunch.

He eased up to her without so much as a sound. "Hi, Ms. Fleming."

"Hello. I know that voice anywhere," she replied in a whisper.

"I had to stop by and see you in action." Lester said.

"Well, it's good to see you," she whispered. She motioned for them to return to her desk and they sat down.

"So, how did it go with your evaluation?"

She showed him her official evaluation report. He read it and was pleased. "Congratulations, you won. I'm happy for you," he said, laying the envelope on her desk. Then he looked her over seductively. "I love you."

She pulled back and sat up straight in her chair when she heard her co-worker's voice in the next cubicle. "Shh, don't say that," she whispered and took a deep breath. Then she wrote on a sheet of paper: You won't believe what Mario has done now."

CHAPTER 48

Today, Mario took Paula for lunch at a popular soul food restaurant. She was glad the paternity issue was settled. She urged Mario to go and see Ashley. More than anything, she wanted Mario to pop the question. He always never got to that point, except to hint around the subject.

"You're positively glowing, Paula." Mario waved to the waiter and ordered another glass of wine. He needed to change the subject.

"I believe last night's lovemaking did the trick darling."

"Good. You were as good as always, you know."

Paula continued to stare at him. Six years had done him nothing but favors—he was more handsome than ever. His body was nicely muscled and his washboard abs showed nicely through his yellow ribbed sweater. He'd grown into a man, with knowing dark brown eyes, full, sensual lips and a smile that would melt a stronger woman than her. She'd remembered his smile and his c___ from the past. She'd taught him well and he gave unbelievable pleasure—enough to blow her off this planet when she climaxed. How lucky can one woman get? This time she decided to put all of her eggs in his basket.

Mario started to tell her about his friend, Lester. "I'm not quite sure what's with the guy these days." Probably, up to no good, he thought. "However, I want to introduce you to him."

"Really, tell me about him."

"Besides my favorite tennis partner, he's a cop, married and divorce at least two times. At least, that's what I heard. Now, he's playing in dangerous territory."

A momentary look of discomfort crossed her face. Thinking she knew what he meant by that, she said, "I read somewhere that if the first marriage does not succeed, people will say that you were young and didn't know what you were doing. A second time around, they say, well you're entitled to make a mistake. The third time, people start to wonder what's wrong with you," she replied.

"Is that right?" Mario asked.

CHAPTER 49

❀

Cara walked inside her kitchen and thought, "You won't win this one, Mario," she said, and started to pace the floor. Deciding to skip dinner, she walked to the bedroom, got undressed and snapped a plastic hanger in two pieces trying to hang her blouse. How dare he try to take Ashley from me? She yelled.

She plopped down on the bed. A few minutes later, the thought hit her that Jennifer hadn't returned her last two phone calls. Cara hoped it was because she had come to her senses and left Duncan. She'd promised to keep in touch and Cara worried about her.

At 6:35 she dialed the Tate's number, letting it ring eight times. She waited fifteen minutes and dialed it again. This time she left a frantic message: "Jennifer, call me. It's important."

She tossed and turned for a few moments filled with worry. Right or wrong, she'd decided to go and see Jennifer the next day. Then the phone rang. She didn't look to see who was calling, figuring it was Jennifer.

"Hello," she said, letting it ring only one time.

"Ump", she heard the deep male voice blurt out. Then she heard a dial tone.

Fifteen minutes later the phone rang again. With her back turned to the phone on the nightstand, she was almost asleep and barely heard it.

"Hello," she snapped.

"Hi, it's me. Did I do something wrong?"

"I apologize, Lester. No, it's the hang up calls and everything else on my mind."

"That's understandable. Have you eaten?"

"No, I wasn't hungry after I got home." She sensed he wanted to tell her something, but for her, she just needed to be close to him, to have him sit and hold her and make it all go away, if not for but one night. Only to herself would she admit that.

"Great, expect me around 7:30."

"See you when you get here." She took a shower and changed. The apartment smelled fresh. The furniture was dust free. Cara knew her bed had been made with fresh linen, the kitchen floor tile would be shiny; the carpet and rugs had been vacuumed; her laundry would be neatly arranged in the drawers or closet. Within fifteen minutes she dressed in a pair of perfectly fitted jeans and red top.

Lester arrived nearly on time at 7:39. He walked in, holding a steaming hot pizza.

"Hi, thought you might like something easy and Italian tonight?"

"Thanks." She gently grabbed the pizza. "If it's okay with you, I'll put it in the oven.

"Exactly what I had in mind." He had to smile at her words, while reading something altogether different from them.

When she returned to the living room, Lester was sitting, leaned back with his head resting on the top of the sofa. Both hands tucked prominently behind his head. She sat down a few feet from him, Indian-style.

"What's on your mind?" She asked.

"Seems I've caused a problem for you. Mario knows about us. I would bet my life he followed us Sunday."

"What? Why would he care? By all indications he's hooked up with Paula again," she spat.

"I wish I knew why, Cara. For both our benefit, I just felt you should know."

"Well, that would explain why he wants custody of Ashley."

"Gee, this puts a new spin on things."

Hearing the words, Lester started to worry. What if Cara decide to cool it between us until after her divorce? I can't imagine not being around her, not ever. A man in Mario's situation could be motivated as such, only out of revenge or because he's jealous, he thought.

"It seems I under estimated the guy, Cara."

❧ ❧ ❧

Cara arrived at work the next day trying hard to deal with too many uncertainties and unanswered questions. She knew before she could move her friendship forward with Lester, she had to get down to the core of her larger problem. She would do better to listen to her inner voice.

Soon after she'd checked her phone messages and department memos, she used her cellular to call her lawyer. Waiting to learn something new about her case had become unbearable.

"Mr. Garnell, this is Cara Fleming. How are you?"

"Oh, there you are, I'm fine. I just left a message at your home number. We've got a court date. The bad news is the divorce settlement papers aren't signed. And, we know why?

Clearly, she did. "What happens now?"

CHAPTER 50

While Cara sat at her desk, she took a call from Lester. He explained his involvement with another murder case. A young black woman was found dead at her home this morning from an apparent overdose.

Are you sitting down?"

"Yes, why?"

"Where did you tell me Jennifer lived?" he asked.

"In Pill Hill? Oh, my God, you aren't going to tell me it's Jennifer you found?"

"I'm afraid so, Cara. The first officer on the scene found her note. I have it. I'm so sorry.

There was a long pause and as Cara struggled to fight back the tears, she managed to ask Lester if she could call him back. When she pulled herself together she asked Grady for permission to leave and told him why.

Thirty minutes later, Cara drove away from her downtown office headed to Jennifer's house. Although the body had been removed, she needed to get another glimpse of the house, to be close to her again.

She parked three blocks down on Jennifer's street and she told herself to be strong as she got of her car. She walked up to a point where she saw the yellow police sign.

A scene still busy: Police personnel going in and out of the house, several squad cars blocked the street, and several onlookers standing and talking to each other. Cara stood outside the line in a state of disbelief. Too angry to react, she looked up at the sky thinking Jennifer had to be up there and out of her misery. All she could think about was Jennifer was dead, and Duncan was alive and free, free to do what he wanted now.

Moments later, she saw something that made her take a deep breath. A man resembling Duncan walked out the house with two officers. Immediately she wanted to scream out at him, but didn't. He looked worn and haggard. He stood along with the officers on the circular walkway, talking for a few minutes. She wondered what he told them. More importantly where was he when it happened. Had he spent the night away again?

The officers took turns shaking Duncan's hand, patting him on the shoulder before they walked to the cars. She felt another surge of anger, turned around and began to walk back to her car.

Just then her cellular rang. It was Lester.

"I was worried. Are you all right?"

"I'm okay. She gave him a full-blown report. "I'm just sick about this," she bleated feeling cold and angry.

"You and Jennifer were close. I can understand how you must feel?"

"Yes. And I feel like I failed her." Fresh tears welled in her eyes.

"Come on, now. Whatever was troubling her, you didn't cause her to do this."

"True, but still, I wished I could've done more."

"I'm sad that you're sad. Listen, you're not alone, I'm your friend, too. And, this friend loves you."

"Thanks, our friendship is important to me," Cara replied.

"I've got to work later than usual this evening. I'll check on you later," he said.

"I understand."

She decided to go back to work.

When she arrived home later that day she walked inside her apartment feeling only marginally better. Even though Jennifer's situation was one that justified her state of unhappiness, it certainly had been totally unnecessary for her to end her life. Maybe Lester will show her the note. Perhaps, reading it would bring clarity and closure.

Exhausted, Cara dropped her body to the couch and fell asleep. When she woke up she felt the urge to call Naomi and tell her the sad news.

"My friend, Jennifer was found dead today.

"Good Lord."

"She was the only girlfriend I had here. She was in a very unhealthy, unhappy marriage. According to Jennifer, her husband was mean, and extremely critical. If you ask me, it was a sign that he wanted a divorce.

"Why couldn't she have left him and started over like you?"

"I don't know. I practically begged her to do that.

"Don't beat yourself up too much, okay? Just pray that you find strength and wisdom out of it. There's something to be learned from every situation."

"I will, Mom."

They talked for a while and she felt a sense of relief. But not the sadness and the void she would her feel for a long time to come. She felt it was time to change the subject and talk about her situation. She hoped it wouldn't cause Naomi to worry.

"If my lawyer can work a miracle, I'll be divorced soon," Cara said.

"Oh, yeah. Is Mario giving you problems?"

"Of course. First he started paying child support. No sooner than he did that, he told his lawyer I wasn't fit to raise Ashley. I've got to fight to keep my daughter, Mom.

"No way he can do that," Naomi screamed. She paused for a moment. "What payments? Why didn't you tell me?"

"I'm sorry, I meant to. So much is going on." Cara explained told Naomi about the college fund she'd set up for Ashley. "There's more I haven't told you." Cara blurted before she'd thought clearly how best to tell Naomi what she'd been up to. "I met a stranger over the Internet. It turned out that he's Mario's brother. He's the kingpin behind the frame-up."

"Have you mentioned this to anyone else?" Naomi asked.

It suddenly struck Cara that her mother's reaction was not what she'd expected. She seemed to know about the Fleming secret, possibly more. Or was it her imagination? For a moment, Cara couldn't figure her mother. Somehow that didn't seem to matter.

"Well, my brave daughter, you have been busy. I can't believe you actually took off to Detroit to meet this woman. What was she like?"

"Aloof, nervous and yet poised. At best, she doesn't want the alderman's career destroyed.

"I bet. At least you got her to tell you the truth."

"What good does it do me? *The man who ruined my marriage is my brother-in-law.* What I want to know now, is why did he do it?"

"Think carefully, were you able to determine if the alderman knew he was Mario's brother before the frame-up?"

"No. I'd be surprised if he did."

Naomi let it all click around in her brain. Cara knew too much, too much. To keep her safe means keeping quiet about the Fleming secret. But, in doing so, her daughter could lose custody of Ashley.

"This could get sticky for you, Cara. If things don't go as you plan, are you prepared to live without your daughter?"

"No, I'm not and neither are you, Mom. No matter what, I'm going to fight these charges with all I got. I won't lose her."

Naomi hated reneging on a promise, especially the one she made to Mary Lee and yet she knew what she had to do. But, first she'd try something on her own.

"I'll talk to Mary Lee. I'm sure we can work something out."

"Why would she want to, Mom?"

CHAPTER 51

❀

Cara put two tickets to the pastor's ball in her purse. Initially she'd planned to go with Jennifer. But that was before she met Lester. Jennifer was gone and now, the time just didn't seem right to be seen with Lester in public. As a gesture of good faith she stopped by the church before she went home. She would ask Barbara to donate the tickets to someone who couldn't afford them

When she entered the main lobby she glanced Barbara coming out of the mailroom.

"Hello, Cara. I'm surprised to see you."

"Hi, it's you I'm here to see," Cara said.

Since the strange looks Barbara threw her sitting along Lester at church a week ago, the chill between them had grown noticeable.

"I won't be attending the pastor's ball. It's such a shame to let them go to waste." She passed the envelope to Barbara containing two tickets. "Please, give them away to whomever you desire."

"Sure, thanks. It's been quite awhile since we talked. How're things going for you?" Barbara asked.

Cara detected a thawing in her tone. Instantly and for some reason she felt vulnerable. "I'm okay. You?"

"Oh, I'm hanging in there and doing it my way," Barbara said. "It's not everyday I get to see you except, on Sunday. Can I have a word with you?"

"Sure, I have only a few minutes before I must get home," Cara said, and gestured to the empty two-seater to the right of the security station.

Both ladies pranced over and sat down. Cara looked at Barbara with a calculating expression waiting for her to take the lead.

"There's something bothering me. I can't think of anyone I know to ask this question." Barbara's body slumped forward as she flipped the thin stack of mail in her hand.

Cara started thinking, Oh sure. Where had she heard someone throw her a lead like that? She told herself to give the lady the benefit of the doubt and listen. She might learn something. Out of sheer habit, she crossed her legs and folded her arms around her.

Barbara exhaled a deep breath and continued. "I'm a single woman who's been roped around as far as men are concerned. I'm the wiser because of it. The problem I have is how do you tell a friend that the man she's involved with has a sketchy track record without hurting her feelings. If it were you, what would you do?"

"Don't tell her what she should know about this guy," Cara snapped, letting the words leap from her mouth. She wouldn't want to hear it. Maybe, you could slip her an article about doing background checks. She could check him over before she commit her heart, if not her body."

"You're so wise for your age."

Cara smiled smoothly, betraying nothing of her annoyance. She knew exactly where Barbara was coming from. "Was that it?" Cara asked.

"Yes. On second thought, I could use a good buddy to go places with," Barbara said, nudging her shoulder toward Cara.

Playing the devil's advocate, Cara figured Barbara knew Detective Miller and worst of all, they were once lovers. If not, why the need for a forewarning? Cara thought.

Cara remained composed and she checked her watch.

"I have to get home. See you Sunday."

❧ ❧ ❧

Alderman Bennett relaxed in his ward office at 6:35 that evening, relieved to know his political career in Chicago was out of harm's way. He had but one more goal to achieve—build an ordinary friendship with Mario. His problem was finding a way to do that without revealing they were brothers.

It didn't take much to let his imagination induce a likely scenario: *At a small gathering of politicians and community folk, he meets Mario. They find time to chat and get acquainted. He learns Mario interest in tennis. He decides to take lessons and is soon ready to hit the ball well enough to play with Mario. Later they would become more than sports buddies. Their friendship grows to a point where they're close enough to be brothers* __. Bennett had it planned to the last detail.

The sound of the phone ringing interrupted his peaceful fantasy when he heard his mother's uncontrolled voice.

"Giles. We gotta talk."

"Hi Mother, how are you?"

"Cara's mother knows you're my son. After your father died, I had to talk to someone I knew I could trust. I'm sorry, the secret wore me down."

"Oh, no. Did something happen? Has her mom talked to anyone?"

"I don't believe she'd do that without telling me. But she could. I don't want to chance it any more than you do. Instead, she's asked for a favor."

"What is it that she wants from you?" Alderman Bennett asked.

"I've got to get Mario to stop his fight for custody of Ashley."

"Do you get the feeling she knows more?"

"Yes, and, it didn't come from my mouth. Cara can prove she was set up to look like she cheated on Mario. Don't ask me how, 'cause she didn't give me details."

Alderman Bennett didn't like the sound of that. In secret, he feared a bigger problem. One he wasn't about to tell her about. But still, he realized there could be a fatal flaw in his plan. His connection to the frame-up and what he'd done to help Cara may no longer be tightly wrapped.

"Well, give the lady what she wants."

"Good deal. I'll talk to Mario."

Mary Lee had given Mario a hundred thousand dollars. She figured the money would keep him under her control.

"But, what if it doesn't work?" She asked.

"I'll have to pull some political strings. Don't worry, Mario won't know anything about it." Alderman Bennett figured he could sway the judge to rule against Mario, if it should become necessary. She promised to work on Mario and report back to him right away.

"I love you, Mother. Call me once you have news. Good or bad."

Alderman Bennett hung up and he sat in his chair to think about his next move. Thoughts about how Cara could've discovered the truth, flashed across his mind: Clearly, the loopholes had been sealed. No way would anyone from his ward or Alderman Tucker's ward talk about this matter.

Could it be Cara was bluffing? He wondered.

CHAPTER 52

On Wednesday Mario had left the Chicago Hilton after an all day athletic conference. He arrived at Due Drop Inn at exactly 5:00 p.m. He looked dazzling and successful in a three-piece camel colored suit, the first thing he bought with his newfound wealth. He loved buying nice clothes, almost as much as Cara did.

Then he concentrated on his future. Part of it was anticipating Paula's arrival in Chicago that weekend. She was packed and ready leave Memphis. She quit her substitute teacher job, settled her debts and located a one-bedroom apartment at Sixty-First and Michigan.

Suddenly his cellular rang.

"Hello, Mama."

"Mario. I need to warn you about something. It's about your divorce. Naomi told me Cara has the proof she never cheated on you. She's threatening to give this information to her lawyer and use it at the divorce hearing. There's more, but I can't tell you about it just now. So you'll have to trust me."

"I don't believe this. And, why can't you tell me the rest?"

Mary Lee wanted to say something like, have I ever lied to you before. But she didn't because that very statement could come back to haunt her someday. "Mario, do this one thing for me, please?"

"You mean I have to drop the charges and let Ashley go?"

"Yes, that's it. It's not like you won't have visitation rights. She'll always be your daughter."

"This so-called proof, do you know what it is?"

"No, Naomi told me as much as felt she could without hurting Cara's case. You can understand that, can't you?"

"I suppose. I need a little time to think about this, okay?"

* * *

Lester left a murder scene involving a drive-by shooting on Thirty-Fifth and State Street that afternoon. He'd telephoned Cara at her office primed to tell her the truth about his past.

Nobody was ever entirely honest about themselves when they first met another person, were they? It took time to build a relationship—and for some reason, mere mention of the word relationship didn't bother Lester nearly as much as it usually did.

* * *

Cara was at Brookins funeral home on Ashland Avenue viewing Jennifer's body. The body was elegantly garbed in a white nylon, long laced sleeve gown, her hand perfectly formed to hold a small black Bible. She looked as though she slept peacefully and without worry or misery. Cara stood close peering down into the brown shiny vault for a long time letting heavy drops of moisture fall down her face. Quietly, the words parted her lips with questions to never be answered. "*Why Jennifer? Did I not do everything I should have to save you? Was there something you didn't tell me? Did Duncan do this to you? I need to make some sense out of this, Jennifer, for me, if not for you. I'm so sorry. I miss you. I pray your soul is taken in heaven. Rest in peace, my friend.*"

A few minutes later, Cara walked out, unaware of her tear stained face, looking over the crowd of folks seated in the Chapel. Duncan sat holding his head down and never looked up.

Thirty minutes later she was on the Ryan expressway headed straight to her job. She remembered her conversation with the woman caller before she left for work that morning:

"Hi, can I speak to Lester?"

"Sorry, Lester doesn't live here."

"Is this his girlfriend?" The woman asked, sounding genuine and yet calm. Cara remembered thinking, now what?

"I'm a friend. Who are you?"

"His wife," the woman said."

"He didn't tell you he was married?"

"No," Cara said in a dull and troubled voice, thinking it had to be someone playing a joke.

"Not many people do. Not even his friends."

"What's your name?" Cara had figured it was time to get some answers.

"Brenda. He married me three years ago. I walked out on him because living with him was impossible. He became angry and filed for the divorce. Since then, we've been wrangling back and forth between our lawyers over petty stuff."

Cara asked her why she was still married to him.

"He wants me to pay his legal fees and give up my share of the condo."

"Is that right?"

"There's more you need to know. The reason I'm telling you all of this is because my mother persuaded me to warn you hoping to spare another woman the same suffering."

Cara's feelings for Lester now damaged. The man who'd satisfied her beyond her wildest dreams. Strangely she was addicted to him. Of course, she had only Mario for comparison. Needless to say, by now, Cara's heart had been torn apart once again. She could feel the sensations dwindling down to her stomach and didn't want to hear another word from this woman.

"Well, Brenda, I suppose I should thank you." In truth, she felt ill and light-headed.

"You're welcome. Women nowadays have to look out for each other, you know."

"Yeah, don't remind me," she said thinking back to Jennifer and how she'd probably failed her.

Cara remembered hanging up the phone feeling partly grateful and yet more angry than hurt at the moment. This woman has burst my bubbles and the sound can only be heard from within, she thought.

After arriving at her desk, she sat down holding a heart already broken by Mario and now, thanks to Lester, her soul crumbled in a thousand pieces, like sunflower seeds in a jar without air. Somehow she managed to let her mind drift back to the work stacked on her desk. She could never remember letting anything interfere with her work. She clutched the blue pen in her hand and struggled to finish one more report before she clocked out on time.

Forty minutes later, she pulled up in front of her apartment. Interestingly, she noticed Lester sitting inside his car parked in full view of her living room window. As she approached the entrance to her building, he quickly got out of his car and called out her name.

"Cara, hope you don't mind me stopping by. Can I come in and talk?" His voice faded losing its masculine edge.

At the sound of his voice, she lifted her head. "Hi, Lester. Sure, you might as well."

She glanced at the parked cars and then stopped to think, Oh, what's the use? Mario is probably somewhere licking his chops thinking he's got me cornered." Plainly, she was just tired of the rat race. At this point she couldn't care if he parked to spy on her.

Lester followed her inside and sat down on the sofa next to her. His face looked tired, eyes ravaged.

"You okay?"

But Cara diverted his gaze and nodded. Because of him, Jennifer and everything else she had to deal with, she found enough strength not to shed a tear. She was tired of crying. Ravaged with emotions piled higher than the Sears Tower and the lack of sleep, she was exhausted and tensed.

"I can't believe you couldn't tell me you're still legally married." She bit her lip until it throbbed like her pulse.

"What?" Suddenly his eyes grew wild. "How did you find out?" His voice was like an echo from an empty tomb.

"You say that as though I shouldn't have found out. After all I slept with you. For me, that's serious business."

She wanted to bring up Barbara Rhodes. Force the truth from him about their relationship. Obviously Barbara had put Brenda up to calling me, she figured. Maybe I should thank her, too. However, I'm not in the mood to thank anybody for breaking my heart.

He stared at her for a long moment. He reached out, swinging her around to face him. "Yes, you do have a right to know. Part of my reluctance was because I couldn't risk losing you. Knowing how you are about dating married men, I just couldn't. Think about it, would you've let things get this far between us if I'd told you?"

Pulling away slightly, she narrowed her eyes at him, suspicious of his ability to read her mind. Nevertheless, she supposed there was still far too much left unsettled between them to let it go just yet. I could forgive him and possibly reconsider the relationship. But now isn't the time to think about that, she thought.

"Why don't you tell me now? I want to hear all about this marriage you left hanging out there."

Lester explained: "She was materialistic. Later, I discovered Brenda was financially insecure and was after what I had. She stayed in the streets leaving me to fend for myself. When she walked out on me, I realized I didn't really love her after all."

She remained silent and pressed her hand over her face convulsively. Had Brenda been totally truthful? How can I forget I know his past and continue on like I didn't?

"It seems we're both in the same boat, paddling our way to face a judge. Considering our situations, it's best you and I don't see each other again."

A glazed look of despair began to spread over his face. Cara, please don't give up on me. I'll make it right."

When she didn't answer him, "Did you hear what I said?"

This time she just nodded.

Then Lester stared at her for three seconds, his fingers circled around her chin. "Maybe I'm chasing a dream that has no legs," he stammered. His expression stilled and it grew serious.

"How are things with your divorce?"

"Nothing new."

"With what you know, can't you fight this thing with Mario?"

"I'm considering my options."

"Do you need my help?"

"This is something I have to do alone." She got up and raised the window and breathed the fresh air.

He stood and walked to the door and turned around to look at her. "Well, my lines are always open to you, Cara. You've got the power and it rests in the keypad on your telephone."

She walked toward him, ready to close the door.

Suddenly, he pulled from his shirt pocket, a white envelope. "I almost forgot. This is something I promised you."

Cara took the envelope and swallowed the lump in her throat. She offered him a polite smile. She realized it was from Jennifer.

"Oh my goodness." She stood there, blank, amazed and very shaken. She couldn't help to search his face for a hint about the contents.

"It's a copy. The original belongs to the C.P.D. According to the autopsy her blood alcohol level was .31, added to that were traces of an antibiotic. It's the primary diagnosis in 20% of the cases where suicide is the cause of death."

She thanked him.

"Oh, don't breathe a word about this," Lester asked.

"My lips are sealed." A pulsating knot within her demanded more, but she just breathed deeply and waved him goodbye as she stood at the door.

She laid the envelope down on the coffee table waiting for a calm moment to open it. She paced the floors reflecting on her life. I'm sure I've traversed this territory before, and yet nothing is looking the least bit familiar.

CHAPTER 53

Behind the scenes, Naomi and Mary Lee had both been busy, trying to prevent life-altering calamity in both families.

It was Mary Lee's turn to head it off. She'd talked to Mario last night and she remembered his exact words: "Mother, I'll agree to your demands, only if Cara shows me the proof."

An hour later she called Naomi again.

"Hello," she answered. She had set the table for dinner before the call came in. Frank checked on Ashley's temperature.

"Mario won't bulge unless he gets some information. Is Cara willing to talk to him?" Mary Lee panted.

"I don't see why not.

"Then call and ask her. Let me know her answer right away."

"All right. I know it wasn't an easy thing for you to do. Thanks, my friend." Naomi replied and hung up.

* * *

Naomi called Cara 6:15 p.m.

"Hi dear, how're things going with you?"

"Okay, considering." Cara replied. Actually they weren't and she wasn't about to reveal the reasons to her mother. She asked about Ashley instead.

After Naomi assured her Ashley was going to be fine, she relayed Mario's message..

"I won't do it, Mom. The proof I have is not for Mario's eyes or ears. He's created a brick wall between us. Mary Lee will have to be one to talk to him."

"I was afraid you'd say that. Okay, dear, I'll give her your final answer."

"Mom, I'm tired of this merry-go-round. Please do."

"I'm sorry, this frustrates you. I promise this will end once and for all."

After Cara hung up she opened the envelope and braced her back against the back of the sofa and read Jennifer's note:

> *"Cara, this is goodbye. My life has come to nothing and it's not because you didn't try to save me. My deepest dark secret I couldn't admit to you or anyone was that Duncan and Cecil are lovers. I know because I caught them at the house one day when I got home early from work. Yeah, that's right. He is sleeping with other women and this man, too. Don't tell anyone, please. Love you, Jennifer."*

* * *

Mary Lee reached Mario at exactly 10:15 the next morning. A woman answered and said he wasn't home.

"This is his mother calling. Ask him to call me ASAP."

Then Mary Lee phoned Giles. She told him they had big problems and that he had to face his brother.

"It was the only way you can avoid political shame."

"Mother," he uttered and paused. "What went wrong?"

"Everything, and besides that, Cara knows too much about your past and your true heritage. That's not all. She knows you framed her."

"You have any idea how she discovered the truth?"

"Yes, I'm afraid so."

There was a long pause. All too quickly he had run out of diversions. Giles knew his world was about to explode, and he knew it was time to stop hiding. "Are you disappointed?"

"I'd be lying if I said I wasn't, son. However, I'd like to believe you had a good reason. Please tell me you did."

"There's much more I want to tell you. I'll have to explain later, okay."

"Well, I know one thing for sure. You didn't know Mario was your brother before this happened. Otherwise, you wouldn't have done it. Right?"

Deliberately, he voided her question. She gave him Mario's phone number, just in case.

Oh, by the way, I tried reaching Mario before I called you."

"And," Alderman Bennett asked.

"A woman named Paula Coles answered. I'm sure it's her."

It was unmistakably all the encouragement he needed, because after he hung up from talking to Mary Lee, he picked up phone and dialed Mario's number.

He heard the faint voice say, "Hello."

Alderman Bennett inhaled a deep breath, clearly anxious about deciding one way or the other, what he would say.

CHAPTER 54

It was Veteran's Day and Cara merely turned over. She'd had a difficult time sleeping the night before. Recurrent dreams of Jennifer had left her feeling comforted. She began to shake all over again as the images, vivid and disturbing, formed in her mind. She remembered Jennifer calling out her name, smiling the entire moment as she waved from the clouds, and softly repeated the words, *"I'm happy now. Don't worry, you be happy."*

Once she was fully awake she turned the lamp on. She rolled her body across the bed and reached for her bible. She read a few verses from the book, Ecclesiastes. She started to accept what had happened but not exactly okay with Jennifer's decision.

Then she turned on the television in her room. A late breaking news story interrupted the morning weather report on Channel 5 News:

"Alderman Giles Bennett was a victim of a drive by shooting last night outside his ward office. According to police, he sustained multiple gun wounds and was rushed to Hyde Park Hospital where he's heavily guarded. No word on his condition or motive for the shooting. His deputy chief, Joe Michaels was with him and luckily escaped injury."

Oh no! She thought. Oh my God. What? How did this happen? She gasped and realized shivers of panic while pacing the floor. In failed attempts to reach Lester, she realized it was a workday and figured he might be in the shower. She got busy going through her daily routine. She made coffee, toast, and a poached egg.

At 6:45 a.m., she sat down at the table and suddenly, pushed the toast and boiled egg to the side. A quick and disturbing thought entered Cara's mind. What if he doesn't make it? Who would want him dead? She bowed her head in a praying moment.

Afterward, she took a big sip of coffee and instantly, she speed dialed Naomi.

"Mom, it's me. Someone shot Alderman Bennett last night."

"My Lord, is he going to make it?" Naomi asked.

"I'll call Mary Lee," Naomi said, and paused for a moment. Oh, one more thing, sit tight and leave the police work to the professionals."

"I will. Talk to you later."

Immediately Cara hung up and reached for her cellular and called Lester again. This time he answered and he knew about Bennett. To her surprise, Lester was unofficially involved. It was commonplace among police friends to help each other on the side. Luckily, he was given permission to give undercover assistance to Bennett's case.

"I'm glad you're involved." She breathed a sigh of relief. What is his condition?"

"He just got out of surgery. It's too early to tell," Lester replied. "It's a madhouse here." The area was filled with several police investigators and anxious news reporters with cameras and microphones, some holding clipboards taking notes. "How're you doing?"

"I'm all right. There's something you need to know. I'm getting a strange feeling about the shooting. Mario's mother leaked the family secret to my mother. They're aware how much I know, which is basically everything except why I was framed. Together they decided to use that as leverage to convince Mario to drop the charges against me. Mario has agreed to the deal providing that I give him the proof that I never cheated on him."

"This thing with Bennett can't get any worse," Lester bleated.

"I don't know. I'm thinking someone forced him to frame me. The person felt threatened in some way. It's the only logical answer. A dead man can't talk, right?"

"Right, Miss Detective." He couldn't quite halt the chuckle that escaped him. "I'm just kidding. You got any ideas about who we should be looking for?"

"Well, I've given it a lot of thought since my meeting with Loretta Bennett. It's a long shot, but it's worth it. Can you do a background search on someone named Odessa Grant?"

Lester remembered reading the name from Cara's printed chat session with MattIwas. "She's the ex-prostitute who gave the alderman shelter during his teen years. What specifically are you looking for?"

"Her family tree, mostly her sisters and brothers' names, where they reside, stuff like that," Cara said.

"I'll get someone on it right away."

"Thanks, Lester."

"You're welcome. By the way, you got the day off, right?"

"Yes, why?"

"No reason, just stay inside and keep your cellular on. I'll call you later."

She said goodbye to Lester and decided to do something she'd wanted to do for a long time. Mario had obviously been checking on her indiscreetly and following her around lately.

Thinking that, what's good for the goose was good for the gander, she decided it was time to do what she liked to on the computer, surf the street where Mario lived. Although he lived on the third floor, just by chance, she believed it would help her in some way to drive by and take a look where he lived. She might spot the rat.

Shortly after she defrosted a pork chop and finished her third cup of coffee and cleaned the breakfast dishes, she left the apartment.

Twenty minutes later, she arrived in Hyde Park. She turned off on Fifty-Second and Vernon. The street was mounted with a few high-rise complexes, a renovated mini-shopping center, offices and restaurants.

Five minutes passed before she figured the way to Mario's street. She slowed to pinpoint which building fit the number jotted on her notepad. She drove too fast to get a good look and decided to drive around a second time. On the return trip, she slowed, stopping in the middle of the street momentarily. The sun flickered on the man's blond hair as he jogged on the sidewalk. A blue jeep turned the corner. It moved slowly up the one way street, then found a place on the other side to park. She had noticed the same jeep on her tail a while back. She remembered how Lester's watchmen would signal their presence. She decided the driver was someone else.

Nervously she glanced at each car parked near Mario's building. She looked carefully and noticed the Thunderbird was missing. Soon she saw a red Camaro that had a Tennessee state license plate. She memorized it quickly saying it over and over out loud and drove off.

Once she'd stopped at the traffic light on 53rd and Lake Park, she scribbled the number on her notepad and drove back to her apartment.

She walked inside and sat down on the sofa to think, trying to figure out had followed her. Her thoughts went rampart: Whoever it was, the person knows every move I made today. *I won't let it scare me.*

The cellular rang and she was glad it was Lester.

"Hello."

"Cara, hi. Are you staying put?"

"No, that's hard to do, considering. I admit I was by his place. I had a hunch and it panned out. A red vehicle with a Tennessee license plate was parked in front of his apartment." She gave him the number.

"We'll run a computer check. The license bureau will have a picture. I'm sorry I forgot to mention someone had been assigned to cover you today. It was for your own good, you know."

"Oh, my. That's a relief." She breathed a deep sigh. Did you learn anything about Odessa?"

"Yeah. Here's what we've found: Ms. Grant never married, grew up in Tennessee, moved about a lot and is currently living in Detroit. She's got a sister, Paula. No brothers. Odessa has a long arrest record for prostitution, but no convictions."

"Now we're getting somewhere. Clearly, Paula got Alderman Bennett to set me up. She wanted Mario free. The one damaging piece of evidence was my birthmark. Mario had to mention that to Paula. There's the motive and thanks to you, we've linked her to the alderman. But, how do we prove it? If Bennett dies, she'll get away with her crimes."

"Not if I have anything to do with it," Lester replied.

Amazingly impressed, he realized how bound and determined Cara was. She could make soup from just stones and water when she sets her mind on it, he thought. And, he wondered what he would have to do to keep her from making another move that would surely put her in harm's way. But in truth, he believed her thinking was right on.

"Let's see what comes back on his license plate number," he said, and his thoughts reeling. "Talk to you later."

"Sure, I'll be waiting for your call."

As someone quite adept at reading between the lines, Lester sensed she still cared for him. And, as encouraging as the thought, he was sure Mario would soon realize he'd made the biggest mistake of his life. Although his grounds with Cara were shaky at best, for some reason believed the future still belonged to him.

CHAPTER 55

Precisely at 11:32 a.m. the next day, Mario picked up Mary Lee from O'Hare. During the drive to the Ramada Inn on Lake Shore Drive, they rode in almost complete silence. As hard as he fought it, he couldn't help but remember their conversation over the phone the night before: "*Mario, I'm flying to Chicago tomorrow. I need to talk with you face to face. My plane lands at O'Hare at 11:05 tomorrow.*"

He drove them from the airport in forty minutes. She hardly said anything while she checked in. Finally, they entered her room and while he placed her baggage carefully on the floor inside the closet, she plopped down in one of the wicker-backed chairs, both hands clutching her purse.

"Since I can remember, I've never seen you like this, Mama," he said, as he walked over and knelt on the floor in front of her. "What is this about?"

She became afraid and wondered what Mario would do, what he'd say to her. Would he still adore her like most sons do their mothers?

"It's about a family so dear to me, that my heart is going to break telling this story to you. So here goes:

Once upon a time, thirty years ago to be exact, this man and his wife were raising their family in Mississippi. There were two sons, one had just turned five years old, and the baby boy was only four months old. Happy to have beautiful boys, they gave them names beginning with the same initial as the mother. Their lives were complete. But one dark day in September in 1969, something dreadful happened to the oldest boy. The mother took him with her to the grocery store and then to get some gas for the car. She locked the door, left her son inside the car while she went in to pay for the gas. When she returned, her son was gone and never seen again. The man and wife were devastated. The man nearly lost his mind. Somehow he decided that to keep from destroying himself and others around him, it was best to cut their losses and relocate to another state. As crazy as it sounds this man figured the only way to do that, was to put the lost son out of his mind, acting like he never existed. So, the man swore his wife to a lifelong secret. And, like an obedient wife, she kept the secret. To this day the younger son was never told."

Mario stood up and sat down on the bed. "Mama, for some reason I get the feeling this story is about us. Is it?"

"Shhh. Don't interrupt." By now, she'd imposed an iron control on herself. No longer able to sit comfortably, she stood and walked to the window. The sun was still high in the sky. Boats sailed far out on the lake and cars were speeding along the outer drive.

She turned to look at him again. "Since I've gotten this far, let me continue."

"Okay, I'm listening." He got up and joined her.

She took a deep breath. "Remember the old cliché: "What goes on in the dark, must someday come to light?" She asked in a deep husky voice.

"Yeah."

"Well, something miraculous happened: The wife, with extraordinary luck and help from someone close to her, found the older son over the Internet. To make this long story short, they reunited and got to know each other. Again she wanted to tell the younger son he had a brother. Above all else he deserved to know."

"Why didn't she, Mama?"

"For reasons unknown to the mother, her older son made her promise never to reveal his existence. Seems he has a shady past. He managed to put it behind him. He started a new life and a respectable career as a politician. He feared losing everything he'd worked so hard to accomplish. The mother was again held to the secret, and so the lie continued."

He shrugged to hide his confusion. "Is that it? Why was it so important to come here, look me in the face and tell this story to me, Mama?" He panted in terror hoping his fears were premature.

She looked him directly in his eyes. "Because the mother can no longer keep quiet. You're the younger son."

His dark brown eyes showed the tortured dullness of disbelief and he refused to register the significance of her words. Since he'd never in his life, uttered a word of disrespect to his mother or father, he found himself saying instead, "I, I can't find the words to respond to that." He turned away from her.

"Oh, Mario. Say something. Say anything. Curse me if you will, I'll overlook it." If only he knew how much she wanted him to do something. Anything.

For a moment Mario stammered around in bewilderment and then he plopped down on the bed and bowed his head to his opened legs. Nearly five minutes passed before either of them spoke.

Finally he raised his head when Mary Lee got up to turn on the television. He appreciated that the volume was at a reasonable low volume.

Then he slowly he stood up, stumbled over to the mini bar and pulled out a tiny bottle. Just as he tore off the top, he looked back at Mary Lee, and let his eyes drop in shame. Then he stomped off to the bathroom and without hesitation, flushed the contents. Deep down he'd realized something he'd known for a long time. Drinking wouldn't cut it this time. Seconds later, he came out and as he approached her, she stood with her arms opened wide. He grabbed and held onto her tightly and they both cried openly.

Finally he spoke again. “I have a brother, I’ve always wanted a brother,” he said, pulling away. “What is his name?”

“Matthew is the name we gave him.”

“Where does he live?”

Just then, late-breaking news interrupted the Jenny Craig talk show. They sat down alongside each other on the bed facing the television. The news anchorman said, “Unknown to the police and the media, Alderman Bennett is missing from the intensive care unit at Hyde Park hospital.” Then a scene with a male reporter talking to the attending nurse was showed. She stated how baffled everyone at the hospital was that such an important patient could be removed without so much as a whimper.

The news anchor continued: “Hospital administrator, Shayia Glass, has assured us that everything had been done to locate the alderman. According to police officials, it’s their belief the popular alderman was removed for safety reasons, which case no one knows where he is. Stay tuned for more updates as we will bring you more information as soon as we know it.”

“What a mess,” Mario said, feeling unnerved by the tragedy. “I hope the guy makes it. He’s one hard-working politician.”

“I hope so too,” she said, and returned to her seat, moving her head, side to side. “I hope and pray he makes it.”

“You seem awfully concerned, Mama.”

“Yes, and for good reason. He’s your brother,” she told him, gently holding his hand. “Alderman Bennett is my son, too.”

“I don’t believe it. How can that be?” At that moment, Mario leaned his head toward her and gazed into her eyes, not trusting himself to speak and he lacked the strength to sit still.

Pacing the floor like a crazy man didn’t help either. He asked her to turn off the television. Then he let his body drop down on the bed in a straight position and he stared around the room. He’d heard more than he cared to.

“Mario, are you okay? Talk to me, son.”

He opened his mouth finally. "But his name is Giles. Did he change that too?" While he lay there, she told him the rest: The little she knew about the people who raised Matthew, his life growing up as a Bennett, the sordid lifestyle he led, the prison term, and that he turned his life around and made something out of himself.

"Does my brother know our father died?" He eased his body back on the bed to hear some more.

"Yes, he was too afraid to come to the funeral. But he came to the hospital the day after you. It was sad for him. He took pictures of Bradley lying there unconscious. And, he asked me to take a picture with his face cheek to cheek with your father. In case Bradley didn't wake up, there would be a picture to hold onto forever."

"What about daddy?" Did he know, too?"

"I convinced your father to call Alderman Bennett and he did. Bradley suffered the heart attack shortly afterward.

"Wow," he stirred his body up awkwardly. "What about me?"

She searched for the best way to tell him. "Many times he talked about how he wished you could be told the truth. He'd even worked out a plan to meet you, hopefully for the two of you to become the best of friends. He would've treated you like a brother."

"How touching, except I would've still been in the cold," he replied, shaking his head in dismay. "But, mama, once the secret was out between you, surely in time I could've understood his plight just as you did. There was no reason for him to fear me."

"Right, and I guess it's time you know the rest. It's about the proof your wife has." He flopped back on the bed and closed his eyes waiting for the ton of bricks to fall on him. And, she continued. "Someone did frame her and somehow she traced it all back to Alderman Giles. She feared hurting our family and decided to sit on it. Now you see why I pleaded for you to let her have Ashley?"

"You got some aspirin, my head hurts." It had all started to make sense: The anonymous phone call. Why his brother feared the truth.

Of course why else would his brother need to keep their relationship still a secret?

By then, it was nearly 4:00 in the afternoon.

"I'm sorry," she began to cry again. "My heart aches for you right now, son."

"It's okay, Mama. I just need some time to digest it all."

"You must be starving. Can I get you something from the diner?

"No thanks, I'm not hungry," he waved his hand in a gesture of dismissal. He hunched over, and rested his arms on his thighs. Neither did he crave a cigarette. But then he'd never smoked around his mother.

"You remember how I yelled to the top of my lungs and said those awful things about Cara?"

Mary Lee sat quietly and nodded.

"Now, I know why you defended Cara. Right now, I'm worried about my brother. He could die and I'll never come face to face with him, never get to say hello. Mama, why do you think he lied to me about Cara? He knew nothing about our family or that he belonged until you discovered each other. So who the hell put him to do such a dastardly thing?" Mario asked, sounding desperate.

"I haven't a clue."

Then the thought occurred to him that the person who shot his brother might try again. "Mama, did Matthew ever mention he had enemies or that he feared for his life?"

"Never. He didn't talk much about his life or his work."

"It's now that I realize how precious life is. Maybe I haven't been spending my time the way I should have." He started to think how if he'd received this information when it mattered, imagine the difference it could have made.

It had been foolish to attack Cara like that, foolish to risk her life and foolish to give her another reason to leave him. It was more than enough to make a grown man cry.

He got quiet again and stayed that way for a few minutes.

"What're you thinking?" she asked.

"Oh, just that I don't have a prayer to lean on this time. It just so happens, I was thinking about Cara, the divorce. By the way, I promised to get back to my lawyer."

Mary Lee stepped to the bathroom giving him privacy. He sat up on the side of the bed and reached for the phone to call the lawyer. He agreed to meet the lawyer the next day.

When Mary Lee came back and sat down, she said, "I'm proud of you son. Hope you did the right thing, finally."

On those words, he let his body drop back on the bed thinking that his mother was so sure of herself. "Don't go giving me that much credit. I haven't behaved like a gentleman. I pushed my wife out of my life and for what, a damn lie?"

Then she sat alongside him on the bed, and asked, "Be honest with me, how you feel about Cara now?"

He grinned, shrugging his shoulders. "She's met someone." His voice was weak and shaking.

"You're kidding, who?"

"Somehow she met my best friend, Lester Miller. He's a homicide detective."

"This friend, could it be that he was just helping her. Maybe, that's all it is."

"I don't know mama. Anyway, I'm just as guilty," he said, sounding desperately unhappy.

"Since you can't be sure she's fallen for him, remember this; it's not over until the fat lady sings."

Mario told Mary Lee about his one time affair and how it almost ended his marriage. Finally, Mary Lee understood Cara's motivation to leave him this time.

Mario adjusted his body to face the wall. "I hurt her real bad this time. She won't ever forgive me."

"Maybe you should tell Cara how you feel," Mary Lee pointed out.

"I can't face her." Suddenly Lester and Cara started to wear on his mind.

"Oh, my God, Cara. What have I done to you?"

CHAPTER 56

❦

Lester arrived at his condo around nine that evening. He was satisfied everything had been done to protect Bennett. Calling in big-time favors, he convinced Michaels to take Bennett to a secure room at the University of Chicago hospital. Getting him away from Hyde Park Hospital had been extremely difficult. Undercover officers dressed in hospital garb eased him without disrupting I.V. and his heart monitor, through a rear entrance and into a private ambulance.

By now, Lester was exhausted and he soaked his tired body in the tub for almost an hour. He thought about his next move as he dried his body and changed into his robe.

At 10:10 p.m., his cellular rang.

"Hello."

"Lester, I need to talk to you."

"Hi, Mario. What's up?"

"My mama is in Chicago. She's told me everything.

"Everything?" Lester asked, voice lowered.

Mario always hated when his question was answered with a question. He felt like yelling at Lester: *I know about you and Cara. How could you do this to me, you son-of-a-b__?* Instead of doing further harm, he said, "You heard me, man and don't act like you don't know what I'm talking about."

"Okay, I see you're upset," Lester replied. "Maybe now is not a good time to talk about this."

"I know about Alderman Bennett. He's my brother. Where is he, Lester? Surely you'd know?"

"Someone did try to kill him. It's possible this person will try again," Lester replied.

"How much do you know about my family's situation and when did you know it?" Mario barked, sounding like he would strangle Lester if he could only see him. "Surely, the police would have some idea. Doesn't our friendship mean anything, anything at all? I mean, why would I want to harm my own brother?"

"What kind of question is that?" Lester asked. Mario's tone aroused and infuriated him.

"It's a simple one, my friend," Mario said, calming down.

"The answer is, yes. I'm still your friend. I'll tell you, but you must promise not to tell another soul. I'm sure you know why."

"Alright, I promise."

"The alderman is barely holding on and hasn't regained consciousness. I'm truly sorry. Bennett didn't deserve to get shot.

"Thank God, he's still alive. When can we see him?"

"I'll call you tomorrow. Can't promise it'll be when you'll see him. But I'll try," Lester said.

"Okay. Sounds good. I'll let mama know he's still alive."

"And no one else, remember?" Lester insisted.

After Lester hung up the phone, he thought about how he would set off his plan. He'd expected Mario to say something all together different. On the other hand, he believed Mario when he said he knew everything. He had to. So, Lester adopted a new policy: *You don't ask, I don't tell. I can play this game, too.*

Before he called it a night, he telephoned Cara and told her what was going on.

❧ ❧ ❧

At exactly 10:30 that same evening, Mario held the phone between his shoulder and head while he made a cold bologna and cheese sandwich. He waited for Paula to answer. The phone continued to ring. She must be out somewhere or asleep. He thought. Maybe it could wait until morning. No. He wanted to find out now. What made her leave the other night before he got home? She'd promised to cook dinner. Why hadn't she called him?

Mario remembered his promise to Lester. Certainly, it didn't pertain to Paula. Why would it matter? In no mood to play games, still, he needed to talk to Paula. He left her a message: "Hey Paula, what's up? Answer the phone."

Fifteen minutes later, when his phone rang, he answered.

"Hi, I bet you're wondering what happened to me." Paula let out a quick sniggle.

"Where were you?

"Oh, no, that's not it," she said with deceptive calm.

"What's the problem then? We had plans for yesterday. When I got home, dinner was missing and so were you."

"Well. To tell you the truth, I started to think you could get too comfortable with things the way they are. I, I don't want to live like that ever again, Mario."

Although her actions had spoken louder than her words, he wasn't ready to deal on their subject with her. "I can't be pushed, anymore than you, Paula. Right now is just not the time."

Paula sensed a clash of wills and knowing Mario like she did, a bad mood left undressed could harden into a bad attitude.

"Can we change the subject, I was just being silly," she said. "Come to my place, I'll do that dinner I promised. We can make love all night long. Please?"

"Tonight is not good for me. Maybe later."

"Why not?" She got the feeling he wanted to be with her but that something serious was on his mind. "Can't you tell me what's wrong?"

"I'm not sure if I should," he spoke louder, letting out an audible breath.

"Fess up, Mario. It's me you're talking to."

"It's top secret. You really shouldn't know. But I know you. I won't get a moment's peace if I don't tell you. You might recall hearing on the news someone tried to assassinate Alderman Giles Bennett."

"Yeah, I heard about it."

"Today, my mother told me that he's is my older brother." He waited for her to respond. "Did you hear me?"

"Brother! How can that be?" Her voice was shakier than she would have liked.

"It's complicated. But what she told me all added up. I've got a brother."

Oh no. This can't be true. Can it?" Paula thought.

❧ ❧ ❧

The next day, Cara arrived home from the Laundromat at 1:15 p.m. The phone rang.

"Hello, Ms. Fleming," Attorney Garnell said. "Seems your husband has stopped the divorce proceedings. I thought you should know right away."

"I don't believe this. What am I supposed to do now?" I wonder what Mario is up to now? Anyone else would've called his wife and discussed such a decision. Idiot!

"I take it you're in the dark about his decision."

"That I am, Mr. Garnell." And she decided it made no sense to inquire if he knew Mario's reasons. Client confidentiality, and legal mumbo-jumbo that she didn't quite understand were likely the reason, she thought.

"I'm glad I called as soon as I did." Garnell added.

"Now, what am I supposed to do?" Care spouted.

"Call him and ask for an explanation. You deserve to know why."

"I was afraid you'd say that. What if I want to proceed?"

"Then we'll file the petition this time. Give it some thought and when you've talked it over and decided what you want to do, give me a call."

After she hung up, she called Naomi.

"Mario knows everything about his family's secret.

"You don't say. Well, we're getting somewhere with this mess. Has he called you?"

"No, you'd think he would have, especially since he's decided to call off the divorce. Sensing that Naomi was about to respond, she said, "Wait, the best is yet to come. I know who got the alderman to frame me.

"Who?" Naomi's breathing had become erratic.

"Paula Coles. She had an affair with Mario when we lived in Memphis. She obviously did it to ruin my marriage. This time she's playing for keeps."

"Who told you?"

"A background search was done on Paula. She's the sister to Odessa Grant. Remember the alderman's prostitute friend in Detroit?"

"Now I get it. My Lord. Wait until I tell Frank. Since I filled him in on everything, he's worried about you. If you get the time, call him this evening. He needs to hear your voice."

"Okay. I need to hear Ashley's voice too."

"How do you feel about Mario withdrawing the divorce petition?" Naomi asked.

"I don't know. Mostly, I'm concerned why he hasn't picked up the phone to tell me. I don't like being left hanging out in left field."

"Mary Lee is in Chicago. Has she called you?" Naomi asked.

"No."

"She's staying at the Ramada Inn on Lake Shore Drive."

"Oh, I see."

"Remember, it's time to stop playing crooks and robbers. I mean it Cara, let the big guys do the work for you this time."

Cara let out a sigh of relief. "It seems I don't have a choice in the matter."

✤ ✤ ✤

After Cara hung up the phone, she started the shower. Minutes later, she stood under the shower massage, and the hot water came pouring down heavy and she rubbed Irish Spring soap all over her body and washed with a soft towel until she felt cleaned and her tired tensed muscles were relaxed.

Then she put on her bra, then opened another drawer and pawed through the panties, looking for a red pair to match her slacks. She checked her appearance and brushed her hair in a ponytail.

Seconds later she thought she heard a noise. Then she heard sirens. At first she didn't pay much attention, thinking they were from the news clip flashing across the television screen. She clicked it off to be sure. The sound became increasingly louder. She'd become used to emergency sirens, fire, police and ambulance in Chicago and wouldn't have paid much attention, except this time, it stop directly in front of her building.

CHAPTER 57

Cara dashed to the living room window. No mistake about it, an ambulance and two police cars were parked in front of her building. Lights flashed. People sprawled along the sidewalk.

Soon, two white police officers pulled a stretcher from the rear of the ambulance. Moments later, two more squad cars arrived and parked in the middle of the street.

Cara wondered if it had to do with Mrs. Walker, as she watched them walk up the front entranceway. She grabbed her keys and walked into the hallway. The men hurried past her apartment door, headed to the floor above. She ran down the steps. As she about to knock, Mrs. Walker stood in the doorway, peeping and trying to listen.

"Hi." Cara gasped for breath. "I was afraid you were ill or something. I'm so glad you're alright."

"Thank you dear. Won't you come in?"

The smell of collard greens cooking permeated the room, and voices streamed from the television. Cara turned around to face her. "What do you think happened to Louis?"

"It's not him," Mrs. Walker said. "He left a week ago for Florida."

Mrs. Walker stepped back to the door to look again and Cara followed her. A police officer was walking down the steps with white gloves and a mask on.

Cara spoke first. "Excuse me officer, what happened up there?"

"We got an anonymous tip to check out the top floor apartment. Apparently gun shots were heard."

"That's odd," Cara said, giving Mrs. Walker a quick glance. Then she looked at the officer who seemed in a hurry. "Did you find anyone up there?"

"Yes, I'm afraid so. A young woman was shot to death. That's all I can tell you, ma'am." The officer turned around and walked out the building.

"Did you hear what he said? That's terrible. Who would do such a thing?" Cara asked.

Mrs. Walker didn't answer and quickly locked her door.

Both ladies rushed to look out the living room window. They stood baffled and mostly in silence watching until they saw two officers move the body out of the building.

"I can't believe it," Cara said, managing no more than a hoarse whisper. "It's the first time I've been this close to death."

"Come, let's sit," Mrs. Walker said. "It's times like this my body goes limp."

Cara followed Mrs. Walker and sat down on the sofa. She wished she'd thought to bring along her cellular. She couldn't afford to miss any calls.

"Do you think it was gang related?"

"Probably. It's not uncommon around here. I'll make us some tea," Mrs. Walker said.

Later, they sat for a while talking about the situation. Mrs. Walker watched Cara with a keenly observant eye.

"I wonder who they found dead up there," Cara asked. Louis had so many women. Maybe it was a girlfriend.

Mrs. Walker explained: "I had a hard time keeping track. Mostly they'd come and go. But my guess is that the dead woman was the one who stayed with him off and on. She'd come over whenever her husband beat her up. He gave her keys to the place. And, when he got tired of her, he'd put her out."

"Why?" Cara asked, sipping some of her tea.

"She was a heavy drinker."

"That's a sad way to live, don't you think?"

"Yes it is. You feeling better now?"

"Yes ma'am. And, thanks for the tea."

"It's understandable that you would be frightened. I've seen so much crime in my lifetime. But then you never really get used to it. Each time is like the first time all over again."

Cara nodded. "Mostly, I'm worried."

"What would you have to be worried about?

Mrs. Walker knew all too well about Cara's regular male visitor. Once he'd worn his uniform. And, she'd noticed men parked on the street watching the building and often wondered why.

"Can I ask you something totally unrelated?"

"Sure, why not," Cara replied.

"The man who come to visit you, is he a policeman?"

"Yes, and to be more exact, he's a homicide detective. His name is Lester Miller. He works out of Area 2 on Wentworth Avenue. He's been a really good friend, looking out for me."

"You aren't in any trouble, are you?"

"No. Compared to most, I'm straight laced, go to work everyday, pay my bills, mind my business and try to stay out of other folks business. What I'm worried about has to do with matters that I can't talk about right now. What I can tell you is that the reason I'm living alone is because I was set up to look like I was cheating on my husband. We're separated and soon to be divorced. My friend is doing what any good male friend does. He's making sure I'm out of harm's way."

"I had no idea, my dear. That's explains it. I could never figure why someone so attractive and nice had to live alone. For what it's worth, I hope everything turns out okay for you."

"Me too," Cara said.

"You mind if I give you some old folk wisdom?"

"No, I could use some more."

"People who lived the longest are independent minded. They don't pound themselves fretting about other's opinions. They do what's right to them."

"I appreciate what you just said. It couldn't have come at a better time." Cara stood up from the sofa. She dangled the door keys. "I guess I'll go home, she spoke loudly. "I'm expecting some calls."

"Okay, I'm so glad we had this talk. I'm here if you need me. Remember, you're not alone. Consider me as an angel on your shoulder," Mrs. Walker said.

♣ ♣ ♣

Once she was sure Cara was inside her apartment, Mrs. Walker locked her door and sat down to re-think everything that had happened that morning: It was around ten that morning when a strange man and woman pulled up in a red car and parked across the street three apartments down from the building. She sat inside the car while he got out of the car and entered the building. He was short and medium build and wore a cap pulled too far down on his head. She heard footsteps through the building entrance. Looking through the peephole gave her a good look at his face. She heard him tiptoe up the steps. She opened the door and saw the man go into the third floor apartment. A few minutes later, she heard muffled sounds and she closed her door. She eased back to look through her peephole and saw the man darting out the building. Later he ran across the street, got back in the car and sped off. She remembered making the anonymous phone call to 911.

CHAPTER 58

Around five that afternoon, Mario got a call from Mary Lee. He'd just arrived home in time to prepare to meet with Lester.

"For God sake, Mario, don't mention this call to anyone. It's a matter of life and death," she said, breathing out of control.

"Whose life are you talking about?" he asked.

"Cara's," she said. She got him to think about whether he could've slipped and told Paula about Cara's birthmark.

If his life depended on it, he could not explain how Paula would know about Cara's birthmark. But every nerve in his body was rattling, telling him he must have told her. "Oh, my God, it's possible, but I didn't mean to." He felt as if his breath was cut off. "Are you suggesting Paula got to my brother and forced him to frame her? How could she? Giles and Paula don't know each other."

"Oh, yes they do." She gave him all of the details.

At that moment he wanted to strangle Paula. His chest felt like it would burst. "Well, I'd be d-----." I'm headed out the door to meet Lester. I'll call you later, Mama."

Lester was waiting at a small table in the corner when Mario stepped in. Prepared to tell Mario what he wanted to know, hoping

Mario would help nail Paula, he'd braced himself for the fight of his life.

Mario went straight to the bar and after a few words with Freddie he joined Lester. That Mario didn't order something to drink surprised Lester.

Lester stood up to welcome Mario, his hands extended for a handshake. A wave of apprehension swept through Lester, but his fears were premature. Instead Mario did likewise and sat down. He had the strangest look on his face. He seemed calm and he smiled easily.

"Hi. Thanks for meeting with me."

"You're welcome. How you doing?" Lester asked.

"I'm hanging. It's just that I never expected things to end up like this. I've known about you and Cara a short while, but since yesterday, even that has taken a back seat in my mind."

"You're being too kind," Lester answered quickly over his choking, beating heart. This guy sure isn't slow to spill his guts, he thought. "If I may, I'd like to explain a few things about me and your wife."

"Sure, why not," Mario said.

"I didn't go searching for her. She found me. You want to know why? She was having a hard time dealing with not knowing what the caller told you. I listened and asked questions. Anyway, after we talked, I had doubts about who to believe. Strange men started to follow her around the city. I traced the license plate to your brother and another one to his political chief, Joe Michaels. I even broke department rules to keep her under surveillance. I took time off to go to Detroit to check Bennett's background. One thing led to another. I found the woman he referred to as mother. Loretta Bennett is her name. But it was Cara who took everything I learned, added to what she'd discovered over the Internet and put it all together. Then without telling me, she took off to Detroit and talked to Mrs. Bennett and that's how she learned the alderman was a Fleming. The rest of what happened is history. She never gave up trying to prove her innocence."

Mario sat without moving an inch, his head bowed at times.

"Sad to admit, but later, things changed," Lester added.

We got closer. If you will recall, you made it clear it was definitely over between you, no matter how many times I tried to get you to reconsider. I hate that it happened. Now, if that makes you my enemy, then I'm sorry, man. I'm so sorry." Lester kept all expression from his voice as he apologized.

"Okay, okay, I hear you," Mario said and paused. "After all we've been through, okay __. You made your point. You were a good friend to Cara, even when I was too stubborn to be that for her. I'm at least grateful for that."

The tension between them seemed to melt. Lester moved his head closer. "Are you sure you're all right? You seem different."

"Maybe I am. I was hit with a wake up call the other day. Believe it or not, I see things differently." Mario replied.

"So, does this mean you can put what's happened aside and help me nail the real culprit?"

"I'm ahead of you on that one."

"How did you figure it out?" Suddenly it hit Lester that Mario hadn't reached for a cigarette.

"It was mama. She called before I left to come here."

Smart lady, Lester thought. But he knew better. Somehow, between Cara and her mother, the idea had been planted with Mario's mother. Knowing Cara, protecting the family mattered most.

Lester looked at Mario. "I got a question for you. Can you account for Paula's whereabouts the night Bennett was shot?"

"No. I figured she was home," Mario said.

* * *

They left the Due Drop Inn for a sneak peep in on Alderman Bennett. The two men drove in their cars to the University of Chicago hospital, with Lester in the lead.

Just ahead of the rush hour traffic, they arrived fifteen minutes later and entered through a rear door. They took the stairs to the fifth floor. To the right was a room with double doors. Inside, it was semi-dark, cold and quiet and there were mostly discarded equipment: copiers, inoperable patient beds, weigh scales, chalk boards and sealed boxes were stacked ceiling high along the walls.

Lester walked through the organized clutter and Mario followed him inside the adjoining room that had a sign on the door in red letters: *No Admittance.*

Inside, the room was dimly lit and the telecommunication hum of onlookers had been smoldered behind the closed door with a dark window. A black nurse sat alongside Bennett's bed reading a book. She lifted her head, revealing a face that was more interesting than attractive, with strong cheeks, a square jaw and a wide mouth. Lester waved a hello and she continued reading.

"Why don't you have a few moments with him alone," he said, looking at Mario.

Mario eased to the bed. Bennett's breathing was labored and his face was pale and it was there Mario saw a picture of his mother. Her facial shape, mouth, contour of his eyes and he looked older than he'd imagined considering they were five years apart. He held the alderman's hand for a few minutes. Then Mario silently spoke to God, promising he would change his ugly ways and be the man their father had wanted him to be.

Finally, he opened his mouth and whispered, "I'm the baby brother you didn't get to know. Stay alive and come back to me from wherever you are."

CHAPTER 59

Still very afraid, Cara sat in her apartment around eight that evening. Frozen in time, thinking about the dead woman and the fact she had been murdered in cold blood. Would the police knock on her door and ask questions. If so, she had none to give. She figured Mrs. Walker had the answers. She knew everything. Cara dared not consider what would happen next.

It was then she remembered to call Loretta Bennett.

Paula had given up trying to reach Mario at home and on his cell phone. She figured by now the news of Cara's death had reached Mario. Even so, why hadn't he called to notify her? She let her mind drift back to that day she accompanied Ralph, the assassin to the building on Exchange. He came cheap, a crack cocaine user for years and he was hard up for money. He'd bungled the assignment to kill the alderman and this time she believed this mission was a done deal. She remembered lifting Cara's address from a pad on Mario's dresser: *7714 South Exchange, 2nd floor. Ralph said the woman was dead when he left the apartment.*

So what else was she to think or do? Paula was already up to her neck in trouble, and one more wasn't going to make too much of a difference. Still the thought occurred to her to get in contact with Ralph to be sure. She reached him at his low-income housing apartment on State Street.

"Hello," the husky voice answered.

Loud rap music was playing in the background. She wondered if he could hear her. "Ralph, this is your little friend in the red Camaro.

"What's up?" He voice was higher than needed.

"I was thinking about ___, would you turn down that music?" She spoke in a loud, sarcastic tone.

A few seconds later he returned to the phone. "Are you satisfied lady? What can I do for you this time?"

"It's about the woman you took care of. Do you remember what apartment you went to?"

"That's better," he said and cleared his throat. "Yeah, I remember, why?"

"Good," she spoke eagerly, taking half breaths. "So it was the 2nd floor you went to, right?"

"Lady, whatcha trying to do to me? I heard you say the 3rd floor."

"You mother f----. You shot the wrong woman. I don't believe this?" Paula screamed.

"Oops, seems I forgot to mention I lost my hearing in the right ear from a gang beating three years ago. What'll you want me to do about it now? I can use another five hundred."

"I'm broke, you fool." she uttered with quiet emphasis.

"Hey, whatcha you want from me? I asked you go with me."

CHAPTER 60

❦

Shortly after midnight, the clock found a 25th hour. Hours had passed and Cara hadn't eaten all day.

She rushed to the bathroom thinking she was going to be ill. Sitting down on the floor and leaning against the tub, she wondered about Mario and Lester. Had they forgotten she existed and needed answers? Calling Naomi or trying to reach Mary Lee was useless.

A few minutes later, Cara thought she heard noise around her apartment door. She pulled herself up and quietly eased to the door. She looked through the peephole. At first she didn't see anyone. She continued to watch a few seconds longer and decided it was just her imagination.

Then she stretched her body on the sofa facing the door. She noticed the doorknob turn one time. She looked around the room, everything in it moved like a slow merry go round, carrying her along for a ride. Deep down she'd always been afraid. Now it gnawed away at her courage to keep a brave face. Immediately she reached for the cordless phone and dialed 911, and whispered, "Send the police to 7714 South Exchange now, someone is trying to break in my apartment. Please help me."

Feeling secure inside with two double locks on her door, she had time to find something, a knife or a hammer to grab onto, while forgetting she had mace hidden in her purse. She rushed to the kitchen and grabbed a knife from the silverware holder, walked back to the living room praying the police would get there like yesterday. Two knocks at the door. Maybe it's the police, she thought.

She dashed back to the door and took another peep, this time a rough looking black guy, young with huge eyes wearing a long bibbed black cap, stood there. His eyes darted around the hallway in frustration.

"Who are you? What do you want at this time of night?"

"Oh, hello ma'am. You don't know me. Your husband, Mario, he's been shot. You need to come before it's too late."

"What did you say your name was?"

"I didn't say, ma'am.

"Where is he? How did you know where to find me?"

"I can explain all of that, if you would just open your door."

"I'm not going to do that, so just tell me." She snapped at him.

The cordless phone in her robe pocket rang. She walked away from the door and answered.

"Hello," she spoke in a suffocated whisper.

"Cara, honey, this is Thelma Walker. I heard a man's voice coming from up there. Don't let him in. He's the one I saw in the building the day that woman was murdered."

"Oh, my God. No."

"Listen, your detective friend knows about him."

"He does, when __?" She'd known fear before, except this time it was as worst as it could get. She thought about the police. What's keeping them? She accidentally pushed the off button as she rushed back to the door. There was no time to talk. I'll call her back later, she thought.

Leaning on the door and still holding the phone, she put her eyes to the peephole. Her eyes were eyeball to his. Afraid he would shoot a bullet straight into her, she jumped away and to the left side of the door and ran toward the sofa.

Just as she moved away, "Bang, bang." Balls of fire pierced through her door. She thought the shooting would never stop as a third gunshot went off. Reverberation of feet trampling down the steps. Immediately, she heard more sounds of feet on the stairs above her apartment. Her mind swirled causing her to drop the knife to the floor. Then there were sirens from both directions on the one way street. The sounds grew louder. There were persistent knocks at her door.

She heard a male voice. It was familiar. "Cara, open the door. It's okay, it's me, Mario."

"Mario," she said and ran to take a look. She opened the door and fell into his arms. "I thought __." Mario, I'm so glad to see you," she cried and he held her close to him.

"Thank God, you're okay."

He walked toward the sofa with his arms still around her. He carefully put his gun on the end table. "He won't get too far. One of my bullets hit him."

Hearing the word *bullets*, she lost consciousness in his arms.

* * *

Twenty minutes later, Lester had arrived at her door and Mario let him in. He stepped inside. Cara was lying on the sofa as though she was in a peaceful sleep and Mario sat down beside her.

"We got him in custody." Lester tried to steady his breathing. "Is Cara okay?"

"She fainted in my arms not long after I got inside the apartment. I guess the drama was too much for her. The hit man tried to get her to open the door. Told her some lame story about me being hurt. Of course we know how he knew my name. I can't think about what would've happened if she'd opened the door. Anyway, she refused to let him in. It's my guess he shot his gun thinking she was still at the door."

"I once remember you said Cara stayed miles ahead of everyone."

"Right, and this time it saved her life."

"The guy was carted off in one of the squad cars. Soon he'll be singing like a bird down at the station, if not before." Lester said with authority.

Mario exhaled a deep breath while he continued to look at her. "Good. It's what we need to haul Paula in."

"His name is Ralph, and he's a first class, hoodlum. The kind that comes cheap." Lester remarked as he ran his fingers across the two bullet holes in the door. Lester gazed down at Cara again. "Are you planning to stay with her?"

Mario spread his hands. "Absolutely, I won't leave her like this. Where will you be?"

"I'm headed to Miss Coles' apartment. Under cover surveillance should be in front of her place as we speak."

Mario walked him to the door.

"Talk to you later, buddy," Lester spoke with staid calmness.

"You bet. Call me here."

A wry but indulgent glint appeared in Lester's eyes.

Mario locked the door and returned to Cara's side. Only now that he was finally alone with her did he dare to relax. He dropped his head down wishing she'd wake up. When she didn't he started to hum a familiar sweet tune, while he gently rubbed her forehead and around her face.

In a matter of seconds, Cara woke up bringing her arm up and above her head. "Mario, you're still here. What happened?"

She blinked feeling lightheaded and her lips were dry.

"How you feel?." His dark brown eyes softened, watching her with concern. She sat up. He gently grabbed and held her. Willingly she let him hold her for the second time.

"I was so scared. Did they catch that man?"

"Yes, and now you're safe," he said, pushing stray tendrils of hair away from her cheek.

"Tired. I haven't slept or eaten since yesterday."

"Can I get you something to drink or eat?" He pulled slightly away from her. His stare clung to hers, analyzing her reaction.

"Thanks, just some water."

He returned with a tall glass of water from the refrigerator. She straightened her body up, letting her feet fall to the floor and she drank all of it.

"Feel better?" he asked.

"Yes, I do." Cara gave him the glass and she slowly curled her body back on the sofa. "I am grateful that you were outside watching over me."

"When I learned you were Paula's next target, you were all that mattered," Mario said.

In her mind she knew he was totally up to speed. For a moment she wondered what was really going on in his mind. She also realized that he and Lester had somehow put aside their differences and maybe it explained Lester's absence.

"I heard footsteps coming from the third floor. That must've been you."

"Yes, keeping an eye on him at the same time, too. If you only knew how much I wanted to let him have it when I saw him turn your doorknob. Lester advised me what to do. I had to play it by the book. He said if I had to shoot him, don't kill him."

"Really? How did you and Lester know someone would come after me?"

"Our friend, Lester is a remarkable guy. Anyway, we met and talked. He filled me in on the urgent call he got from your downstairs neighbor. Apparently she traced Lester to the 2nd District station. Somehow, they decided you needed protection. In the meantime Lester had a hunch and put a wiretap on Paula's phone. That led the police to the hit man. The rest is history."

"You did this for me." She hesitated, her brow lifted. "I don't know what to say." Cara lowered her voice for dramatic effect.

"Say nothing, except ___." He froze, letting a hot tear roll down his cheek. I hope, someday, you can forgive me for not believing you. Mama told me everything, Cara." He fought to control the tears. "I know how you risked your life to prove your innocence, and how rough things must've been for you. I'm so sorry." His head dropped and body slumped and paused for a moment. "I just needed to say that and it's okay if you can't find it in your heart to forgive me. As it is, I'm finding it hard to forgive myself."

She sat up and put her hand on his shoulder. "You came to rescue me, that means so much to me. Maybe now is not the time. What I really want to say is, don't be so hard on yourself. Hasn't this mess done enough to both of us? And, your family, too?"

Hearing the words from Mario seemed punishment enough. Cara didn't bother to wipe the tears that started to trickle down her face. Listening to him just now reminded her how he was when she married him. Loving, thoughtful and protective. She started to think that if God can forgive us, then we ought to forgive each other. The past seven months had helped her learn many things about life and people. Empathy and flexibility were a few.

She looked at Mario and forced a smile. "It means a lot to hear you ask me to forgive you. They won't erase what happened between us, but you know me, I don't have it in my heart to hold grudges. You have to answer to the God you believe in, not me. And, so it's for that reason that I can once again forgive you."

After Mario racked his brains for a subtle way to say what he needed to tell her, he sat up straight, looked deeply into her eyes. "For what it's worth, I needed to hear you say that. In fact it's eating my insides raw looking at you, being so close to you, and yet knowing how much I hurt you. You've always been the brave one, Cara. Outside you depict strength, patience and reasoning. But deep down, this must be ripping you apart."

Cara sighed. "Yes, I've been through the mills, sometimes immersed in a lot of pain and other times, filled with a lot of anger.

No question about it, Paula's revenge wrecked our world, affecting so many people. And yes, it was rough for a while, but thanks to your brother I got a bigger paycheck. I could see light at the end of tunnel. It wasn't until later on, that I realized he meant me no harm. He's got a good heart and that's why he did it." She breathed and smiled. You should focus on him now."

"I'm sure you're right."

Little by little, warmth crept back into her body as the tears blinded her eyes and her choking voice. They were tears pure nostalgia. The life and times they had together brought on a sorrow that seemed to weigh her down.

Leaning forward, she peered at him. "Now, do this one last thing for me. Forgive yourself."

"You say that like you really mean it."

"Actually, I do mean it," she replied, and swung her head lazily to the side.

The cordless phone rang and she answered.

"Hello."

"It's good to hear your voice," Lester said. "How are you?"

"Likewise. Thanks for everything."

"No problem, I couldn't desert you. Can I speak to Mario?" She glanced at Mario and passed the phone to him, "It's Lester. He wants to talk to you."

"Lester, I hope you're going to tell me Paula's been arrested?" Mario stared at Cara.

"No, it's just a matter of time though. I'm calling about your brother. He's out of the coma and resting comfortably. He's asking for you and your mother."

"How does tomorrow sound? I'm staying here tonight."

"Oh, Okay.

"Thanks again, man. I'll never be able to repay you."

"Don't mention it. That's what friends are for."

While Cara listened, her eyes were misty. By Mario's reaction and words, she knew the alderman had regained consciousness. She was glad for the Fleming family.

Mario clicked the phone off and put it down on the cocktail table. "According to Lester, my brother is going to be okay. Will you come to the hospital with me?"

She was caught off guard by the sudden vibrancy of his voice. "Oh," she cast her eyes downward for a moment. "Under the circumstances, it might be too overwhelming for him. You and your mother should see him first. I, I'll go with you on the next visit, if that's okay," she answered.

More than anything he wanted her by his side. She was the half that could make him a whole. "I want you there whenever you can come." He paused looking deep into her eyes. "Mama asked about you."

"Good. I hope to see her before she goes back."

Cara smiled at him and looked at the clock on the wall. It was 3:30 a.m. Daylight was just a few hours away. She was glad it was Sunday and counted on sleeping later than usual. She wondered what he would do. Leave her alone or sleep over. She was still afraid but would never admit it.

They both sat in silence for a while and he watched her lean back on the sofa. She started to yawn a little and her eyes drooped some. He was still watching her.

Mario drew his lips in thoughtfully. "Why don't you go and get some sleep. I'll sleep out on the sofa until morning."

"Good, I'll feel better with you here."

She got up to get the spare comforter and pillow she kept in the linen closet. She came back to the living room holding a pink fluffy pillow and a solid magenta comforter. She placed the linen at the end of the sofa.

"This should help you get some rest."

"Thanks, and don't worry, I'm just here to protect you."

She stood motionless in the middle of the room. He sensed her disquiet. "By the way, we've talked a little about everything and nothing about our daughter. How is she doing?" Mario asked. He seemed upbeat for a change.

"Yeah, you're right, we seemed to have pushed her aside for too long. She's getting over a terrible cold. The other night when I called down there, she told me about a new playmate named Chantiera and how much she love playing with her. They call her Tee-Tee and she lives four blocks down the street."

"That's good. I'm planning to go and see her soon."

"I meant to thank you for the child support. Most of it is going to a special college fund for her. The rest, I send to my parents to help with expenses."

"Good idea. I'm glad to do that." Mario plumped his pillow and opened the comforter. "I don't know if I'll be able to sleep much. Would you mind if I listened to soft music.

"No, not at all. Goodnight," she said, and eased to her bedroom.

He kicked off his shoes, and fully clothed, he stretched out on the sofa, pulled the cover over him. He pressed the slim remote to V-103 FM. Following a McDonald's commercial, Nathalie Cole's *I'm Singing My Song For You* played.

He'd wanted passion with her forgiveness, but he knew he had to settle for something a little less carnal for the time being.

CHAPTER 61

Less than five hours later, Cara woke up to the sound of the phone ringing and she reached out groggily, unaware of what she was doing.

"Hello."

"Did I wake you?" Naomi asked.

Cara paused just for a moment to check the time. "Yeah Mom, it's good you did. How you doing?"

"I had a dream last night that you burned in a fire."

"Not quite. Something did happened here last night. Mario rescued me from some gunman Paula hired. He slept on the sofa, and don't go getting any ideas."

"My Lord. Are you all right?"

"Yes, we're safe now. Good news, Mom. The alderman regained consciousness last night. Mario wants me to go with him and Mary Lee, but I passed this time. It'll be too awkward being there. They need time alone. Can you imagine the things they need to say to each other?"

"Oh, yeah, you're right. I hadn't thought about that. How're you and Mario getting along?"

"Okay. Actually, he was a total gentleman last night."

"I hope they catch that Paula soon."

"Me, too. They say it's just a matter of time. Mom, I need to shower and get dressed before Mario wakes up. Call you later. Give Ashley and daddy my love."

She hung up and jumped out of bed, threw on her robe and slipped into the bathroom and turned on the shower.

Meanwhile, on the sofa, Mario had heard the phone ring. The radio was still playing and he turned it off.

Mario worried that it might've been another call from Lester. Just yesterday he asked Lester point blankly, where his relationship was going with Cara. He recalled Lester's words: "Mario, it should be no secret that Cara is one hell of a woman. You'd be glad to know she never said she loved me. Quite frankly, I don't believe she ever will."

The sound of the shower became clearer and he continued to lie there thinking about Lester. Was Lester being diplomatic just to get my cooperation to save Cara's life? Or did something go wrong between them? Neither had Cara given me reason to believe she wanted me back, he thought.

He made a pot of coffee while she showered, thinking she'd appreciate the gesture. He helped himself to a cup and admired the flair for how she maintained a lovely and clean kitchen. Some things never change, he thought.

Suddenly he heard the bathroom door open. Cara dashed out, hurried to her bedroom properly clad with a blue beach towel around her. She'd always been self-conscious about exposing her body, even to me, Mario thought.

Fifteen minutes later, she appeared before him looking incredible. She wore an olive green two-piece skirt suit. Her hair down her back and 14-carat earrings looped in her ears, and with just the right amount of makeup applied.

"Good morning, how you feel?" he asked.

"Hi. I'm better. I smell coffee." Her eyes brightened with surprise.

"That it is," he beamed as he stood up and motioned for her to sit down. He quickly poured the yellow mug to the rim. "Still take one sugar and no cream?"

"Yes. You, remember the formula." She grinned, easing the tension.

He set her coffee on the table before her. She took two sips and smiled. "It's actually good. Thanks."

She sat down at the table facing him. "Have you thought some more about your visit with your brother?"

"Yeah, I did. I did what you always do, I prayed and the answer came to me. I know exactly what I should do," he said.

"Good for you. I'll send up a special prayer for all of you."

Shortly afterwards, Cara walked him to the door. He turned to face her. "By the way, I called off the divorce. I meant to talk about it last night, just couldn't find the right moment."

She blinked, and then focused her gaze down. "I know, my lawyer told me.

❦ ❦ ❦

Twenty minutes later, Cara locked the door and finished her coffee. Then she thought about Mrs. Walker, realizing she owed her a world of thanks. Besides, she needed some answers. She placed the call and they spent time chatting about the whole ordeal.

Cara discovered how Lester and Mario entrapped the gunman: Ralph talked, naming Paula as the person who hired him to commit murder. He further told the police how she promised him an I.O.U. to go back to get the right one. Mrs. Walker admitted that it had been difficult to keep quiet about what was about to go down. She'd even taken an afternoon nap to stay alert later that evening to carry out her part in the plan.

"I can't thank you enough, Mrs. Walker. You've been more than a good neighbor. You were like an angel on my shoulder." Cara wanted to reach through the phone and hug her.

"I'm glad to know I was able to do some good," Mrs. Walker boasted. It's times like these, we have to really look out for each other."

"True. And, as long as I'm living in this apartment, I'll to be your angel," Cara said.

They talked some more and then Cara glanced at the clock on the kitchen wall. "I've got to leave for church. See you later after I get back."

"Oh, yeah that reminds me, I met your husband. How will you ever choose between them?"

CHAPTER 62

Around 9:30 that morning Lester and a slew of plain clothed cops had Paula's apartment surrounded. Lester had been there since daybreak. He climbed the steps to her third floor apartment and knocked on her door twice. He waited a few minutes and knocked again, calling out her name. "Ms. Coles, this is Detective Lester Miller, Chicago Police Department."

After waiting for five minutes he walked halfway down the steps. He connected with a cop waiting in the alley: "Detective Miller here, there's no answer, apparently she's out."

"I can see why," the officer replied. "She's pulling out of the garage as we speak, and I'm on her tail."

Immediately, Lester scurried to his unmarked car and drove off behind three squad cars down Seventy-First and Cornell. Paula was able to get slightly ahead driving faster than the speed limit allowed. She managed to avoid colliding with the cars in her path. She passed through two traffic lights in the knick of time, crossed the rail track and drove west to Jeffrey Boulevard. She nearly hit the car speeding through the light when she turned right on red.

On South Shore Drive, it was their luck the traffic on the four-lane outer drive was light. Passing every vehicle ahead of them, Lester could clearly see Paula's car. Soon he realized that she was about to approach the dangerous curve near the Museum of Science and Industry. By then the speedometer in his car had reached 80 miles an hour.

Traffic from 57th street poured on the Drive at normal speeds. The driver in the gray UV aiming to turn left and the black sports car veering to the right on green swerved in the same direction heading south on the Drive.

Suddenly she veered her car toward the Lake. Instantly she plowed into the cement wall flipping over into Lake Michigan. Sounds of steel banging and tires hugging the street brought a line of southbound cars bumper to bumper. One vehicle burst into flames and drivers close by, scrambled to get out of their cars. Some rushed over to the embankment.

Lester pulled over a few hundred feet away and parked in the emergency lane. Within a matter of minutes, three fire trucks, four ambulances and more police cars appeared on the scene. Several tow trucks arrived shortly afterward. Gapers were then ushered away further from the area.

Once all unaffected vehicles were out of the way, Paula's car was lifted up from the water. The windows were rolled down. Soon the paramedics rolled the stretcher down the pavement, the body covered with a white sheet. He wanted so much to bring her in alive, but in this case he didn't seem to mind that they didn't get to her in time. Bennett's anonymity would be preserved. Case closed.

He soon pulled off and veered southbound on the drive letting the area police handle the matter wondering how Mario would react.

People waiting to enter the church started to pour in and fill scattered vacant spaces on the pews. It was during the morning hymn and everyone stood singing robustly, *My Faith Looks Up To Thee.* Cara rejoiced feeling grateful about the sudden turnabout of events in her life. Mostly she was grateful to be alive and she sensed a suitcase of emotional baggage had been lifted from her mind and her heart. As she sang, she thought prayerfully about Mario's family.

As more people scurried to find a seat, she peripherally glimpsed Barbara, dressed in the navy blue usher's uniform, stop in the aisle directly alongside her pew. Suddenly, she looked up and saw Mario coming toward her wearing a warm smile on his face. Before he could ease past her to stand to her left, Mary Lee scrambled to stand on the right of her. Cara stopped singing and hugged her mother-in-law.

"Hi, Mother Fleming. What a surprise to see you guys here," Cara softly whispered.

"It's so good to see you," she whispered in Cara's ear. Mario couldn't sit still to do anything today. He just had to come to your church."

"I'm glad you're both here." She continued to hold Mary Lee's hand as she started to sing again. Then on impulse, she looked at Mario. He gave her a quick glance and he reached out and clutched her hand, singing the words like he meant it.

After the song ended, they sat down. Mario leaned over and whispered, "Hope you don't mind, I'm here. Oh, I asked the usher to take us to where you were sitting."

Cara smiled demurely, thinking Barbara ought to be happy with her church guest this time. "Oh, of course not, it's good to see you, Mario. The choir will rock the church. And, the sermon is always good."

He gently withdrew his hand and folded both his hands down to his lap, seemingly braced to enjoy the service.

Fifteen minutes later and during the sermon, Mario's pager pulsated inside his shirt pocket. He waited a few minutes and slowly pulled it out and pushed the message button: *Been trying to reach you. Paula drowned in Lake Michigan trying to flee the police on the outer drive. More later. Lester.*

Mario dropped his head for a moment and then he looked at Cara thinking the nightmare was over. He nudged his hand against hers. When he got her attention, he slid the pager in her hand. She looked at him and glanced down to read the digital read out. With a stunned look on her face, she shook her head and looked back at him. He pressed the pager button off and returned it to his shirt pocket.

CHAPTER 63

Mario opened the main door to let Mary Lee and Cara enter the University of Chicago Hospital. He'd persuaded her outside the church to come with them. They walked to the desk and Mario gave their names and relationship to the patient. The clerk issued them guest passes. They took the elevator to the 4th floor, room 4002.

Cara stood back and let Mario and Mary Lee entered the private room.

Bright sunshine streamed in through the big windows in his room. Bennett was alone, awake and his bed was tilted slightly upward. Mario opened the door as quietly as he could and the threesome tiptoed in. Bennett's eyes sparkled with pleasure. He folded his hands peacefully.

"Come in. It's about time. I was hoping you'd come." He smiled, looking first at Mary Lee, then Mario and finally Cara.

Mary Lee took a few steps to his bedside, and bent to kiss him on the cheek. "Hello, my child. Don't ever give me a scare like that again. I thought I'd lost you all over again." He wrapped his arms around her and held her for a few moments.

"For the second time Mother, I'm glad to be back." She smiled at the alderman. Then she looked at Mario. He was standing on the other side of the bed.

"Hi, big brother. I'm Mario. He leaned his head down low and their faces touched. "I'm so glad to finally meet you. Thank God, you're alive." He said, holding his brother's hand.

"Likewise," Alderman whispered. He breathed in shallow, quick gasps.

"Try to take it slow for now. I'm not going anywhere. We got nothing but time to talk."

Bennett paused to breath deeply until he calmed again. "You were just a baby when I last saw you. It seems that all my prayers have finally been answered. There's so much I want to say to you. I'm so sorry. I didn't know you were my brother. Paula threatened me with everything I worked so hard for. I'd given it all up for my family, if I had known you were my brother. Do you think you can forgive me?"

Mary Lee couldn't resist rubbing his shoulders gently. She looked at Mario seemingly anxious for him to say something.

"You bet I can. And, this time I want the world to know you're family. No more hiding, no more secrets, okay? Mario said proudly.

"Okay, it's a deal. That's a mighty big load off my shoulder."

"You must know I'm not angry with you. Mama told me what happened two days ago. So, yes, I can forgive you." They gave each other the thumbs up gesture.

Cara stood more than a few feet away from his bed, watching everything. Perhaps, it was simply her uneasiness. Then Bennett gave a slight nod at Cara and smiled.

She took that as encouragement to come closer. She'd heard and seen it all and she smiled back at him. Slowly she came closer and stood alongside Mario. Amazingly, being face to face with Bennett reminded her she knew him on four levels—a chat room buddy, a politician, a church member and now her brother-in-law.

"Hello, Alderman Bennett, I'm Cara. How're you feeling?" She asked, gently.

He had glanced at her for a sign of objection. “Better now,” he said taking a deep breath. “Seeing the three of you together like this has given me all the reason to want to get well and get out of here.”

Alderman Bennett reached and softly held her hand in gentle grasp.

“I can't help wondering what you of all people must think of me? I know I caused you pain. For that I'm truly sorry.”

“It's okay.” There was a faint tremor in her voice as though some emotion had touched her. “Please, try not to worry about that now. You've more than made up for the harm you caused me. I'm praying you get smashingly well and get back to helping the people in your community.”

“I'll hold that close to my heart, sister-in-law. You're as smart and optimistic as you are beautiful. I'm grateful for your understanding.”

Cara noticed he appeared drowsy and that he wanted to say more. She looked at Mario and whispered in his ear, “Why don't you stay with him. He'll appreciate the company, besides it'll be a good time for you to talk. Ease his mind some. Tell him Paula won't be blackmailing him anyone ever.”

“What will you and mama do?” Before Cara could answer, Bennett was even more awake than before.

“Stop whispering, you two.” That brought some laughter to the room.

He looked at Mary Lee and asked her to sit down and relax. “I've got one more thing to beg for.” He folded both hands with his head bowed and eyes closed. When he opened them, a smile found its way through the mask of uncertainty for how he would speak words of wisdom to Mario and Cara. He needed to be sure his bad deeds wouldn't keep them apart forever. The time was now or never, he thought.

“Giles, go on, we're listening,” Mary Lee urged him.

He looked at Cara. Remember what I wrote you in my last e-mail?”

"Yes."

"You didn't know who I was at the time and yet I knew you. It's just that I needed to say something to give you hope and belief in yourself. It went something like this: There's hope when something has died; There's hope when you think you're down and out and have no where to turn; There's hope when you've been lied on and had to give up your happiness and peace of mind." He unfolded his hands and blazed his eyes up into hers. "Did it help you?"

"Absolutely."

"Good. Now, I'm moved by the spirit to say this to you and Mario:

People are sometimes mean and difficult; forgive them anyway. If you're successful, you will win some false friends and sometimes enemies; succeed anyway. If you find serenity and happiness, they may be jealous and want what you've got, be happy anyway. What you spend years building, someone could destroy overnight; build anyway. The good you do today, people will often forget tomorrow; do good anyway. Give the world the best you have even if it's not enough; Give your best to the world anyway. You see, in the final analysis, it's between you and God; it was never between you and them anyway. Life is measured by the moments that take our breath away. Don't waste your breaths pretending you don't love each other. God put you together, let no man keep you apart."

Bennett looked at them, one by one, smiled happily and closed his eyes.

CHAPTER 64

Mario sat quietly by Alderman Bennett's beside that afternoon, thinking deeply and dreamlessly this time, with no thought of the future and no fear of the past. There was only the present. He tried to cope with the idea he might lose Cara. For a man who was fighting an uphill battle for his marriage, he might as well been clinging to a straight pin. He was tired, discouraged and needed a whole day of sleep.

Then he remembered unfinished business about the case. Had Lester located Paula's sister in Detroit? Other than her girlfriend in Memphis, and no one else to call, the thought came that someone had to make arrangements for a funeral and burial. At no time had Bennett sat up in bed and opened his mouth to talk again, so he eased out of the room to call Lester on his cellular phone around 3:45 p.m.

Lester sounded groggy from only four hours of sleep in two days. Mario was relieved to know that Paula's body was at Jackson Funeral home on Cottage Grove. Her sister, Odessa was on a Southwest airline flight to Chicago to make arrangements to have Paula's body prepared and shipped to Detroit for the services. And, most disturbing was that Loretta Bennett had called and asked for Lester's help to arrange a private visit with the alderman.

"Does Mrs. Bennett know my mother is here?"

"Yes and she backed off," Lester replied.

"Good, for once she made the right decision."

Mario couldn't begin to imagine what meeting the woman even by accident, would do to his mother. He was all too aware that the woman who stole his brother had in the end helped Cara find the needle in the haystack. Just thinking that if none of that happened, he would still be in a relationship with poisonous Paula. He owed Loretta Bennett a debt of gratitude.

CHAPTER 65

❀

On her way home, Cara had decided on a complete take-out meal from Kentucky Fried Chicken. Mary Lee talked about meeting and getting to know Giles, and apologized to Cara for having to lie about needing Matthew's screen name.

"It's all water under the bridge, Mother Fleming. We should count our blessings for the good that came from it," Cara replied.

"What did you think about Giles? He wants you and Mario to work things out, you know."

"Yes, that was quite clear. What he had to say was touching. I can see that he's your son. I'm so glad he came back to you."

"Except for a different name and a new life, he's back in the flesh, mind and soul. I just wished Bradley could've live to see him."

They both got quiet and Cara tuned the radio to a station that played gospel music. Mary Lee took comfort in a song by Yolanda Adams.

Cara thought about Lester and how he'd removed himself to help everyone. It hadn't mattered so much now that he had been deceitful. He was above that, a good man and a good friend to her and Mario. *Truthfully, he was the wrong man at the right time in her life.*

Oh, sure he'd reminded her about passion and romance and he gave her the best sex she'd ever imagined was possible. He took her to the mountaintop. She'd seen what was possible and yet she knew he was not the man to share the view with. To do so would've been nothing less than going from a frying pan to an inferno. She'd learned enough to fill a lifetime. She felt a gap in her heart wider than the Grand Canyon.

Cara pulled up in front of her building and Mary Lee helped her take the food inside. While she changed into a pair of jeans and a yellow v-neck sweater, Mary Lee put the large box of chicken, mashed potatoes, biscuits, cole slaw and greens inside the fridge. Mario was expected within an hour or so.

Then Cara took Mary Lee downstairs to meet Mrs. Walker. The two older ladies liked each other right off the bat, and surprisingly, Mary Lee took her phone number and promised to call her later.

Then before Mario arrived, they talked and reminisced about the good-old days in Memphis, how Ashley was growing by leaps and bounds, finally Mario. Mary Lee was careful not to push Cara's feelings or plans about her future.

* * *

Mario arrived at 4:30 p.m. They got the food ready and the three of them sat at the table and while they ate, Mario gave them a glowing report about Giles. He woke up around 3:15 p.m. They talked for a long time about the years he spent away from home. They promised to start acting like brothers. There were reporters waiting outside the room and a surprise visit by Joe Michaels. Giles introduced them and Mario left shortly afterwards.

After the meal, Mary Lee insisted that Cara and Mario take a moment to talk alone in the living room. She cleared the table and made the kitchen tidy again. Mario pulled out his cellular and called Ashley. They took turns talking with her, Naomi and Frank.

Cara looked up fifteen minutes later as Mary Lee entered the living room holding two glasses of white wine. She gently took a glass.

"Thanks Mother Fleming. Sit down and relax."

"Did I hear him call out Ashley's name?" she asked in amazement and passed a glass to Mario.

"Yes," Mario answered.

"What has Ashley been saying to you guys?"

"Oh, just that she loved us and how she can't wait to come to Chicago and be with us." Cara wondered how her father must've reacted was when he heard Ashley say that.

❧ ❧ ❧

Later that evening Cara retrieved an electronic greeting from Lester. He obviously remembered her screen name from the investigation. She clicked on the greeting while her head started to spin. It was a happy birthday message, two days early. It wasn't that she'd forgotten she just didn't take the time to think her birthday. Lester's message was sweet, brief and not binding. She sent him a thank you reply.

CHAPTER 66

Two days later, Giles had been released to recuperate at home. He could return to doing light duty at his office in a week. Michaels and Bennett's housekeeper made sure he was comfortable, the house was kept immaculate, and meals served on time. The day before, Mario and Mary Lee were given the grand tour the same day he arrived home. Mary Lee found the photo book lying on the curio table. She explained to Mario how she'd kept pictures of him over the years.

During the ride back to the hotel, she remembered all she'd done since Sunday to plan a surprise party for Cara. It had taken some doing, but in the end she managed to convince Frank and Naomi to bring Ashley on an all expense paid trip to Chicago. They would come on a Greyhound bus. Expected arrival time was 5:40 p.m.

Fifteen minutes later after leaving the hospital, Mario pulled up to the hotel entrance.

"I'll see you later, mama."

"Okay, try to get some rest. You want to look your best."

Cara woke up immediately realizing it was her birthday and the phone had been silent all while she got dressed for work. She arrived at the office at 8:50 a.m. and waiting on her desk was a bouquet of flowers. The card read:

"Happy Birthday, Cara. We wish you all the best." She smiled and was pleased the staff thought as much to remember her birthday.

Suddenly, Shirley Carr peeked her head from the cubicle a few feet away. She seemed unusually sneaky but friendly when she greeted Cara.

"Hi, Shirley. You guys shouldn't have," Cara beamed, looking at the pink, purple and blue floral arrangement.

"It's just a little something from us," Shirley said. Grady stood close by and Shirley nudged him slightly. He appeared bashful and smiled.

"You have plans for the evening?" Shirley probed.

"No, none that I'm aware of."

"Terrific. At Mr. Dunlap's request, I made reservations for a group dinner in your honor tonight. I can pick you up around 7:30 this evening?" She asked, eagerly waiting for Cara's answer.

"Oh, my goodness, all this for me? I'll be ready," Cara said, totally surprised. She felt like member of staff finally. By now, she had expected her parents to call. Surely they wouldn't forget her birthday.

❦ ❦ ❦

At exactly 5:15 p.m., the Slater family arrived earlier than expected. It was Frank's first time in the windy city.

They waited outside the terminal for Mary Lee to take them to the hotel. Ashley was hugging the brown teddy bear Cara bought her, Mr. *Chocolate*.

It wasn't long before a taxi pulled up and stopped. Mary Lee got out and gave each of them a warm hug. Once they were comfortably seated, the driver fought to get through the Loop traffic. Mary Lee filled them in on the remaining details. Naomi and Frank seemed satisfied Cara's nightmare was finally over.

As they rode on, Frank joked around and got everyone laughing right away. Then he looked back at Mary Lee. "You've gone to a lot of trouble. I sure hope this plan of yours work.

"So do I." Ashley had leaned over on Naomi and fallen asleep. "More than anything, it's for our granddaughter's sake that I want them back together."

"Here, here," Naomi added. "She's talked about nothing except coming to Chicago. Ashley brought her coloring book to show her mama and daddy. That child painted pictures yesterday until she almost dropped."

Naomi couldn't imagine how she would tell Ashley her parents didn't live together.

CHAPTER 67

Expecting to be greeted by her co-workers in the main dining area, Shirley led Cara to a private room.

No sooner than she opened the door and looked up, there was Mario. She looked into his eyes once again. She thought she had worked out what she'd say when their paths crossed again. He looked smashing and handsome. Finally, his eyes told her what she needed to know.

"Happy birthday, Cara," he beamed, and stood with his arms stretched out in her direction.

Startled, and suddenly feeling like someone who mattered, cared about her, Cara embraced him without restraint. "Thank you," she whispered while still in his arms. She pulled away slightly. "You've outdone yourself this time. In my wildest imagination, I can't figure how you pulled this one off."

"That's for me to know and you to figure out, isn't it?" Mario said, still holding her.

As he whisked her to the middle of room, Shirley joined several waitresses who stood near the string combo. They sang happy birthday to her as the music played softly. She slowly looked around the large room, beautifully decorated. A banner that read: Happy Birthday, Cara, 29, sparkled in red and yellow, like a neon sign. Suddenly she realized Mario and Lester had truly patched their differences. Shirley and Grady were part of the plan.

Shirley beamed as she snapped pictures of Mario and Cara as they danced slowly to romantic music. Cara looked at him and smiled, yet, baffled by his latest action. She once thought he didn't love her anymore.

Mario noticed the onlookers were staring at them. They were all smiling broadly. Mario decided, as long as he was giving everyone a show, he might as well make it a good one.

With a deep breath for courage, he turned to look at Cara. Remember me? I love you more than ever. Even if you don't want to stay married, please believe that." Tears welled in his eyes.

Understanding softened her face. Suddenly she remembered how painful it could be when the one you really love was hurting too.

He pulled a small black box from his pocket and opened it. She stared at it, with a look of wonder as it winked and sparkled. "Cara, will you wear this ring as my wife again?"

She lifted her tea-filled eyes and smiled. "Yes, Mario. Oh, yes. I still love you, too." He held her tight, closing his eyes to savor the moment as everyone cheered.

A few seconds later, the music stopped. Mario and Cara turned to look in their direction, as everyone started to leave the room one by one and thanked them. Shirley tiptoed over to Cara and hugged her. She gave Mario a handshake and left the room.

Just then, a closed door opened and all the family poured into the room screaming *surprise, surprise!* Frank helped Giles, sitting in a wheelchair, into the room. Cara behaved like a starry eyed contestant who'd just won a national beauty contest. Mario had to hold her up to keep from falling. All together, they sang the happy birthday.

"Ashley, Mom, Dad," she screamed their names, bouncing around. She grabbed her daughter, taking her into her arms. "Hi Ashley, you surprised me."

"I love you mommy. You look pretty." Ashley laid her head on Cara's shoulder. Naomi and Frank stood close by and put their arms around Cara while she still held onto Ashley.

"Happy birthday, Baby Girl," Frank said.

"Are you happy, darling?" Naomi asked.

"Yes, Mom. I'm so glad you came. My God, I am so happy." She hugged them again.

Mario stood close by and heard what they said. Cara gave Ashley to him and he held onto her. "Hi daddy, I missed you." Ashley said, laughing.

"I missed you little one. This time I promise you will stay with us."

Then Frank and Naomi joined Mario and Ashley. "Welcome back to the family son." The handshakes suddenly changed to warm hugs. Ashley held tight to Mario.

Then Mary Lee joined Cara standing not far way. "Welcome back, my sweet daughter-in-law," she said and hugged her.

"Thanks for everything, Mother Fleming. You've been amazing through it all."

When it was Bennett's turn, he offered his congratulations to the happy couple. "Hey little bro, I'm glad your plan worked. We're one big happy family now."

"You got that right," Mario said. I've got more to do to clean up my act. Thanks for being there for me big brother," Mario said, and hugged him.

"I've got a really big surprise for you and Cara."

Mario raised his eyebrows in wonderment.

"Don't even ask, I won't tell," Bennett replied, and smiled. Then, Mario pulled Cara closer to him. All they could do was smile at each other again. Mario looked back at Bennett. "Me and the Mrs. can wait for the surprise."

Everyone had a good time eating from the lavish buffet of seafood and chicken. Frank and Naomi were pleased to finally meet Bradley's oldest son. Frank urged him to come to Memphis to get acquainted. Alderman Bennett promised he'd come soon.

Family members talked and laughed, mostly listening to Frank talk about his first trip to Chicago and the long bus ride.

"Next time, maybe you'll get on a plane," Mary Lee quipped.

"Hell no, you'll have to sedate me before I do that." He threw back his head and laughed. He looked ten years younger when he laughed.

An hour later, Mario and Cara finally had a moment alone. They sat holding hands unable to take their eyes off each other. Happily exhausted, and still very excited about their new beginning. The others had almost vanished to their rooms. Joe Michaels had arrived an hour ago and took Alderman Bennett home.

Cara and Mario agreed to stay in the room Mary Lee reserved for them. After hugging and rejoicing with their family, Mario and Cara walked inside their hotel room and were surprised again. Mary Lee had arranged for an overnight basket containing sleepwear, robes, toiletries, and clothes for Mario and Cara to wear the next day.

Cara took notice and smiled, standing close to him. "Your mother is a champ, wouldn't you say?"

"Yep, that's Mary Lee for you. She's a busy body, but she means well." Mario drew Cara close and held her gently for a long time. "Let's renew our vows. This time, I'll get it right. Please say yes."

Succumbed with happiness, "Yes, oh, yes. Let's do it again."

"Then it shall be done," he said.

Exhausted, they plopped down on the bed and held each other some more. She was a glowing image of fire, passion and love. In a raw act of possession, he grabbed her and they kissed slowly. A hot tide of passion raged through both of them.

As much as they wanted to make love for the first time in a long time, Cara pulled away for air a few minutes later, "Let's savor the moment, count our blessings and ___."

He interrupted her. "And, save the best for last?"

"Yes, how did you know that's what I wanted to say?"

"Because, not only do I love you, I know you like a book. Throw out the stuff I said about you. You're a lady, my grand lady," he said. A smile lingered on his face.

Hearing those words, she thought, everything is going to okay again.

Later, they showered, and dressed for bed. They toasted each other with some of the wine Mary Lee had chilled for them. Mario told her about the inheritance from his dad's estate, the landscape business, and his decision to put most of the money in savings and CD's. All of it welled up inside him, including the desire to tell her about his surprise plan to buy them a home in Chicago. He wanted to blurt it all out, but he wanted the news to be his gift to her later.

"Really. You're doing the right thing this time. I'm proud of you."

CHAPTER 68

A month later, Cara and Mario renewed their vows. Alderman Bennett had managed to work magic behind the scenes and got Luther Vandross to sing at the wedding. Luckily, the star had a two-hour lay over at O'Hare for a flight to Atlanta.

Among the one hundred plus guests were: Cara's co-workers: Dexter Grady, and Earl Dunlap; Thelma Walker, Alderman Tucker, Renita Dates, Captain Hayes and his wife, Duncan Tate, Cecil Hawkins, Barbara Rhodes, and several of Lester's police buddies who watched over Cara. Loretta Bennett had promised Giles she'd come unannounced but changed her mind at the last minute. She was not ready, if ever, to face Mary Lee.

And, to everyone's surprise except Mario and Cara, Frank made an unprecedented move at the last minute. He insisted that Lester walk his daughter down the aisle. When Frank had heard the whole story behind his efforts to save and protect Cara's life, nothing else mattered to him. Besides, he'd already given Cara away to Mario at their wedding six years ago. Mario had been in total agreement with the decision figuring it was a price worth paying knowing he was going to have one more chance with Cara.

Traditionally the bride and groom's family sat opposite each other. This time the family chose to sit together. Filling the gap left by Bradley's death, Frank sat alongside Naomi and Ashley, and Mary

Lee. By now they were all impressed that Mario had learned to control his anger, his jealousy and his out of control behavior toward the woman he loved.

With everything and everybody in place, the organist started to play soft music in a Vanessa Williams tune. Mario stood at the altar along with Alderman Bennett, his best man. They wore dark gray Gucci tuxedos. Shirley Carr, the matron of honor, walked in first. Ashley looked beautiful as the flower girl, sprinkling petals of peach colored roses as she walked down the aisle.

Then everyone applauded loudly when Luther was introduced. He stepped proudly to the microphone dressed in a glittering two-piece black suit. When he started to sing the bridal song, *Here and Now*, everyone suddenly turned completely around to look at Cara standing at the door.

She wore a strapless elegant off-white gown with embroidery and crystals on the bodice and train she found at Saks Fifth Avenue less than six days ago. Diamond earrings and a beautiful diamond ring Mario sparkled. Hand strung peach, and blue-diamond flowers adorned her hair. She carried a bouquet of peach and white orchids and dahlia.

Thirty minutes later, Mario held her hand and looked at her: "Your love is loyal and it has deathless wings that never fails to rise to triumph. Your love has turned my heart of shame to one of honor and gladness. Cara, you make so very happy. There shall never again be failure in my commitment to you. From this day forth and with God as the center of our lives, I promise to love you faithfully and trust you perfectly."

When he was finished, Cara cited her vows: "Mario, I love you and there's nothing anybody can do about it. Though we've walked the road as all lovers and married folk have traveled; in wild and secret happiness we stumbled. But, you're still so utterly mine. True happiness is being with only you. Yes, I can return to you as your wife, promising to love you faithfully and trusting you perfectly. Together, with God in the center of our lives, and our little girl, Ashley, we will move forward from this day, keeping the promise we made six years ago to love and respect each other until death due us part."

There wasn't a dry eye in the church when Rev. Lewis said, "On their words, and by the grace of God, I give you, Mr. & Mrs. Mario Fleming and daughter."

❧ ❧ ❧

A commercial wedding planner had decorated the church's annex in blue and peach colors. Cocktails and a three course catered dinner of shrimp, and prime rib were served. Everyone looked lovely and they seemed happy for the couple.

After the meal, a popular jazz band kept a lively mood in high gear. Mario and Cara danced to the Kenny G classic, *Forever In Love*. Mario had privately asked Bennett and Lester not to interrupt, as it was his public moment alone with his wife. He released her to dance with them briefly after she danced with her proud and glowing father.

Cara and Mario posed for tons of pictures and on all of them Ashley stood in the middle.

Meanwhile, standing huddled together in the crowd, Duncan Tate commented to Cecil, "I'm glad that story had a happy ending. You should feel lucky."

"Yeah, let's keep our fingers crossed the rest of it will stay buried."

Across the room, Mario stepped away from Cara's side to speak to Lester. She looked across the room at each person she'd met over the past few months. Her thoughts of each one slipped through her mind and she remembered the aftermath. She wondered what they were thinking.

When Mario joined Lester, he was sipping on a drink called the Stockman's Blues, a blend of Russian made vodka, blue curaco and pineapple juice served in a martini glass.

"Hey, we pulled it off, man. Congratulations," Lester greeted him and they gave each other a manly hug.

"Thanks, you're the best friend I've ever had. It took a lot for me to realize that."

"Don't ever forget it man. I wish you and Cara nothing but the best." He nudged Mario to look at Duncan and Cecil. "That's the couple I told you about. The one with the straight hair was the *anonymous caller.*

"Oh yeah, any other time, I'd called him-a-you-know-what," Mario chuckled.

They both laughed. "Seems like old times, uh," he said, putting his arm around Lester.

"Yep, and I'm glad, buddy."

"Now, let's keep our fingers crossed my brother's past and his involvement stays out of the press. His career depends on it," Mario said, firmly.

CHAPTER 69

An hour later, Mario, Cara and Ashley had changed into traveling attire. Goodbyes and hugs to everyone were exchanged. Then Cara stood and embraced her parents for a few moments.

Holding Mario by the hand at the top of the steps, "I'm ready," she said. Mario took the small bag from her hand. The rest of their luggage was already in the limousine trunk.

"Then let's go and start that life we always wanted," he said.

Amid rice throwing, hand blown kisses, Mario ushered Cara and Ashley down the steps and into the limo parked in front of the church. Ashley sat between her parents on the back seat. They turned to face the crowd and waved goodbye. The driver would take them to O'Hare to board a plane to the Cayman Islands. Mario had secretly made the plans right after Cara agreed to stay with him. They would spend the Christmas break on a real honeymoon, *but not without their daughter.* It was the way the couple wanted it. Helping things along, Mary Lee would fly there the next day to keep Ashley occupied.

Once the driver was about to turn the corner, Ashley turned and looked at Cara and then Mario. "Mommy and Daddy, that was fun. What's next?" Mario and Cara laughed heartedly.

Mario sat Ashley on his legs and she faced them both.

"We're going to get on an airplane and fly up and away to a beautiful island where there's a lot of water, beaches, sun, trees, peace and happiness," he replied, smiling.

"Oh boy, I can't wait, can you mommy?" Ashley's eyes sparkled as though she was playing a game.

"No, darling, I can't either," Cara replied, and kissed her on the cheek.

Once they were on the Ryan expressway headed straight to the airport, Mario looked at Cara. "I love you, my grand lady. This time we're going to make it."

"I hope so, Mr. Fleming."

0-595-24817-9